JUSTIFIED

SAGA OF THE NANO TEMPLAR - BOOK ONE

JON DEL ARROZ

SILVER EMPIRE

ONE

Dots of light flashed on the planet Nemayr, followed by swelling plumes of destruction rising from the atmosphere. The end result was a giant cloud of dust covering every location that once held a major Sekaran city. No more. When Drin's dropship hit dirtside, there would only be fire and destruction.

The dropship entered the atmosphere, rattling on its way down. Drin held onto one of many dangling chains so he wouldn't flail around the cabin. Not that he would go far, as the dropship was packed with his fellow Templars. They all had the veneer of the armor the nanites provided them, though none had formed weapons in the close quarters of the dropship.

To the average Sekaran eye, the technology they used looked like magic, but Drin understood how the tiny machines created the weaponry. A dangerous technology if it fell into the wrong hands, but fortunately, the priesthood had tight controls on its programming. It took the will of one Templar to bestow nanites upon another, and one only did so with the blessing of the priesthood.

The nanite technology had been brought by Lord Yezuah over a thousand years ago. Its secrets had been safely kept for the faithful by the Elorians, who would one day retake Eloria from the Sekarans. The Elorians' vile enemy spread like cockroaches across the galaxy. System after system, they pressed forward corrupting civilizations with their heresy and creating subjects to bow to their false prophet. Just thinking about it made Drin clench his fists. He turned to look at the others. Most had their battle armor fully formed—jagged helmets with reflective visors so the enemy couldn't see their faces. But the chaplain stood in robes, walking the small center aisle between all of the Templars, and showering them with holy water. His scaly green Elorian skin shone, and his black ponytail swayed behind him. Drin regretted cutting his own hair, seeing long hair as a sign of strength, but even with the assistance of nanites, it tended to get in the way during battle.

The chaplain muttered prayers aloud as they came closer to the ground. Drin had heard it a thousand times before, but he was too focused on the pending battle to listen to the words.

"Power and glory to Yezuah!" all of the Templars shouted in unison. That rousing cry was enough to quicken the pace of Drin's heart.

The orbital bombardment had softened the planet for Elorian invasion, but there would be enough Sekaran fighters to greet them that it would be inadvisable to underestimate them. Drin only hoped he wouldn't see an EMP-suicider, one of the crazed Sekarans who sacrificed himself in order to disarm the nanites temporarily. He'd met with one before, and though Drin was a perfectly capable warrior without nanite assistance, he didn't relish the thought of fighting against Sekaran hordes or meeting a battlemage, without his armor.

The dropship landed with a jolt. The whole left flank of the cabin dropped and clanged onto the ground, creating its own ramp. The Templars pressed forward, shouting and crying out to Yezuah to deliver them victory. Their battle armor flashed and shimmered as they departed the craft, adjusting to the dirt-brown of the dust that littered the air, providing camouflage for the warriors. Their helmets filtered the air for breathing, another tactical advantage against the Sekarans.

Drin's face reflected beneath his visor as it adjusted to night-vision mode. His face looked somber, high cheekbones, a strong chin, and dark eyes far too solemn for this glorious occasion of liberating a world. His frame was wide enough that with the armor, he had to sidestep through the small opening in the craft.

He gazed ahead at what had once been a population center. Great skyscrapers were now rubble. Buildings had collapsed, toppled, or cracked into single walls. Nothing could withstand the Elorian bombardment once planetary defenses had broken. God willed their dominance. The Sekarans relied on their vast numbers and ruthlessness to counter the Elorians' precise strikes. It was the difference between barbarism and civilization, or so Drin had thought before trudging forward with his compatriots.

But the destruction he saw here broke his heart.

Not just buildings and infrastructure, but people lay littered on the ground. Civilians. Dozens of them were spread out before him, trapped in the rubble of what once had been tall buildings. Women grabbed onto their former lovers, bloodied and crying their eyes out. Children cried with them. Dirt and blood were caked everywhere. Some had missing limbs. The devastation could pierce through anyone with a soul.

Was this what God meant when he said he'd bring peace to all? Would those who converted outweigh the cost of life here? For the first time in Drin's life, he wasn't sure.

A slap jolted his shoulder, the clang of armor on armor ringing through the air. "Hey, buddy. Let's keep going. Gotta wipe out the rest of these Sekaran scum so the missionary teams can come and rebuild," said Jellal, a Templar who had been raised as an apprentice knight along with him. Anyone who had an aptitude to control the nanites was plucked away from their parents at an early age, sent to seminary and knight-training. Control of the little machines required an incredible mental aptitude as well as physical prowess. Those who couldn't control them succumbed to the machines and died horrific deaths. Drin had never seen such a case, but he had heard of them.

"I'm coming," Drin said, his voice shaking despite himself.

"Good. Scout units say there's a platoon of them up ahead," Jellal said. He formed a light sword in his hand. From hilt to blade, it pulsed with energy and would be deadly to the touch. "I look forward to severing a few of their heathen heads."

"God protect us," Drin said. He concentrated and formed his own light sword with the nanites' assistance. They projected energy and also drew in heat and sunlight from the world around him. His stores were full. He was ready for action.

Several of the Templars pressed forward, using boosts from their suits to leap over piles of rubble, speeding toward the purported Sekaran army holdouts. This dropship and a dozen others like it would secure what was left of the big cities on the Nemayr colony world. The world had been held by Sekarans for more than two hundred years. It would finally be restored to balance with its people learning to worship the one true God.

Drin followed the others, charging and leaping over piles of rubble that had once been buildings. He recalled playing a hopping game as a child. What had it been called? An odd thing to think of in the middle of combat. Twelve Square. That was the name of the game. Each square represented one of the twelve tribes of Eloria. The adults at seminary encouraged the game as a way for the young Templars-in-training to memorize their history and heritage. The kids enjoyed it because hopping from square to square proved challenging. It was only a meter or so at a time between those squares, but Drin recalled failing more often than not. As an adult with nanites, he didn't even strain himself as he stepped over twenty times those distances.

"Woo!" Jellal shouted ahead of him. His friend had far too much fun with this. Just like a child, he thought of these battles as a game.

Drin had seen enough death to never consider warfare a game. They had a sacred duty to perform. Glory would come later, but it would hurt in the present. That was the way it should be. And even though holy war was not considered murder under doctrine, Drin would seek confession from Father Cline and ask forgiveness for each and every life he took. Assuming he survived the battle.

The Templars bounded into one of the few standing sections of the formerly great city. The scenery had gone from rubble to intact buildings, though these had their windows blown out from the blasts. Glass shards lingered everywhere on the streets.

Drin slowed his step, watching the others as they moved forward. Some had assault rifles on their shoulders, others held their light swords. Primary weapons were ordained, not used by chance. Drin's proficiency with a light sword meant he would have to move to the front line before they engaged the enemy.

A rumbling came from a block away. The Sekarans came flooding around the corner. They cheered and shouted in their own language, invoking their own false god as surely as Drin and the others invoked the true God.

Faith brought strength. Faith brought victory. Couldn't the Sekarans see the folly in their ways?

They would once the Templars made them.

With a deep breath, Drin charged. Several of the other Templars moved with him. Their paces matched each other perfectly as a refined unit. They had equal space between them, packed tightly enough that an enemy wouldn't slip through their ranks without meeting a light sword's blade. The Sekarans, by contrast, were disorganized, untrained. While they had superior numbers, they didn't have the mental faculty or the discipline. The warlords and battlemages used these poor men as pawns in service to them, nothing more.

The Sekarans opened fire with their laser-repeaters. Small beams of light and energy pelted the charging Templars. The armor adjusted for the weapons' frequencies and provided adequate shielding. All it would do was drain a little bit of their energy. That could prove dangerous over time, which was why Drin moved in for a swift kill.

He leapt into the air, rising far above the cluster of Sekarans. Some raised their laser-repeaters to fire on him, but others concentrated on the rest of the group. The move served to split their weapons' fire. He landed in the middle of the enemy and spun around. His movements were fluid like a dance. The twirl of his light sword severed the heads of a dozen Sekarans with one stroke. Their screams of pain blended into one senseless cry as their bodies hit the ground.

The action disrupted their ranks and caused the remaining Sekarans to spread out. One shouted something, a phrase Drin recognized. "Focus fire!" He'd heard it before. It was the only way their laser-repeaters would be effective against a Templar. They didn't focus on him, however. They focused on Jellal.

The other Templars cut through the Sekarans, but even as they made progress, another wave of enemy soldiers spilled around the corner. Some threw rocks, but most had more traditional energy swords with metal hilts. Electric charges sizzled as their blades met with the fluid energy of the Templars' light swords.

A shock stick pierced the armor of another member of his unit. Drin tried to cut his way through the Sekaran soldiers to get to him, but by the time he arrived, the Templar's nanites flickered out, leaving a naked man to get stabbed, kicked, and beaten to death by the mob of Sekarans. Drin chopped at the assailants with his light sword, but his brother had already lost his life. When he finally came to the body, he saw it was Antun. He muttered a prayer for the man's soul.

Anger welled in Drin. One of the faithful had been killed. At least he had died in God's service, but it didn't take away the sting. Drin growled in a guttural rage.

Even though they had taken down one of the Templars, the Sekarans weren't equipped to fight them. They were just fodder, sacrificing themselves to slow down Drin and the others. He knew what was to come. They were being softened up for the real battle.

Drin pushed forward, even though he had doubts. He was in the midst of the fight. There was nothing he could change. He rounded a street corner and, this time, the Sekarans ran from him. Drin gave chase, using his armor to leap beyond the fleeing enemy. He passed them, sliding in the dirt street to halt his advance and cut them off.

Fear filled the eyes of one of the Sekarans before him. The man had no weapon, nothing that could put up a true fight against Drin. But he had been part of the horde in resistance against the Templars. It was his choice. He could have laid down his arms before, repented, and accepted the mercy of the missionaries to follow. Instead, he chose death in the name of his false god.

"*Eltu enswa,*" the Sekaran muttered, and then said it again. *My God will fell my foes.* It wasn't so different from the Templars' battle cry.

Drin hesitated. He should strike down this heathen. But he couldn't. Not a disarmed man who shivered in fear and called out for his god. What would be the point? "Go. The true God will have mercy on you. Repent and you'll be saved," Drin said.

The shaking Sekaran stared at him as if unsure. He likely didn't understand the Elorian language, but he certainly understood he'd been spared. He took off running in the opposite direction.

"You spared one of the faithful. Perhaps Eltu will show you compassion in the next life." A deep voice, speaking in Drin's language, came from behind him.

Drin spun. A battlemage loomed before him, the most dangerous of all the Sekarans. These were the ones who led the holy war against the Elorians, driving his people from their own world in ancient times. They had their own techno-magic, a Sekaran counter to the strength of the Templars.

The battlemage didn't look to have any armor. His eyes were dark, without pupils, as the foul magic he wielded consumed everything about him, to the loss of his eyes and his soul. He had no hair, head shaved as some sort of sacrifice to Eltu. The metallic implant above his right eye bestowed the battlemage with his powers. He wore long, purple robes, with a repeating design of a star, and a long V drawn down the back—the symbol of his false god.

Drin wouldn't cower in fear. He willed his nanites to change his light sword into a burst of energy. He pushed his hands forward to direct the energy. Bright and deadly light shot from his hands toward the battlemage.

The light spread across some invisible shield in front of him. The attack dissipated. The nanites reformed into their little metal components, dropping to the ground as if they had been poured out of a salt shaker. The battlemage grinned. "Your powers are nothing. Your God has failed you," the battlemage said. "You should have learned your faith meant nothing when you lost Eloria to my people. The rest of the galaxy will soon follow, but you won't be here to see it."

The battlemage conjured his own energy, a blue ball that grew in his hands. He waved his arm and it pushed forward like a wave.

Drin braced himself, willing his energy shield to strengthen. The wave hit him, causing him to stumble back. His energy field held. No damage. He pushed forward, but as he did, his energy monitor blinked in his visor. The nanites' energy drained. Ninety percent. Eighty. Seventy. It kept going down. The attack had an effect after all. This was a magic he hadn't encountered before. Drin's armor flickered into nothingness, leaving him naked.

The battlemage grinned. He stepped forward casually, as if about to greet a friend. When he came close, he reached out and grabbed Drin by the neck. The Sekaran pulled him in close to where they were face to face. "The superiority of Eltu's warriors will be the last thing you remember, infidel."

Drin squirmed. He tried to strike at the battlemage, but an invisible shield stopped him. He hadn't been prepared for the spell that drained his nanites, and he was going to die because of it. *Please, forgive my sins. I pray my fight has been pleasing to you, o' Lord.* He hoped his life hadn't been wasted.

Another ball of energy formed in the battlemage's free hand. It grew in both size and brightness until it became a force large enough to knock Drin's head clear from his body. The battlemage cocked his arm back.

Then the battlemage gasped for air. His grip around Drin's neck went slack. The ball of energy dissipated in his hand. He fell to the ground.

Drin fell as well. His knees slammed on the hard dirt. Without the armor, it hurt, but not as badly as it would have if he had been hit. He looked up.

Jellal stood less than a meter behind the battlemage, with a Sekaran laser-repeater in his hands. With the battlemage distracted by Drin, he'd been defenseless against an assault from behind. Jellal moved forward and kicked at the battlemage's body. It didn't move. "You have to be more careful against battlemages, brother," Jellal said. "Head-on assaults rarely work in our favor." He offered his hand to Drin.

"Thanks," Drin said. He took Jellal's hand and struggled to his feet.

The street in front of them was clear of Sekaran soldiers. Bodies littered the road ahead. Dust still filled the air from the orbital assault. "The *Justicar* reports the sector is secure. This battlemage was going to be their last hope. Good work distracting him," Jellal said. "It's ready for the rebuilding missionary team. We won. Glory be to God."

"Glory be to God," Drin said, still in a daze. He'd almost died. And for this? He wished he believed the words he just said.

TWO

DEKLYN'S CAPITAL CITY OF PYUS STRETCHED INTO THE FORESTS of the central continent as far as the eye could see, as did the centuries-old trees that covered the entire region. Even from Anais's balcony in her family's company palace far above the tree line, she could see little but the lights trickling through the leaves of the tree-tops. A few buildings jutted from between the trees, but nothing coming close to the way the palace loomed over everything.

They had codes, which stated no building could stand taller than the palace. It came from the rules of Deklyn's planet-wide kingdom, meant as a symbol of the merchant-lord's power. That symbol meant nothing in the age of space travel. It was antiquated and idiotic, just as many of the rules governing her life. How much better could they serve the population if they allowed more upward building?

Anais sighed as she watched a shuttle launch from the clearing at the edge of the horizon. She could see the transport's lights flicker in the distance as it disappeared into the atmosphere. Many a time had she seen transports take off, and just as many she'd wished she could be on one to see what it was like among the stars. Her people never left their world.

She turned back into her room, a spacious cell, but still a prison in many ways. Lush silks adorned her bedposts and fluffy pillows covered the bed itself, which was carved from the finest emberwood in the local forest. She even had a personal terminal for virtual reality games and communication, a luxury few could afford. Still she felt trapped.

A full length mirror was opposite her balcony, and she stared into it. White fur covered her face, unblemished and with consistent coloration. It made her blue eyes stand out, giving her an innocent quality she often used to get into dance clubs without paying. A pink dress came down just above her knees, accentuating her curves perfectly. It had better, with how much it had cost. Her legs were long and slender, though she still didn't think she was quite as pretty as her best friend. *Speaking of whom...*

"Computer, call Lyssa," Anais said.

She waited as her comm unit tried to connect with her friend.

"Hey," Lyssa's voice came through her room's speakers, audio only.

"We still going to sneak out tonight? We can go dancing down at Shimmies Club." Anais asked.

"You have to give me a couple of hours. My parents have people over and they're still here."

"It won't even be worth the cover credits if we go that late."

"I'm trying, okay?" Lyssa laughed. "You're always in a rush and on the move, aren't you?"

"You know me," Anais said cheerfully.

"I'll call back in a bit. Don't leave without me."

"I won't."

With a *bleep*, the comm signal clicked off.

Anais sighed. She really should be more careful about sneaking out like this. Though she was not a direct line for inheriting the family company, there was still a need for security. Often in Deklyn's history, where members of the most powerful merchant-lord's family had been used in hostage situations, things had ended very badly for the royal merchants. But times had changed, hadn't they?

What could she do? Her long ears twitched in irritation. She flopped face-first into a giant body pillow on her bed. There were the games on her tablet, but none of that sounded appealing. Why was everything so boring?

Her keen hearing picked up the sound of hurried footsteps outside her door, down the hallway. Who could be coming her way at this hour?

Someone kicked the door in. Anais screamed and clutched at her pillow, as if that would provide any semblance of defense. Four men holding guns burst through the doors. These weren't Deklyns. They didn't have the long ears or thin eyes with large pupils that her people did. They wore armor and helmets, but the designs wouldn't accommodate such features. The shields over their faces revealed beady red eyes and pale yellowish skin. She'd seen this race before in her schooling vids. These were Sekarans. But what were they doing here?

"Hands up. Get off the bed," one of the Sekarans commanded her in his language, something she had learned as part of her schooling for trade negotiations.

Anais clutched at her pillow even more tightly, digging her nails into it. This couldn't be happening. Where was the palace guard?

As if understanding she wasn't about to comply, the other men pressed forward. They grabbed her by the arms.

Anais kicked at them, squirming as much as she could. She screamed at the top of her lungs, over and over, until one of the Sekarans ripped some of the silk lining off of her bedpost to tie it tightly around her mouth and gag her. She still screamed into it, but found that the energy she was expending quickly outweighed the small amount of noise she made.

The men moved her out the door of her room and into the hall. What she saw made her eyes go wide. The entire palace was filled with these Sekaran soldiers. How had they all arrived here so fast and without alerting anyone? Where was the rest of her family?

The lead Sekaran met up with another. "Is the palace secure? Are there any others?"

"A few women to take back home. Many fine jewels. The sheikh will be pleased." He gave a leering glance over Anais. "Very pleased. This one he may even take as a wife."

The leader laughed. "We'll see about that. Perhaps I'll be granted a promotion and be allowed to take one of my own!"

Anais squirmed again, trying to shake herself free from the invaders. When she did, she caught a view further down the hall. The palace guards had all been killed, their bodies piled on the floor, blood splattered along the walls and tapestries. Horror filled her. She wanted to vomit. She didn't know which person was which, but she thought of Tyrin, her personal guard, and the two young gentlemen at the stairs, who had always complimented her on how pretty she was. She'd never hear from them again.

Then it really struck her. What happened to her father, mother, and brothers? Were they bound like her? It sounded like she was some sort of prize to be won rather than a simple hostage. What did that mean for the others?

"Can someone help me with this one? She's feisty as all get out," one of the Sekarans said.

She had to escape, had to find help somewhere. She broke from the Sekaran's grip and stumbled onto the floor.

When she looked up, another guard smacked her in the skull with the butt of his laser-repeater. The world spun and blinked out.

WHEN ANAIS AWOKE, it was cold. She was on a floor of some kind, metal or tile, it was hard to tell, but it wasn't comfortable in the least. Her head throbbed. She probably needed a medic. Would she have a concussion? She at least seemed to be able to think.

She groaned, turning to her side, her muscles stiff from being left so long in an awkward position in such an uncomfortable space. The lights were low but it wasn't too dark. The room was bare, industrial in appearance. Some lights blinked on a panel on the far end of the room, but it was impossible to tell where she was. It certainly wasn't the palace.

The gag still held in place in her mouth. Her hands were bound behind her back, limiting her movement.

A large circular door made a mechanical groan as it opened, revealing two Sekaran soldiers. "That was almost too easy," one Sekaran said.

"They never saw it coming," the other said. "I came on a merchant transport. You?"

"Same, three months ago. Fifteen in our group."

"Twenty in mine. My commander said we had more than twice the amount of troops as these soft traders do by the time we arrived." He laughed.

"Look at what we have here," the first said, trudging toward her. His heavy soldier boots pounded on the floor, reverberating where her head hurt the most with each step. "Damn. She's a fine one."

"Yes, she is," the second said, circling around the other side of her. "Forty like her would be a fine reward for our service when we reach the Prophet's gardens."

"That's only for martyrs," the first said. "If we aren't able to die in battle, we won't get anything of the sort." He ran the toe of his boot up Anais's leg, which pushed the fabric of her dress upward to expose her thigh. Her fur stood on edge. "That's why I think it's best to take what we can get now. Shut the door behind us."

It dawned on her exactly what they were talking about. No, this couldn't be happening. Anais thrashed about, trying to loosen her bonds any way she could. Why her? What had she ever done to deserve this?

The second Sekaran looked annoyed, impatiently moving back to the door and hitting the flashing lights to close it again behind him.

The first reached down and ran his hand up her calf and over her thigh. His skin was thick, calloused, and sweaty. It felt disgusting to the touch.

Anais kicked at him, connecting with his gut.

The Sekaran stumbled backward and laughed. "Looks like we're going to have to hold her down after all. You hold her first."

"Why do you get to go first?" the other Sekaran protested.

Anais couldn't even fathom how disgusting this conversation was. How could they be talking about another person in this way? This was impossible. It had to be a nightmare. She had to wake up. Someone would come and help her. They couldn't have taken out all of her family's guards. She pushed her feet on the cold floor, sliding her body away from them. It burned where her body dragged, but it would be worse to be closer to those disgusting creeps.

"Stop arguing. We don't have a lot of time," the first Sekaran said. He righted himself and scrambled after her. It was as if her fear made him more voracious. He grinned, chuckling at her helplessness. He caught her by the ankle and dragged her to him. "Now, stop fighting, honey. It'll be a lot easier for you if you just have fun, too."

The second moved over from the door. "Fine. What do you want me to do?"

"Hold her shoulders and head down," the first commanded.

The second Sekaran put his big hands on her, too strong for her to resist. She was stuck. The first pinned her legs down with his own. Her arms were still bound. Her weight nearly crushed her hands under her. It hurt almost as bad as her headache. There was nothing she was going to be able to do. She made one last struggle, trying to push the Sekarans off of her with every ounce of strength she had, but the Sekarans were too big, too strong. Any movement was futile.

She resigned herself to them, slumping her shoulders. They would take what they wanted. It didn't matter. Tears streaked down her face. Her lips quivered.

"That's better," the first Sekaran said. His hand moved up her thigh, all too close to her private parts.

Anais closed her eyes.

The sound of the door opening came again.

"The hell," the first Sekaran said, surprise in his voice.

The second lifted his hands off her shoulders. "No one's supposed to be here. It's late shift," he said.

The Sekaran commander stood at the door. He looked none too pleased. He had no helmet, but his rank markings on his armor were ones Anais clearly remembered. He had a laser-repeater in his hands, pointing it at his soldiers. "Fools!"

"Sir!" the two Sekarans inside said. They moved away from her as quickly as they had come upon her, standing at attention.

Anais couldn't believe it. Had she been saved?

"This is the sheikh's property. You would dare defile it?"

"We were just checking on the prisoner," the first Sekaran said.

"You know the rules. The prize of the hunt is always returned to the sheikh. He will get first bid on her before the other nobility can take her. If she is no longer a virgin, she'll be worthless. Why would you ruin this property?"

"That's not—"

"Silence!"

The room echoed with that word, and the two guards said nothing.

"I cannot have this kind of insubordination within our unit. You both are a disgrace to Eltu," the Sekaran commander said. He quickly aimed his laser-repeater at one of them and fired.

The Sekaran's head blasted to bits. His body convulsed a few times and collapsed on the floor.

The second Sekaran attempted to run toward the commander, as if to try to fight him. Before he made it halfway across the room, three laser bolts vaporized his torso. The rest of him fell to the floor. His body smoked, smoldering from the damage done. The burning flesh smell made Anais gag.

The commander shook his head, lowering his weapon. He moved and kicked at his soldiers' bodies, ensuring they were dead. He paid her no heed. Why would he? As he had said, she was property. As much as the two men had just frightened her, the worst might be yet to come.

"Eltu bless them. Lead them to the next life. Give them the reward for their service," the commander said. He reached for a comm device on his belt, unhooking it, and speaking into its mic. "Ry'ik here. We have two dead in cargo bay four. Will need clean up and disposal."

He stopped to look at her, frowned, and then spun on his heels and left again.

Anais sat there in shock for a long moment, staring at the dead bodies in front of her. She couldn't believe what had just transpired. The pure disregard the commander had for his own men's lives was almost more horrific than what they'd been about to do to her. The Sekarans were a cruel and terrible people. And she was going to be a slave to one of them.

She curled up on the floor and sobbed until no more tears would come.

THREE

DRIN WOKE IN A COLD SWEAT, SITTING UP AS FAST AS HE COULD. He'd had nightmares of the battlemage again—the third time since the *Justicar* descended on Nemayr. Each night, the dreams became more vivid and more destructive. This time, the battlemage in his dream had a light sword to his throat, singeing the skin. Drin could recall the smell of burning flesh as if it were real. He reached for his throat and found nothing but stubble from not having shaved in a couple of days.

The quarters were dark, shared with three other Templars. A small light in between the bunk beds kept it from being completely pitch black. None of the other three stirred. None had the same problems with sleep that plagued him.

When he'd returned from Nemayr, Drin went to see Father Cline, both to confess his sins and to assure himself that he truly was doing God's will in his fight. Thinking of how easily he'd slaughtered so many Sekarans in his last battle rattled him. It never had in the past. He couldn't explain what had changed in him. Perhaps it was seeing so much devastation, so many helpless men, all willing to go to their deaths in order to slow him down. They had no hope of defeating him, but they fought hard all the same.

Father Cline told him that it was God's will. The only way to ensure Yezuah's triumphant return to rule over the galaxy would be for His soldiers to make disciples of all worlds. They had to prepare the way before they could reclaim Eloria for his glory. Without fighters like Drin, the universe would never see God's desired plan.

But why did it feel so wrong?

Drin slid his feet back over the bedside, letting them dangle for a while before slipping down from the top bunk. He wore a long nightgown, but the nanites still pulsed through his blood. They could create a façade of clothing or armor, which left him no need for any form of material possessions. It was why the Templars shared rooms with the others. First, their shared space reminded them they were there to sacrifice everything, to not focus on the physical but the spiritual. Their fellowship in close quarters was pleasing to God, or so Drin had been taught from a young age. Second, it provided accountability. It was harder to sin when three other strong Elorian men were present at all times.

Baifed stirred from the bottom bunk. He sat up quickly when he saw Drin's dangling legs. "Drin," he whispered. "You shouldn't be up past curfew, scaring people in the dark. You're going to get yourself hurt."

"Sorry," Drin whispered back. With his bunkmate awake, he slid down to the floor, doing his best to remain quiet. "I can't sleep. Nightmares again. Was thinking of taking a lap around the ship."

"You need to get your rest. Big day of training tomorrow. Sparring tests."

Sparring tests were physically demanding, pitting the Templars in combat with one another for a full day. Last time, Drin's muscles had ached for days. He could barely walk from the strain. It was better than getting injured, but he still hated those days. "Thanks for the reminder. Maybe a jog will wear me out enough to sleep."

"Suit yourself. Just be quiet on your way back," Baifed said. He laid back down and put his pillow over his head.

Drin stepped carefully until he reached the door, not wanting to make more sound and wake up the others in the room. He tapped the control to open it, shielding his eyes from the bright hallway. When he stepped into the corridor, it was empty, eerie, with only the hum of the ship's engines in the background. Suddenly aware of the fact that he still wore his nightgown, Drin summoned his nanites to form his suit of battle armor around him.

The nanites swirled, and soon, his body was covered in a way that felt more proper for being outside of his bunk. But he still didn't feel comfortable. His face dripped with sweat, still rattled from the nightmare.

Once in the empty corridor, Drin ran.

He ran hard, as if it were a part of a battle readiness drill or formal workout. He ran from all of his frustration, his anger, his hate for all of the destruction the Templars caused in their holy crusade. Could it be that what they were doing was truly an affront to God rather than something that was right?

Drin didn't know what to think anymore. But he knew he needed a change. Once out of breath, he stopped, doubling over to get himself the oxygen he needed. The running relieved his stress to some degree, but most of his doubts and fears still remained.

What were his options? He glanced around to get his bearings. A large set of double doors stood before him. He'd stopped right outside the drop shuttle bay. Was this a sign from God? Did he need to leave the *Justicar* to find peace? The ship was in hyperspace. It would be dangerous to take a fighter or drop shuttle. More dangerous when the others caught wind of his treachery and followed him. Traitors were executed. There could be no dissent in the ranks of the holy.

Leaving would be crazy but, for some reason, the thought compelled him. He couldn't stop thinking about it. What if God's will for him was to leave this life, enact a change that started inside? The holy book did speak of changing the way of the warriors to one of peace. Yezuah himself ended the fighting on Eloria so long ago. But it didn't necessarily mean the passage applied to his personal situation. Drin needed space to think.

He scanned the corridor. No one was around. It was far too early in the morning. There would be a skeleton crew monitoring crucial systems but everyone else would be peacefully asleep in their bunks. At worst, should he decide to flee the ship, he would have one tech to deal with in the shuttle bay.

But could he do it? Could he exit the ship and abandon the way of life he'd lived since his youth? A sinking feeling overwhelmed him. On the other hand, he had been trained to be decisive. Templars had no choice but to act in the moment, go with instincts that were given by God. There were stories in the holy book about men who felt called, who were too scared to heed that call and ended up punished for it. Could this be one of those moments?

Drin frowned at the shuttle bay doors. He searched his heart. The mental images of killing Sekarans filled his mind again. They'd had no chance against him. There was no way such disproportionate force could be right. He bit his lip and entered the shuttle bay.

The bay was huge. He'd been in here several times before, marching into one of the many troop transport dropships deployed on missions to Sekaran worlds. The bay also held more than two dozen vipers, fighters the Templars used for space combat. It was easier to launch one of those small ships. A viper would also be a little harder to strike than a dropship, with such a small surface area to hit. If he were going to depart on his own, that's what he'd have to fly.

His piloting skills were adequate, but he'd never attempted to take off with the *Justicar* in FTL. He would have to rely on God to keep him safe.

"Templar?" asked a voice from further down the shuttle bay. A maintenance tech in grease-stained coveralls poked his head out from behind one of the dropships. "There's no drop scheduled. What are you doing here?"

Drin had to think of an excuse for being here. Not that the standard ship crew questioned the Templars. Although he held no official rank above the ship's crew, the maintenance staff treated Drin and the others as if they deserved reverence. "I require a viper," Drin said cautiously. Lying wouldn't be a good start to this call if it were something he needed to do for faith. He was glad not to have to.

"We're in hyperspace still. I wouldn't recommend launching—"

"It's important," Drin said.

Disbelief fell upon the tech's face. He glanced back to the fighters behind him. "We didn't really use fighters in the Nemayr assault. All of them are fully fueled and ready to go."

"Good. Then you can direct me to one," Drin said, trying to sound adamant. Was this even the right choice? In a lot of ways, it was stupid. This all came too fast. But then, life hit the great prophets just as fast when they were summoned by the Lord. He recalled the story of the prophet Affed. God woke the man in the middle of the night with an earthquake and made him pack up and leave his land. Though Drin had a bad dream about battlemages, he was faced with very similar signs and portents.

"I should probably contact the commander," the tech said.

"The commander is sleeping. Please. I have a message to deliver." A message of what? And to whom? That was the question. He needed some time to think was more of the truth. He silently prayed forgiveness for his small lie.

The tech considered another moment and then nodded to himself. "Okay, this way. You can take *XG-3*," he said.

At the rate fighters were destroyed in combat, most weren't given names, but a number to signify them, identified by their mothership if in a full fleet battle. The viper in question would be fully identified as the *Justicar XG-3*. Drin grunted his agreement to the young man and motioned for him to lead.

The tech led him to a nearby viper and brought Drin a ladder to assist him into the cockpit. He'd half-worried he would have to knock the tech out to be able to depart safely. It made him feel better not to have to resort to violence.

Drin secured himself inside the cockpit. The controls rested in front of him—a small touchscreen and two joysticks in an otherwise automated set up. Each joystick had buttons for laser fire and, together, they allowed movement in three dimensions.

The cockpit lid shut, hissing as it pressurized. Drin willed his armor suit to form a helmet, adding another layer of pressurization in case something went wrong. Most pilots used special flight suits, but Drin's armor could take care of a number of matters ordinary people required special equipment for. He touched the screen, opening a comm link back to the tech. "Ready to launch."

The tech jogged out of the area and into the launch control room. "Bay doors opening. Maintenance forcefield engaged. Bay is depressurizing. Engaging the sling for a launch in five, four, three, two..."

The XG-3 shot into space, a mass of colors in front of him. The whole universe looked like it was bursting apart at the seams. His heart thudded against his chest. In hyperspace, without clear trajectories, one could find oneself on the wrong side of an asteroid or space debris. The ship's shielding managed to deflect most foreign objects, but moving at these velocities with a random launch out the side of a bay didn't account for everything.

Hyperspace folded into the normal black of open vacuum. Drin moved at normal speeds, about a quarter of light speed. Vipers could jump to hyperspace in a pinch, but only for short jaunts at a time, and only two or three times before having to return to refuel. A lack of fuel was another gamble Drin hadn't considered in this half-cocked plan. Perhaps he should have taken more time to think about this after all. Regret for his decision set on his heart. The silence of space provided him no comfort.

In a fighter, he wouldn't have much of a way to obscure his trail. If the Justicar wanted to find him, it would. At the very least, he would have to land somewhere to disable the tracker installed at the rear of every Elorian craft.

"Computer, scan the system. Where are we? Are there any habitable planets?"

The display screen lit with a special map and information. They were in the Konsin system. Five planets, the second of which was in the habitable zone. It had a large amount of desert and wasn't considered one of the most pleasant worlds to reside on, but the areas in the extreme northern and southern bands had substantive vegetation. They were considered some of the best agricultural growing zones of the galaxy. The exports listed on the screen didn't concern Drin. He could hardly care, as long as he had somewhere he could land and stay away from his Elorian masters.

He was on the outskirts of the system now. A couple of micro-jumps could get him there within hours.

Before he could move his accelerator joystick, the *Justicar* jumped into the system. A red light flashed on his screen: an incoming emergency message.

"Computer, play on audio," Drin said.

"Templar Drin. You have illegally stolen church property in viper fighter *XG-3*. Return immediately to our bay. Confess your sins and explain yourself."

A squadron of fighters poured out of the *Justicar's* shuttle bay, heading toward Drin.

At this point, it was too late. He'd gone too far to be allowed to return without severe repercussions. Drin leaned into the joysticks, shooting his vessel forward. The stars turned to a blur behind him. He hadn't made precise calculations, but he didn't have time for anything more. The *Justicar* followed.

"If you will not comply, we will disable you. Stand down, Templar," came the voice of the *Justicar's* conn officer through his comm unit.

Drin rushed toward the planet. His only hope would be to land there. The *Justicar* would be able to follow him otherwise. Konsin II had a burnt red-orange hue, with green bands around it, just as the computer had described. He guided his viper directly toward the planet.

The planet spun slowly but wrapping around the eastern side

came two capital vessels. Their looming designs jolted Drin to his core. He'd seen them many times: Sekarans.

Drin jerked on the controls, pushing his viper to a trajectory that would take him to the right and above their plane. There was nowhere for him to run. He was trapped between his own people and the enemy.

A volley of laser fire came from the Sekaran ships.

They could hardly target Drin from this distance. The bolts shot past him, toward the *Justicar* and its deployed fighters. His people returned fire, no longer focused on Drin.

With the Elorian comm channel still open, Drin could hear the *Justicar*'s conn officer barking orders to his fighters. "We're not prepared for a fight against two Sekaran dreadnaughts. Fighters pull back. Leave Templar Drin to meet his fate for betraying God."

Betraying God.

Those words stung. He wanted to speak into the comm and contest those words, but it wouldn't do any good. The whole reason he was out here was that he trusted God and wanted to do more to follow a new path the Lord provided him. It had to be better than to continue endless missions of slaying people, even if they were foreign heretics.

Drin hit the accelerator again. His only chance of survival was to get to the planet and get off this ship. It was good his people followed him and provided a distraction. He'd have to hope the Sekaran dreadnaughts would ignore the lone fighter and pursue the *Justicar* long enough for him to hide. No, he wouldn't just hope. Drin mouthed a silent prayer. *Lord, if this truly be your will, keep me from harm so that I might serve you.*

The planet grew in front of him, soon filling his vision from the cockpit. The Sekaran ships ignored Drin just as he'd hoped, pursuing the larger vessel and its squadron of fighters. They continued their barrage of laser fire as they advanced in what appeared to be slow motion, the capital ships dwarfing the fighters with their hulking size.

Something struck his viper. It should have been impossible at this range, with the Sekaran ships behind him, but a stray laser bolt must have come from the *Justicar's* fighters. Impossible odds or not, he'd been hit, and his console flashed red. The *XG-3* flashed a code for systems trouble. Its engines were failing.

Instead of a smooth transition into the atmosphere, Drin shook at the full resistance of going from vacuum to the thick atmosphere. Konsin II had a windy climate in the upper atmosphere, which didn't help as his fighter was thrown by several meters in his descent. The viper shook and rocked through the air as he futilely tried to regain control.

Worse was the heat from the reentry. He barely noticed it at first, his nanite armor protecting him from the onset, but something must have gone wrong with his viper's shielding. The whole front of the craft heated to a reddish color, as if he had entered metal into a forge. This was bad. He'd taken the wrong trajectory, perhaps an even worse error than not having planned a proper hyperspace departure.

He prayed again. Even though he might be asking God for too much, surely if this was His will, Drin could yet survive this hardship. Sweat poured down his cheeks. The flight controls became hot to the touch. The fighter wouldn't be able to take much more punishment.

He pierced through the upper atmosphere and into the clouds. The *XG-3* cooled as quickly as it had heated. But the controls were dead. Down he went, far too fast for a safe landing. He slammed his fists into his joysticks, which seemed to reactivate them. Desperately, he tried to pull the ship's nose up, which worked to a small degree, but the ship still fell far too fast. He had to hope for a flat landing somewhere.

The landscape ahead had a few mountains, rocky and desert with a full spectrum of different red and orange colors to it. It would have been breathtaking if he could have concentrated on the view. He looked for somewhere he could let the craft drag and not get killed from hitting something in the process.

Drin turned hard to the right, spotting a flat area in the desert. He passed a few huts and buildings before passing into a view of nothing but open desert sand. This was where he would land.

The fighter hit the ground in a loud *crash*. It slid across the sand, dragging across the desert on its side, kicking up more dust than he'd seen in the aftermath of explosions of the Nemayr invasion. His cockpit clouded with dirt, making it impossible to see. The windshield cracked.

Drin held on for dear life.

FOUR

Sᴡᴇᴀᴛ ᴄᴏᴠᴇʀᴇᴅ Aɴᴀɪs ᴡʜᴇɴ sʜᴇ ɴᴇxᴛ ᴀᴡᴏᴋᴇ, ᴍᴀᴛᴛɪɴɢ ʜᴇʀ fur in the most uncomfortable manner. A sandy fabric clung to her. Even with her sweat, the heat made her want to crawl out of her skin. How did it get so hot? She opened her eyes.

As before, she was on a floor, but this was certainly no longer the cargo hold of a transport vessel. The floor was rough compared to the smooth surfaces she had once been on. It was made of stone, and the walls were some sort of plaster. It looked almost unfinished. Everything around was dirty, worn, and dusty. Up about six meters in height hung a few slotted windows, allowing soft light to trickle into the room.

When her head unclouded from the rough sleep, Anais noticed she wasn't the only person on the floor here. There were at least a dozen others locked in this room. All women.

The space had a wooden door on one end, no handle on this side. Each of the women wore a very thin garment that covered them neck to toe. The clothes were sheer, revealing the detailed curves of their bodies. She noted a couple of ear-lines of the other women. She appeared to be the only Deklyn among them, but several other species were present. All of them were beautiful in their own ways, fit and with curves in the right places.

The other women hadn't woken yet, still knocked out by whatever force or drug these barbarians had set upon them. Anais scooted herself into a seated position, bringing her knees to her chest. Someone had dressed her in the same garb as the others. The fabric itched, worsened by her sweat and her movement. It was so hot and stuffy. It was hard to breathe despite the open windows. She had to get out of here. The last few days of a nightmarish life kept getting worse.

Another woman stirred. She rubbed her eyes and sat up, looking directly at Anais. The fabric looked strange against her Elorian features of green-hued skin and blue-black hair, a mismatch to say the least. Even with looking out of place, the woman had an attractiveness about her that made Anais feel inadequate. Not that she wanted any of her captors to note her as one of the more attractive women here. Anais crossed her arms across her breasts.

"Deklyn?" The woman asked her, speaking in galactic common. "I didn't know many of you traveled outside your home system."

"We don't," Anais said softly.

Understanding grew in the other woman's face. "Ah. My condolences. Such is the way of the universe. It will not be forever, though. This is only temporary. My name is Tarryh."

"Anais," she replied. Were condolences supposed to make Anais feel better? She peeled her eyes from Tarryh and looked to the door. "We have to get out of here somehow. These men captured me, said something about being taken as a wife for a sheikh."

Tarryh chuckled. "I would make no sheikh's wife. To them, I have been used." She shrugged. "But you should know, there is no escape. This city, this entire world, is controlled by the Sekarans. You with your strange eyes and ears would stand out like a glo-rod in a dark cavern. The best you can do is comply with them and hope you, indeed, get paired with some nobility as a lesser wife. You can't guarantee you'll be treated well, but at least you'll have some comforts."

"I'm not going to be anyone's wife," Anais protested.

"You say this now, but you don't want to end up like me."

Anais opened her mouth to ask what she meant but closed it again.

"I've been traded and sold as a slave several times." Tarryh shook her head. "You're not from here. I know. My family sold me as a young girl. Sometimes, it must be done to survive. I understand. You will get used to it soon enough."

Anais frowned. The woman stopped talking, and a couple of the others woke. She couldn't let herself become anyone's slave, minor wife or no. The prospect sickened her. There had to be something she could do about her situation. If she had been taken to some distant world as Tarryh said, it made her situation worse. It meant none of her father's mercenary guard would be coming to save her any time soon. She didn't have any resources on her own. There had to be some hope, someone who cared.

Tarryh stood moved closer, draping an arm around her. She lightly rubbed Anais's shoulder. "There, there. It's not so bad. There are worse fates in this universe."

"I just want to be back home," Anais said in a manner that came out much more like whining than she'd intended. This woman had been sold multiple times as a slave, and yet Anais felt sorry for herself. Her lip quivered, and she sobbed, pulling her knees closer to her chest and dropping her head onto them. This wasn't fair.

She could hear some of the other women asking what was wrong with her. Tarryh waved them away, strangely protective.

Even though she didn't know this woman, having a friendly touch brought her some comfort. Being held by a friend was more than she'd had since she'd been captured. Her sobs lasted another few minutes until her eyes went dry again. She had to stop crying all the time. All she did was wear herself out, which would leave her in no position to take advantage of any escape opportunities. Even if Tarryh said it was impossible, she had to try. Which meant having the energy to seize the opportunity when the time came. With one more sniffle, Anais nodded to herself.

Before she could fully regain her resolve, the wood door creaked open, and then slammed against the back wall. Two Sekaran guards bounded in, wearing full armor and holding their laser-repeaters pointed toward the women slaves. Another Sekaran followed them, one without armor but wearing a long, flowing black cape.

The caped Sekaran surveyed the women. "All of you, it's time to get up. You'll need to wash your faces and your hands in the bowl outside. When you're done with that, you will line up single file and get yourselves ready."

Anais's ears grew hot. She wanted to claw at this man so badly, but doing so wouldn't end well. One of the guards narrowed his eyes on her as if sensing her violent thoughts. But who did this caped man think he was, to order her like she was livestock?

Tarryh must have noticed her rage. She squeezed Anais's shoulder as if trying to calm her or warn her.

"Well?" The caped Sekaran said, voice impatient. "Move it! The sheikh is waiting!"

FIVE

THE SHUTTLE SKIDDED TO A STOP. BY THE GRACE OF GOD, DRIN didn't crash against one of the hard rocks out in the sand. His body hurt, ached beyond anything he could have ever imagined. The harness had held him in but burned against his skin, rubbing through the fabric of his nanite-constructed flight suit. If Drin had concentrated harder, he could have had his armor protect him, but he had focused on the task at hand, setting down the viper and surviving the crash.

He was on the ground. Now what? Drin let out a breath as he considered what he'd do. He had to get out of this fighter, or the Sekarans would find him.

Drin pulled on a lever, manually popping the cockpit, opening his space to the air of this world. It was hot, stale, worse than the environmentally controlled fighter that he had been in, even with the life support mechanisms blown. This was what Sekaran worlds felt like. Oppressive. Hot. But coming here was his choice. He had to deal with it.

Pushing the top, Drin slipped out of the fighter. He plopped onto the sand, the grains of the earth below covering his toes when he landed. What was his best course of action? God would have to provide for him. Drin closed his eyes and prayed. Which way should he go? Where did God want to lead him?

Keeping his eyes closed, Drin walked, leaving behind his downed fighter. He would have to give up the relative comforts of the Elorian Templar fleet. Until now, standing under a beating sun, walking through the hot sands alone, he hadn't considered how blessed his life had been. The scriptures had always told him to be grateful, but it took leaving comfort to understand what those words meant. His mouth already felt dry after a few steps. Would he even survive?

Drin kept walking, spending hours traversing the sands until they turned into hills, and then grasses. It was still hot, but the scenery changed rapidly. Perhaps he wasn't as lost as he had thought. But still, he found no water, only more land. In the distance, Drin saw what he thought was a fence. He squinted to make sure. Was that a settlement? It was hard to tell in the unending daytime heat.

He pressed forward, even though his body screamed at him to stop. The alternative was to lie down and die. He couldn't allow that, not now, not after all he'd given up getting here.

As he moved closer, Drin saw he had been correct in his assessment that a fence lay ahead. It was wooden, erected several years ago by the looks of it. Beyond the fence lay tall grasses with domesticated animals, ones he didn't recognize, having never been on this planet before. The large creatures browsed on those grasses. Past the grazing animals was a small pond, almost brown in color, where other animals drank. They seemed so peaceful. Drin squinted and looked further. He saw some buildings. A farm?

Drin jogged toward the fence and put his foot up on the bottom plank so he could hop it. It felt freeing to get out of the desert. Perhaps he would live after all.

He pressed forward, bringing his hand above his brow to shield his eyes from the sun. His calves ached, hamstrings protesting every step after the hours of trudging through the sands. He needed water but dared not drink that brown dreck the animals used. He was parched, his mouth so dry his tongue stuck to the roof of it.

Each step became harder. One after another. He had to focus to keep himself upright, even with his nanite assistance. They were drained from all the strain he'd placed on his body these last several hours. Was he being punished for his betrayal of his people? Drin's vision blurred. The animals around him seemed to mock him with the strange noises they made. But still, Drin refused to give up. Sweat dripped down his face, pouring into his eyes until he could no longer see.

His breath became labored. Heatstroke. It was too much for him. It would take more than just water to survive—shade was crucial as well. He smacked his lips, trying to get any moisture into his mouth, into his eyes.

"Mister?' A small boy stood in front of him, perhaps eight years old, dark hair flowing into his face. Where had the boy come from? Was he a hallucination?

"Water," was all Drin could mutter.

"I'll get you water, sir, hold on," the boy said. He ran away from Drin.

Drin reached out a hand, trying to stop the boy. *Don't leave me.* That's what he wanted to say, but couldn't. If he were to die, he didn't want to die alone. The world spun, blurred even further, and then went dark.

WHEN DRIN AWOKE, he was in a barn. Old wooden boards hung almost haphazardly to comprise the walls, with very little attention to detail or craftsmanship. Rays of light poked through holes where the wood had warped or rotted out. He lay sprawled out across some hay, with some domesticated animals situated nearby. Drin pushed one's face away from him.

"Pa, he's awake!" the boy shouted.

Drin recalled where he was. He'd left his ship and passed out just outside this boy's farm. The boy saw him and offered water, and that was the last thing Drin had remembered. He had a splitting headache, and he was still parched. How long had he been out? In this heat, even in the shelter of the barn, he could have dehydrated and died just as easily as he had woken again.

The boy offered him a canteen.

Drin grabbed it and drank, shaking as he poured it over himself, sucking in the water as if he might never taste a drop again. It spilled on his face and down his chest. The lukewarm liquid felt like it was heaven-sent.

An older Sekaran man came into the barn, towering over him. The man had a laser-repeater rifle in his hand. He pointed it directly at Drin. "What are you doing here, Elorian?"

Drin dropped the canteen. It clanked on the dirt beside his place in the hay. Instinctively, Drin formed a shield of energy around him. Orange light flickered where the nanites pushed to their maximum range.

Panic filled the man's eyes. He fired.

The burst of laser fizzled against the nanites' energy.

"Don't try to attack me, you'll just burn out your weapon," Drin said. He tried to maintain his calm, forcing himself to his feet. He kept his palms up toward these strangers to show he was no threat. "I'm not here to do you any harm."

The boy scurried behind his father, clutching at the man's leg. The older Sekaran kept the weapon fixed on Drin. His hands shook. "What do you want with us? We've heard stories about you from the sheikh."

The sheikh must have been their local leader. These people didn't look to be much of a threat. Just a man and his boy. Honest workers. The type of people the Templars brought torment to when they descended on worlds. Was it worth it to convert people living in such fear? Drin frowned. "I don't know. I was just trying to get someplace safe. I need shelter."

The older Sekaran laughed. "I never thought I'd hear that from an Elorian soldier-beast. You have your fancy technology that keeps you from having to do real work."

"I do real work," Drin said, crossing his arms.

"Like slaughtering my people?"

Drin frowned. "Those are not my ways. I wish to pursue peace."

"Those are words I never thought I'd hear an Elorian say."

"They are true."

Silence hung in the air. Drin's somber countenance must have moved the older Sekaran. The man inclined his head. "Hmph," the Sekaran said. He let his weapon fall to his side. "Eltu understands work and peace. If you prove yourself through real labor, you can stay awhile. You can sleep in the barn, and we'll feed you, but that's all. I won't be paying an Elorian. You're fortunate you came at a good time since harvest is just around the corner. If you can do some heavy lifting, we can come to an arrangement. Deal?"

Drin nodded. He wasn't sure what path this would take him, but this was obviously a sign from God. Instead of facing death, he'd found redemption. Someone was willing to provide him a livelihood. That was praiseworthy on its own.

A COUPLE of weeks went by. Drin worked as hard as he had promised, which his Sekaran host, Mohiel, took every opportunity to let him know was a surprise. The Sekarans had been taught since birth that Elorians were lazy heathens, something Drin quickly put to rest through his deeds. He maintained his prayers every night that God would let His will be done, guide him in his life. But he found himself unable to pursue much meaningful philosophy. Each day left him weary, after a full day's work of tilling fields, harvesting crops, and tending to animals.

Truth was, he didn't mind the work. It was relaxing. Mohiel, his wife Areya, and his son Yiv were all hospitable people. They prayed to their false god four times per day: once in the morning, once for lunch, once after the day's work, and once before bed. They always were down on their knees and recited the same chants. They told Drin that, while he resided in their house, he would be expected to join them, but Drin refused. He stepped outside during prayer time and watched the skyline.

Several days later, Drin still toiled in the fields under the hot sun. He had a long rake to pull weeds from the crops. Sweat dripped down his face and soaked his clothes. He'd considered removing the shirt the farmer had given him, but he wasn't sure if the gesture would offend Sekaran sensibilities. It might draw attention to have too much of his green skin showing out in the middle of mostly open space.

Yiv dashed out to the fields, waving his arms frantically.

"What's wrong?" Drin asked, leaning on his rake.

"Soldiers, they're coming. My father wants you to hide in the wagons over by our storeshed. Come on," Yiv said. The boy didn't wait for a reply but scurried back toward the farmhouse.

Drin jogged over to the store shed, following behind the boy. He climbed into the wagon, and Yiv covered him with a tarp. Bushels of grain surrounded him, and it made Drin's nose itch. He had to be careful not to sneeze or make noise. The slightest sound would alert the soldiers to his presence.

Footsteps came toward him, and he overheard Sekaran city guards speaking with Mohiel.

"He's a dangerous man," Drin overheard the soldiers say. "A Templar with strange armor. If you see anything, report it to the magistrate. Do you understand?"

"Of course. Eltu be with you."

"Eltu be with you."

Several more minutes went by before Yiv poked his head into the wagon. "They're gone, mister!" he said with a mischievous grin.

Drin dusted himself off and crawled out of the cart. When he did, Mohiel was standing there. "Get inside, boy," he commanded to young Yiv.

Yiv frowned and dragged his feet, but he complied. Drin said nothing, as it was not his place to interfere between a father and his son.

When the door to the house had shut, Mohiel approached him. "Is what they say true? You're not just an Elorian soldier-beast but a Templar?"

Drin didn't hesitate. He had been called by God. It was nothing to be ashamed of. "I am."

The farmer's eyes became dark. Even after these weeks where Drin lived with his family and broke bread with them, anger consumed his face. "Your kind killed two of my brothers at the battle of Tynzee."

"It was a hard-fought battle," Drin said.

"There are some things I cannot forgive," the farmer said, looking away. "I expect you gone this evening. I don't want to see you again come sunrise."

Drin wanted to argue and fight, but something inside him told him not to. Perhaps this was part of God's plan for him to move on. He couldn't find his true calling while staying here at a farm. It had given him time to reflect, time to toil in the hot sun, perhaps a form of penance for his traitorous deeds. But he accepted his fate.

He supped with the family as usual, acting as if nothing was wrong. Yiv was excited about the soldiers visiting the farm earlier, and the way he had helped Drin evade them. He kept talking about it, though Mohiel only frowned when the conversation went that direction. They finished their food and Drin entered into the barn for a final time.

A moon was high in the sky when Drin decided to depart, obeying what the farmer told him. He thought about how he could have used his armor to make them bend to his will, but he was still ashamed of the way he'd so often mowed through the Sekarans without a second thought. There had to be a better way than violence.

Mohiel was there waiting for him when Drin came to the end of the dirt road, the one that turned to go into the city. "Here, take this," he said. He held a cloak and burlap sack. "It's got a canteen, cheese, and bread. You worked hard for us. I can never forgive you, but it's the least I can do."

Drin took the sack and thanked the Sekaran.

SIX

THE SEKARANS DRAGGED ANAIS THROUGH THE STREETS BY chains around her wrists. It would have been humiliating enough, but the sheer fabric draped over her left nothing to the imagination in the light of the giant sun that beat down its rays upon this world, almost as oppressive as her captors. She was led with the other women, a couple dozen in all, through the streets, past peering eyes of merchants, traders, and laborers. They arrived at a gated palace, which stood behind white walls. The main structure was adorned by a golden bulb pointing toward the sky, with a large ruby V etched into it, the sign of the Sekaran prophet.

The group passed the armed guards at the gate before being brought inside to the courtyard. Bright flowers lined the walls in various intricate designs. It created a lush environment, a life-filled contrast to the dead, dirty streets outside.

Inside the main doors was a reception room with lavish rugs on the floors and similar tapestries on the walls. The fine designs brightened the palace with reds and purples. Off to the side, two Skree played music. One had a stringed instrument with a long neck, and the other had a curved flute of some sort. The tones they made evoked a sense of meditation combined with wonder. The background music filled the room.

Several Sekaran men lounged with slaves—all women—tending to their every need. Some women fanned the men with long reeds, others brought refreshments, and more danced and posed for their Sekaran overlords. The men conversed and laughed together while the new crop of slave women was brought before them.

The lead guard stepped before a large man who sat at the center of the room. The man had rolls upon rolls of fat, folding over him to form more of a lump than a proper male form. His hair was neatly tied and braided in the way faithful Sekarans often did. His dark eyes were unfocused and hazy, amplified by the cloud of pipe smoke in front of him. The vapor smelled of aether hashish, something Anais had never partaken of but had seen some of the other nobles on Deklyn try. It made people stupid and lazy. She expected no more of this fat Sekaran.

The large man blew out a puff of smoke. "Watcher Tellah, we were wondering if you were going to make it today."

The guard, Watcher Tellah, prostrated himself in front of the fat man. "Sheikh. Forgive me. These women were slow to rise."

"Eltu is merciful to the faithful, and so am I," said the sheikh. He puffed his pipe again, making an ugly sound sucking in the smoke. The pipe was attached to a tube, connected to a glass base, which had a haze of smoke over the burning aether hashish. "Line them up and tell me what we'll be acquiring this day."

Watcher Tellah rose and motioned for his men to get the women in order. The other guards grabbed the women one by one, setting them on display for the party, mere arm's lengths apart. A couple of the Sekaran men made howling noises and whistles at the flesh on display. Anais never felt more disgusted in her life. She wanted to cover herself from this leering crowd, but she could barely move her arms with the heavy chains. One of the guards prodded her with a stick, forcing her forward.

The Sheikh stood, aided by a couple of the slaves beside him. He was so large that he wobbled, though it might have been the hashish causing him to have trouble standing. He grinned when he righted himself and moved toward the line of new slaves.

Music still played in the background. Most of the men didn't bother to pay attention to the sheikh's movements. Anais glanced to either side. The other women beside her stood straight, eyes forward, almost military-like in the way they held themselves. Were they so beaten down that they refused to resist?

The sheikh stepped toward the first in line, brushing against the woman with his blubber, apparently not concerned in the least about her personal space. He grabbed her by the chin and turned her head to the side. "No," he said, as if inspecting an object.

He moved along to the next down the line. Anais wanted to run, looking for any means by which to escape. Guards manned the doors, and the other direction only would bring her further into this maze of a palace. She couldn't hope to outrun everyone present. There had to be something she could do.

Time proved her enemy as she found the Sheikh in front of her before she could formulate a plan. His body squished against her, and she tried not to stumble backward, not having anticipated his weight. He grabbed her hand, holding it up to inspect it. "Delicate," the sheikh said. Stubby fingertips ran along her palm and down over her wrists. "I like the soft fur."

Anais tensed, but the hand held her wrist tightly, leaving her unable to pull away. The sheikh turned to Watcher Tellah. "This is the one." He motioned around the room. "The others are gifts, spoils of war. Give one to each to the battlemages first, and the leftovers are for the heroes of the Battle of Deklyn. Eltu is gracious this day!" He laughed in a hearty, deep tone before patting Anais on the cheek.

His hungry eyes made her shiver.

SEVEN

THE CITY OF ALTEQUINE BUSTLED. CARTS MADE THEIR WAY through the streets. Sky-bikes buzzed overhead. Merchants traveled with packbeasts or Skree slaves carrying their wares. The Skree had a purple tone to their skin, with three arms on each side of their bodies and a hearty frame, which made them useful for laborious tasks. Drin had liberated many of them who had been sold as slaves to different worlds. Never had he seen so many congregated in one place.

The Skree worked hard for their masters. On many occasions, Father Cline had turned the newly liberated slaves into converts. A trusting people, eager to please.

In his taking time to admire the Skree laborers, Drin bumped into a fruit stand. The stand had fleshy bulbs, which looked like they had been recently harvested. Met with the force of Drin's body, many of them toppled onto the ground. Drin didn't want to draw any attention to himself. He pulled his cloak over him, ensuring the hood kept him in the shadows.

The cart's owner wasn't fooled, scooting from behind her stand in a flurry of anger. Her hands were raised in the air, and she shouted, intent on making a scene. Several of her patrons scrambled out of the way, pushing back into the crowded streets. They bumped into others. Before Drin could react, a circle of angry people formed around him. The crowd pushed and shoved. It became a frenzy.

This was the opposite of what he needed. "Please, calm yourself," he said to the merchant who shouted all sorts of obscenities at him in return. It did no good. The merchant grabbed him by the cloak.

A skinny young child used the confusion to grab some of the fruit, stuffing the bulbs into a sack. He caught Drin's gaze. Those youthful eyes were sorrowful, tired...like Drin had seen in many of his enemies after their defeat. The youth was Sekaran, but only a child. A beggar. Before Drin could even measure the sympathy he felt for the child, the boy ran.

"Thief!" someone yelled.

The merchant spun about and knocked yet more of her fruit to the dirt streets.

Drin tried to slip back into the crowd, but too many people pressed right into the area where he stood. He couldn't pass through them without knocking some of the pedestrians down. This was not how he wanted to start his quest to find God's plan for him.

Someone in the crowd pulled back Drin's hood.

The confusion stopped. Only now, matters had become far worse. All eyes were on him. Gasps and sounds of shock came from people around him. "Elorian!" someone shouted. "Dog," another said. Curses followed.

Pushing also followed. Several people near to him attempted to hit him or throw small trinkets. Drin managed to shove a few of the pedestrians away to give him some space. It allowed him to activate an energy bubble around him and form a light sword in his hand. The Sekarans backed away.

A woman screamed. Others fled. It turned into mass panic and a trampling crowd, unconcerned for their fellow citizens. They feared him. The crowd reaction spooked a packbeast into rearing up on its back hooves. It shook from its bonds and trampled upon a bystander. Bones cracked amidst howls of pain that went suddenly silent.

The death only caused more panic. The congested streets became a madhouse of pushing, shoving. Drin had to escape, but he was caught at the center of the storm. There appeared no way out. If he relied too much on his armor's powers, it might alert battlemages to his presence here. He couldn't risk that.

With the chaos all around him, Drin deactivated his light sword and secured the hood over his head, concealing his face. The best he could do in his current situation was to blend back into the crowd and to keep quiet.

Drin walked with his head cast low, trying not to draw any further attention. Everyone around him appeared to be occupied with their own brawls. The original merchant was more concerned with the thief than him. He managed to put distance between himself and that fruit stand. But now where would he go? Mohiel hadn't paid him in coin, which meant he had to find more work soon if he were to survive. He had accepted leaving as God's will, though he wished he could have spent more time to speak with the farmer and his family, to share God's love and erase the past crimes of his brethren. Sekarans didn't have the propensity toward forgiveness that the Elorians did. Of course not, their false god had not commanded such from them.

But these were still people like any others. Merchants, beggars, farmers, workers. That was Drin's problem with the whole situation. How many of them had he hurt in his time as a Templar? Had it been worth it?

He considered Mohiel and his prejudices against the Elorians. Would the Sekaran farmer have had those if a Templar hadn't killed his brother? The thought made Drin frown. Perhaps they were doing more harm in the universe than good.

He moved further through the open market, making his way into a large square with a running fountain. The crowd thinned out in this area. Several people lounged, ate food, and drank refreshments. Some rested under overhangs or umbrellas to keep themselves out of the hot sun. Two little boys played with a small ball, kicking it back and forth and trying not to let it hit the ground. Drin tried to remember most of these Sekarans were innocent people. It was their leadership failing them. Perhaps this was what he was called to see.

From around the corner came a man, followed by three women covered from head to toe in black garb. The women had chains on them, connected together. When they slowed their pace, the man yanked on the chain. The women stumbled forward. The man cursed at them.

Drin frowned. There was good here, but evil as well. How could someone treat women with such disregard? He thought about intervening before a strong hand gripped him on the shoulder and spun him around.

A Sekaran magistrate and three guards in bone armor plating stood before him. The armor was scuffed and dirtied from the sand. They had round helmets strapped on their heads with reflective sun-shielding visors, as well as three laser-repeaters pointed directly at Drin.

"Elorian," the magistrate said. He met Drin's eyes with anger and ferocity. "You caused quite a scene back in the market row. You will follow us for questioning."

The laser-repeaters hummed as they readied.

Drin considered his options. He could activate his armor and destroy all three of these guards and the magistrate in the blink of an eye. These were local city guards, not soldiers. They would hardly be able to react before Drin could end them. The nanites surged within him, ready for action, charged from his time in the sun with very little use. "I did nothing wrong," Drin said.

"Why are you here?" the magistrate demanded.

"God commanded me here," Drin said.

The guards clenched their teeth. The magistrate's eyes went

wide. "Heresy. You will not speak of Eltu except by the name allowed to the common people!"

"Eltu is not God," Drin said. He clenched his fist. It might not be possible for him to have peace.

The magistrate motioned to the guards. Two of them circled around him while the third kept his laser-repeater trained on Drin. The other two grabbed him, each by a wrist, jerking his arms behind him.

Drin was strong. Even a slight resistance threw the two guards off balance. But he still was torn. Should he fight? He prayed that God would send him a message of what to do. He'd come here to find peace. This situation was anything but the peace he sought.

The guards redoubled their efforts. One planted his foot, with his boot slipping across the sandy street. He found his balance and jerked Drin's arm back. On a weaker man, it would have dislocated the arm from its socket, but Drin's arms were solid as rock. The other guard managed to bend Drin's arm back, as well. Charged cuffs circled Drin's wrists. His hands were stuck behind his back. The nanites could overpower them, but the cuffs would give him a shock.

Was prison God's plan for him? He'd read several stories of the young apostles on Eloria being taken to military prisons. They met their captors with truth, persuaded them to release them and allow them to return to battle. Their stories didn't help him to decide a course of action.

One of the guards pushed him forward.

"Move, infidel," the magistrate said, pacing ahead with confidence. People in the square stared as the guards took Drin away. They whispered. Some scoffed at him. Drin was starting to hate this planet.

DRIN UTTERED prayers in his cell. "Lord God on high, Your name is sacred forever. This kingdom is Yours now, as You have gifted us, and will hold us until You return. Forgive us our sins, as we forgive the sins of our enemies. Never let Your flock go astray, but keep us apart from evil, that we may grow in our faithfulness. Power and glory to Yezuah," Drin whispered to himself.

He had his arms chained to the wall. His left leg had an anklet around it, tied to a chain attached to a heavy rock. Even in this humiliation, the Sekarans had no clue he could activate his powers and bring this entire prison down. And yet something kept compelling him not to.

The other prisoners in the cell looked at him as if he were crazy. The Sekarans in the prison looked like they had lives as rough as the thief boy back in the market. There were also a few Skree, who sat chained with all of their arms bound. Drin ignored them, keeping his head bowed toward floor in front of him. He repeated his prayers. If he focused, meditated on that which was eternal, God would have to show him a way.

The cell door creaked open. The magistrate stood at the door, pushing it further open. The door was heavy and old, in need of maintenance. It looked as antiquated and in need of repair as everything else in this city built of old adobe bricks, sandblasted by the winds of the desert over time. It was a prison, true, but Drin wondered why the free Sekarans allowed themselves to live as they did. They could build with more modern furnishings and have better lives. Why didn't they?

"Elorian," the magistrate said. He moved past the other prisoners to stand in front of Drin. He held a staff and jutted it toward Drin's chin. An upward push lifted Drin's head to force him to look the magistrate in the eyes. "The city guard discovered your craft kilometers from here. They're unsure how you could have walked this far and survived, but they have been searching for you for weeks. You are not just a heathen, but an enemy soldier."

The magistrate jabbed Drin in the neck with his staff.

Drin grunted. It hurt, as it was meant to. In addition to the pain from the blow, the rough wood scratched his face. Still, he said nothing, casting his eyes away from the magistrate. Perhaps God meant to teach him a lesson in humility before fulfilling his purpose.

"Let it never be said that Eltu and his servants are without mercy. We will give you one more chance. In three days' time, we will hold a trial before the sheikh in the square. The whole city will see what the Elorian dogs are reduced to." He paced in front of Drin. "Then you will swear your life to the divine prophet and Eltu. You will beg forgiveness to the sheikh, and he may have mercy upon you by sparing your life. Do you understand?"

"I will never blaspheme against Yezuah, the one true God," Drin said.

The magistrate smacked him across the face with his staff. The blow resounded with an echoing *crack* on his cheek. It jolted his head to the side.

"Silence, infidel! You know what you must do to live, but you will not spread lies in my jurisdiction."

Drin could feel the blood pooling in his mouth, but he said nothing.

The magistrate glared, looking ready to strike again. He glanced to the other prisoners, who all pretended they weren't watching the exchange. "Three days, Elorian," the magistrate said. He turned on his heel and strode out of the cell, shutting the door behind him.

The door closed with a *creak* and a *thud*, sound once more echoing through the dark cell. Drin held silent for a time. When the sound of the magistrate's footsteps faded, he resumed his prayer.

One of the other prisoners next to him watched him. In between prayers, he whispered, "Elorian?"

Drin paused from beginning a new prayer to look at him. A Skree, but one missing all three hands on the right-hand side of his body. Only stumps remained on those long arms. The Skree looked like he'd been flogged with a whip dozens of times. What crime could the Skree have committed to receive such treatment? Drin's mouth had filled with blood, which he had to spit out before speaking. "Yes?"

"Can you tell me about this Yezuah you speak of?"

Drin met the Skree's black eyes. They were pools of eternity, almost vacant. Some Elorians believed Skree didn't have souls. But they could observe and see the wonders of God for themselves, perhaps especially with those eyes. "I would be glad to," Drin said.

EIGHT

ALL THINGS CONSIDERED, ANAIS MUCH PREFERRED THE PALACE to the prison. After being chosen by the sheik, she was ushered by servants to a large, circular bed, with a plush pillow top and several other pillows adorning it. Her room was at the end of a long hallway on the second floor of the palace, and it did have a window to the outside where she could see the light of glo-rods scattered across the streets of the city. Very few walked the streets at this hour, save for Sekaran city guard patrols who kept the peace.

Bars adorned the windows, preventing escape. When she had first been left alone, she tugged at them, hunting for any weakness. The bars held steady. There went her fantasies of prying one or two of the bars loose, slipping through, and tying blankets together to use as a rope to rappel down the side of the palace.

The Sekarans left her alone for a long time after bringing her here. Her fear and worry dissipated into the newfound comfort of the soft sheets and pillows of the bed. She settled into a nap.

She woke to the sound of a loud bell. The noise was so overwhelming that it vibrated several of the objects in the room. It rang five times.

Anais scrambled to her feet. Was it an alarm to warn of danger? She rushed to the window to see what was going on. She recalled all too vividly the night in her own palace back on Deklyn, a night where she had no care in the world. In a few years, she would have stood to inherit titles, land, perhaps even rule of the entire planet if her family company's stock remained high enough. She had been upset about being confined. Now it wasn't all that different, except the Sekarans had turned her from a person to a possession.

She moved to the window to see what warning the bell brought. The few gathered in the streets all stopped what they were doing and prostrated themselves on the ground. They faced the same direction. Even from this distance, she could hear the words they shouted, "Glory to Eltu! Glory to Eltu!"

The chants didn't come from the street alone, but also from the palace, reverberating through the walls. The cultish dedication frightened her anew. But what could she do? Where could she go to get away from it? She prayed silently to herself, not even sure who she was speaking to, hoping someone would rescue her from this.

As if the universe answered, the door to her palace opened.

But instead of a rescuer here to whisk her away, the sheikh stood at the door. He stumbled into the room with a grin on his face, slamming the door behind him. He had to be either stoned, drunk, or both.

Anais wanted to scream, but she stopped herself. What good would making a commotion do other than to summon guards?

The sheikh waddled toward her. She backed away from the window, but there was nowhere to go. The large bed blocked the slightest chance for her to evade him. Before she could react, the sheikh moved faster than she would have thought possible for him. He grabbed her by the wrists and pulled her toward him, pressing his face against her cheek. "I don't think I've ever had someone so beautiful brought to me before. You'll make a great addition to my other wives. Don't worry, they aren't jealous."

Anais squirmed. She tried to rip her hands away from him, but he was much bigger than she was. All she succeeded in doing was pushing herself closer to the bed, which made the sheikh grin even wider. He knocked her off balance, causing her to fall over. He pounced atop her before she could move.

His full weight pressed her against the bed. She could barely breathe. His hands moved over her, violating her. It was too much. She couldn't let this happen!

Anais squirmed to get her hands free. She scratched him hard across the face.

Her nails broke his flesh. Four streaks of blood ran deep across his cheek. It would leave a scar. He brought his hand to his face, horrified. "You whore! What have you done?" His deep, confident voice was replaced by something akin to a shrill child. This was a man used to getting what he wanted and never having anyone fight back.

Anais was unrepentant. When he pulled back, she brought a knee to his crotch, causing him to double over in pain.

"Guards!" the sheikh cried. "Guards!"

This was exactly the sort of thing she wanted to avoid. Whatever he had been about to do to her, the penalty for resisting might be worse. She didn't want to be beaten and brought to submission like the other women who had been lined up earlier. That wasn't her. What horrors could they expose her to, and for how long, before she broke?

The sheikh's stunned pain turned to anger, his eyes from hunger to fire. He struck her across the face in return.

Her cheek stung. A man had hit her. What kind of hell was this? She could never have imagined such a thing happening on Deklyn. She kicked at the sheikh a couple of times and scrambled backward across the bed to get away.

The door opened again. Two armed Sekaran guards burst through. They pointed their weapons at her. Behind them stood a man in white with an ornate gold pattern running along the edges of his clothes. He stared at her in judgment. "Sheikh, I heard your call from the palace. Though I am not on duty, is something the matter?"

The sheikh growled, his hand cradling the wound on his face. Fresh blood dripped from his cheek to the floor. "This harlot thought she might cast some wicked spell on me with her charms. She wished to consummate before holy matrimony and tempted me with her vile ways."

Anais's mouth hung open. Nothing of the sort had happened. "Liar!"

The magistrate inclined his head. "Silence, slave." He surveyed her for a long moment. "Yes, I see that she is uncouth, and that she moves in ways unnatural and wildly improper for a woman of her station. That she should wish to bring someone of your stature into sin is not unexpected. We must make an example of her." He motioned the guards forward.

The two guards lowered their weapons and circled around the bed. They grabbed her by one arm each, lifting her up with ease and pushing her forward. Their hard grips would bruise her wrists. With no compassion or gentleness, the guards pushed her to the floor in front of the magistrate. With hands on her shoulders, she was forced to stay on her knees.

The sheikh moved to the magistrate's side.

The magistrate turned his head to him. "She is your property. I will leave it to you, but the punishment for the wicked attempting to bring Eltu's faithful servant into sin is death."

"Execute her," the sheikh said with a hiss.

What? Anais's mouth went dry. She couldn't die like this. Because a man attacked her. Didn't she get a say? "That's not what happened."

The magistrate backhanded her across the face. "Silence, heathen. Judgment has been pronounced, and it is so witnessed by a magistrate of Eltu, the ultimate arbiter of justice. You will be reverent."

The force of the blow turned her head to the side. Even though she tried her hardest, she couldn't stop the tears from flowing down her face, as they had so many times these last few days.

The magistrate let out a deep breath. "Better. We will bring you to a cleric before the execution tomorrow. You will have one chance to repent and dedicate your soul to Eltu. It will not spare you in this life, but he may have mercy upon you in the world beyond."

The sheikh grumbled. "She deserves no mercy. She should have been honored to be my bride."

"This is the consequence of bringing in heathen races to our worlds without proper conversion training. But fear not, my friend, I doubt you will have any more troubles after the public sees her stoning." The magistrate motioned a finger toward the door, and the guards dragged her out of the room.

NINE

It took several Sekarans to drag Drin into the Altequine Square. The sun beat down on his face. Drin summoned his nanites to bring a film over his eyes to combat the glare. Hopefully, it would be a small enough miracle that it wouldn't be noticed by the Sekarans. His hands were chained in front of him, the tight manacles chafing his skin. The denizens of the city had all gathered for the spectacle. They lined the streets from the door of the prison, mocking, jeering, spitting, and throwing small objects at him.

Drin winced, taking the abuse. He couldn't let this charade go for too long, but there were others to consider. The one Skree who had asked about Yezuah had turned into many among the prisoners. It resulted in a night of relaying the story of how Yezuah had brought peace to Eloria. "That peace can be for all peoples," Drin told them. A few of the Skree seemed as if they believed.

One of the guards yanked on his chains, causing Drin to lose his footing. He fell face first to the dirt street, slamming his chin on the hard ground. The salty taste of blood rose in his mouth. He spat some of that blood onto the street.

The crowd went wild with the action. The Sekarans dragged his full weight through the street, not giving Drin a chance to stand. His body scraped across the ground as he was pulled forward. Temptation to don his armor filled him, but it wasn't the time. He had to endure until the moment was right. He didn't want to tear apart the crowds of civilians, as he had while serving with his Templar unit from the *Justicar*. The whole point of his journey was to do something different.

But would they give him any choice?

The mounting scrapes and scratches burned by the time he reached the square. The crowd's roar grew louder. Sekarans packed into the square, trying to get a glimpse of a large dug-out hole ahead of Drin. The guards pulled him to the lip of the pit, lifting him to his feet. They unclipped the chain they used to drag him, keeping his hands bound together.

A guard pushed him squarely on the chest, forcing him to stumble backward into the pit. Drin spun, tumbling to the ground. Several Sekaran onlookers laughed, others cheered. Several of his new Skree friends were in the pit with him. They looked scared. Of course they did. The Skree had been slaves all their lives, never having anything but torture and pain, and now they were going to endure the worst until the end.

"Will Yezuah save us?" one of them asked.

Drin didn't want to make any commitments, but he closed his eyes and said a brief prayer for their safety.

When he reopened his eyes, another person was being dragged into the pit along with them. A girl. His eyes lingered for a long time, not out of any inherent lust, but because it was such an odd sight to see such a lithe frame in such revealing clothes. The nuns aboard the *Justicar* covered themselves so completely, draping black garments over themselves that one could hardly tell if they were men or women. It was to prevent any of the Templars from stumbling into sin, of course. They were discouraged from too much interaction with the fighting men for the same reason.

This girl had nothing left to the imagination. She had thin silk covering her, which fell just over the top half of her thigh. In the sunlight, the fabric became see-through and revealed everything. He saw every curve of her shapely form. Her breasts, her stomach, even her most private of parts were on display for everyone to see.

Drin turned his head to the side. The Lord must have placed her before him as a test. His vow of chastity must remain true, even in his instinctive thoughts.

The Sekarans threw the girl into the pit. She landed directly where Drin had turned his head to face away from her. When she hit the ground, she did not get up as easily as he did. Drin rushed over to her, offering his hand to help her.

The girl recoiled.

This time when he saw her, he saw not only her womanly curves, but her face. She had large eyes, darkness filling her pupils, and more notably, long, slender ears that poked through her hair and up above her head. They twitched while she lay there on the ground. When she turned, she revealed a small tail on her backside.

"Please, let me help you," Drin said.

She looked up at him, trembling, but she took his arm and let him help her to her feet.

The girl didn't speak.

The Sekaran magistrate stepped to the lip of the pit, looming over them. Several city guards stood with him. The whole area felt like it was going to erupt into violence. People surrounded the pit, holding knives, stones, sticks, or other weaponry. Anger and hatred filled the eyes of many of the onlookers. Others watched with morbid curiosity. Conversations swelled, and the air became thick with tension.

"Quiet!" the magistrate said, lifting his hands. The crowd settled. He lowered his hands to his sides. "We gather to convene this trial, with the guidance of Eltu, the greatest of all. Might he show mercy to us and swift judgment to the enemies of the prophet Sekar."

The crowd jeered and shouted agreement.

The magistrate waited for the cheers to quiet. "There are five here today, standing accused as enemies of Eltu. Three Skree, slaves who, as it is written, are unworthy of name, but must labor and toil for their original sin, as it is written in the Great Book. They have violated the sacred social orders by rebelling against their masters. Is their master here to testify against them today?"

A Skree city guard stepped forward, armor-clad and with a sword holstered at his side. "I am Watcher Tellah. I testify that these slaves rebelled against Sekarans and sought to do violence upon their betters, the superior race for whom it is written they should toil."

Mutters and curses came from the crowd. The magistrate looked on. "So it is testified. Is there a better who contradicts this testimony?"

The square descended into silence. No one spoke on behalf of the Skree slaves. With this crowd, even if there were a witness who thought otherwise, would they? Such a person would be liable to be thrown in the pit along with the prisoners, the crowd looked so riled up. They gritted their teeth and stared at Drin as if he were a devil.

"We need a miracle," one of the Skree said.

The girl with the long ears frowned, dejection in her eyes. "Yeah, well, maybe it's better to just get it over with."

The magistrate raised his arms again. The crowd silenced themselves. "It is my judgment under the power vested in me from the sheikh, and under the guidance of Eltu, that you shall be put to death. May Eltu grant you mercy in the next life!"

The crowd roared. Hundreds of Sekarans shouted for the Skrees' deaths.

When they quieted again, the magistrate pointed to the girl. "You, woman of Deklyn, were set to be wed to the high sheikh, and yet you cast foul magics upon him, trying to seduce him before your proper vows."

"I did no such thing!" the girl shouted.

"If you speak again, I shall cut out your tongue for talking to a magistrate in such a manner." The Magistrate inclined his head. "Where was I? Ah, yes. I witnessed this act personally, as a magistrate of Altequine. Are there any of higher station who doubt my word?"

As with the Skree, no one in the crowd said anything.

"Then it shall also come to pass that this vile temptress be stoned to death for her crimes!"

The crowd went even wilder than before.

The magistrate turned his attention to Drin, his Sekaran eyes cold and beady. This place was terrible, the result of peoples lost among this false religion. This was why the Elorian crusader ships existed. Scanning the crowd, Drin saw only hate and reviling on their scowling faces. Not a compassionate soul among them. The people needed salvation. Salvation from this magistrate, from the sheikh, and from the false prophet.

God had sent Drin here, placed the doubt in his mind about his own people so that he could see the truth. He bore witness firsthand to the horrors of these Sekarans and their backward laws, condemning anyone out of convenience. All for a show. They made sport of stoning a few Skree slaves and a poor woman. And him.

Drin had been so caught up in his thoughts that he didn't hear the charges leveled against him.

"Is there any here of a higher station who doubts my word and testimony?" the magistrate asked again.

Drin made one step forward, meeting the eyes of the magistrate, challenging him. He felt the fury rise within his soul. There was only one way he would save the other victims in the pit. "Yes," he said. "Your words are lies, magistrate. I committed no crime, and by that token, I doubt these people did either."

He fanned his hand across his body, and in the process, activated his nanites. A rush overcame him as they coursed through his veins. They had been there, dormant, waiting. A gift from God, providing him with righteous protection. They formed a translucent energy shield around him. He didn't need to morph them into his full Templar armor attire. This would provide an adequate demonstration. Next, he let the nanite energy flow to his hand, where he formed his light sword.

The crowd panicked at the sight. Most hurried away. Some flung their objects toward the pit. Shouts of "Elorian!" and "Templar!" rang through the square. Pebbles and sticks hit his energy shield and fell harmlessly to the ground. Though he couldn't completely surround the others, he blocked most of the onslaught. The attacks faded as quickly as they came, as few risked prolonged confrontation with Drin. The crowd scattered.

The city guards descended the slopes toward the prisoners, six in all. "Stay behind me," Drin said to the others, using his free hand to wave them back. With his sword hand, he spun his light sword, an act that had little fighting purpose other than to intimidate the enemy.

It worked, causing the guards to stay back in caution. "Stop him," the magistrate ordered. The guards with spears shuffled cautiously forward and jabbed at Drin, trying to use their long poles to keep their distance and advantage. The crude weapons were no match for his holy nanite technology. The spear tips disintegrated when they met with his energy field. The Sekarans drew back in horror.

"Laser-repeaters, fire!" one of the Sekarans shouted.

Drin moved, slicing one of the spears in two with his light sword. He jumped, the nanites assisting his leap over the Sekaran's head. As he descended, he ran the light sword through the Sekaran's body. The guard collapsed.

The others drew their laser-repeaters. They took aim at Drin and fired.

His shield stopped their blasts. They kept firing. A display of nanites appeared in his vision, showing that their energy levels were holding. This was going to be too easy.

Just as he had the prideful thought, a blast ricocheted off his shield, hitting a Skree prisoner. The Skree staggered back and fell. The two others wailed something in the Skree language.

Drin winced. Pride was a dangerous sin. He would have to ask repentance later. It had caused a death. "Watch over this Skree's soul," Drin muttered in prayer. He didn't have time to give the fallen Skree the consideration he deserved.

The Sekarans backed up the slope of the pit, giving Drin ample room to work. With a nanite-assisted burst of speed, Drin drove his sword through one of the Sekarans with laser-repeaters. He pulled the light sword out of the collapsing body and spun the blade for another Sekaran's neck.

The quick deaths of their companions gave the other Sekaran guards pause. One screamed, and the spearmen scurried back up the slope. Two more with laser-repeaters fired but retreated along with the others.

At the top of the slope stood the magistrate, looking on with a disgusted frown. He saw his people fleeing from Drin and grabbed one by the arm before the man could move too far. "Head to the sheikh's barracks and summon a battlemage," the magistrate said.

It had been far too easy for Drin, dealing with these city guards. He'd fought off thousands of these in his time as a Templar. A battlemage, however, brought him to attention. He couldn't hold this pit forever. They needed to escape. He turned to the girl. "We need to get out of here."

"This isn't my sand-hole of a planet! I'm following you," the girl said, long ears twitching.

The two Skree hovered over their companion, who still convulsed on the dirt. They spoke in the Skree language, and tears flooded their eyes. One of them looked up at Drin. "Will Yezuah save his soul?"

Drin wished he could be certain. His gut told him yes, that the Skree had souls just like any other sentient species and, as such, God would protect whoever believed in his great ascension, granting eternal life. The scriptures clearly stated the message. He had to lead these new converts to salvation, however. That was his duty. "Yes," he said. "Pray for his soul, regardless. It can only do good."

The Skree uttered what sounded like prayers. The other Skree stopped moving, and a black tar substance formed on the ground beneath him. The two remaining Skree stood. "We can lead to the city gates if you can get us there," said the Skree with the missing hands.

Drin nodded. "Lead," he said, pointing his light sword forward. "Make sure I stay close. I will extend my shield to protect you the best I can."

The two Skree pressed up the pit slope. Drin and the girl followed.

The square was nearly clear of people, most having rushed back for the markets. Dust filled the air. A hazy cloud filled the sky.

The Skree surveyed the area and pointed to an avenue to Drin's left. They ran for it. Drin followed, taking a moment to scan his surroundings and make sure no enemies pursued. The magistrate and his remaining guards had gone the other way. They had to move quickly. If the magistrate's threat of a battlemage was true, it could prove too much for him to handle. He didn't want to tempt fate, at the very least. Was this the path God wished for him?

Drin had no choice but to follow as the Skree slaves led the way.

TEN

ANAIS COULD HARDLY BELIEVE WHAT WAS GOING ON. HER whole experience on this world still felt like a nightmare, one she couldn't wake up from no matter how hard she pinched herself. These last several days made no sense. How could she have ever wished for a life outside of her comfortable existence on Deklyn? How foolish she had been.

After the guards had taken her away from the sheikh—thankfully before he was able to have his way with her—she hadn't expected to survive. She'd resigned herself to death. It had been hopeless. Then they threw this strange Elorian man into the pits with her. He had bright green skin, making his race easy to recognize on most worlds. Elorians were a strange people, extremely religious, so she had heard. She'd never met one before.

What she didn't expect was the Elorian to be so masculine. His muscles practically bulged from his body like they were going to pop out and form a completely new person. If she had even a moment to stop running, she might have used it to admire him further.

She followed the Elorian and two Skree down the streets. Onlookers rubbernecked, some shouting obscenities in their direction. Her death was supposed to be a sport to these sick people. The audacity of branding her a harlot for refusing the godawful sheikh. It filled her ears with blood and steam.

They reached an alleyway, and the Skree turned into it. The fleeing group took a few moments to catch their breath. Of the four of them, she had to be the most out of shape. She'd kept up appearances, of course, as well as any young Deklyn noble would, but she'd never had any true strenuous physical tests in her life. She found herself panting in the hot sun, her dry mouth tasting of dirt and sand.

The Elorian maintained the most stoic of faces. He didn't appear worried in the least, or out of breath for that matter. He extinguished his strange energy weapon, making it disappear into thin air with whatever magic he used. "What's the plan?" he asked.

Back on the main street, guards ran past the alleyway. They didn't appear to see the fleeing criminals, the party shielded by an overhead awning, providing relative darkness. Too many people cluttered the streets. They were relatively safe, but that wouldn't last for long.

The Skree conferred in their own language, words of a guttural and dissonant tone. As repulsive as Anais found them physically, these were her allies now. Even though the Sekarans might look the most like her of the species she'd encountered on this world, they were far more vile creatures underneath their skin.

"Err-dio has a brother who works in the sky-bike maintenance yard. The sandstorms blow far too much debris into the motors and slaves are needed to clean them out. We could steal some sky-bikes and break for our people's hideaway encampment," the stump-armed Skree said.

The Elorian frowned. "Thieving is a sin."

"When the choice is but to sin or die, what choice is there?" Err-dio shrugged.

Anais had no idea what they were talking about. She wanted to get out of this city, whatever it took, and had no compunction about some perceived sin. Wherever their hideaway encampment was had to be better than here. "I say let's go," she said, trying to channel her father's tone when he wanted to sound decisive to his company men.

All three of the men turned their attention to her. At first, they seemed surprised she'd spoken, but then they nodded their agreement with her judgment.

Was this how her father had established his rule as a merchant lord? By projecting confidence? She would have to consider that implication at another time. "Lead the way...?" she let her last word dangle into a question, fishing for the second Skree's name.

"Sao-rin," he said with a nod. "Descendent of King Sao-dei."

"You're royalty too?" Anais blinked.

"Too?" Sao-rin raised a thick brow.

She shouldn't have said anything. These people were unknowns to her. As much as they were in this escape together, they might decide to use her as a hostage, or worse, if her origin as a daughter of the highest valued merchant lord on Deklyn became clear. She shook her head. "Heat must be getting to me. I didn't know there was Skree royalty, I thought you all were just—"

"Slaves?" Sao-rin laughed at her as if she were a child. "None are slaves by birthright. Not forever."

Anais flushed. The question had been tactless. But she'd never heard of a Skree being anything but a slave.

"Enough talk," the Elorian said. "We've had our rest. It will be dangerous to linger any longer. I can protect you, but it would be better to get away from this city, where my protection may not be enough once their legions or battlemages find us."

Sao-rin motioned them onward, and they followed him down the alleyway. They came upon some sort of outdoor bazaar, filled with people. It would be impossible to conceal themselves amongst so many, the three men dressed in tattered slave clothing, and her in the sheer silk covering that would make anyone stare.

They carefully weaved through the crowd. With such a dense concentration of people, few did more than give them a passing glance, though many of the men's eyes lingered on Anais far longer than the others. The crowd slowed as they trudged along, bottle-necking into a small passage at one outlet. Two Sekaran guards stood watch over the bazaar, not seeming alerted to their presence.

"There wasn't any other way?" Anais asked to Err-dio.

The Skree shrugged but did not look back at her. They continued through the crowd. One of the Sekaran guards caught sight of her and parted the crowd to move to her. He grabbed her by the arm. The others kept going. She yelped instinctively.

"What've we got here? A slave girl? Out dressed like *this* without your master?" the Sekaran said. His companion came over to them.

Anais tried to shake free from him, but she bumped into the other guard. The first released her, causing her to stumble. The second Sekaran caught her.

"A pretty one. She brings great shame to her house, allowing all to cast lustful eyes on her like this," the guard who held her said. His hands slid down her backside.

Every instance since she had been taken by these dreadful people had been the same. Anais cringed. She should have stuck closer to the others and been more cautious. The men escaping with her had themselves to look after and didn't know her from anyone else on this disgusting planet. They had no reason to slow for her sake.

The guard was off her a moment later. She heard a *Hggk* from behind her. A shadow fell over her.

Anais turned to see what happened.

The Elorian grabbed the guard by the wrist and pulled him away. Thrown off balance, the Sekaran guard exposed his full torso. The Elorian took the opening and jutted his hand forward. His hand glowed in light that cut through the guard's body. The guard coughed and then fell to the ground.

"We don't have time for this," the Elorian said.

Anais fought the urge to press against the Elorian, to use him for comfort and safety. She had little dignity left, it was true, but she wouldn't throw herself at someone and lose the rest of it.

The Elorian huffed and gripped her by the wrist. He pulled her along, bringing them into the funnel of people. They passed through the archway, and the crowd thinned again. The two Skree waited for them.

Sao-rin narrowed his eyes. "Where did she go? Did she alert the Sekarans?"

"Not intentionally," the Elorian said, releasing her wrist. "We should make haste, regardless."

Anais didn't get a chance to speak on her own behalf before the men moved forward. She jogged to keep up with them, not wanting to be separated again. It wasn't as if she had much of a choice but to draw attention, dressed as she was, but they wouldn't be sympathetic to her explanations.

They passed through several less crowded streets, passing shops, houses, and smaller markets. All of the buildings were stuccoed, round structures. They finally reached a district that looked more industrial and modern, though it kept the same themes of the sand-blasted aesthetic she had seen throughout the city. They reached a yard, fenced in with a laser forcefield. Depending on the angle, it appeared transparent or a dim orange. Two poles marked the entrance, where two Sekarans stood guard.

"This is it," Sao-rin said. "The yard's inside. We'll have to take keys... individual bikes?" He looked to the Elorian.

"I can pilot." He looked to Anais expectantly.

She waved that suggestion off. "I've never flown myself." On Deklyn, she had had drivers to take her wherever she wanted to go. The life of luxury and servants, one she missed desperately, but now she also wished she'd developed *some* skills. How useless could she be?

The Elorian nodded. "You'll ride behind me then." He stopped his pace, looking ahead at the two guards. "Will they let us through?"

Sao-rin stopped as well. "Yes, they will recognize Err-dio and myself. But we will want fewer guards on the alert when we steal these sky-bikes, yes?"

"Fair point. Get us through, and I'll handle them when you're safely away from stray laser-repeater fire," the Elorian said.

They moved forward again. The Skree took the lead this time. They bowed to the Sekarans when they arrived. "We return with clientele who were being entertained by the sheikh. They wish to see the progress on their bikes," Sao-rin said.

The two guards seemed not to care, motioning them forward and into the yard.

The yard was vast. Dozens of sky-bikes were lined up, packed into the area. Several Skree slaves wiped down sky-bikes with rags and buckets of water. Others moved some of the sky-bikes back to a large warehouse building with an open bay door. Several sky-bikes were inside, some on lifts, and many torn apart as slaves worked to clean the sand out of the engine coils.

"Will the slaves bother us?" the Elorian asked.

"I doubt it. We'll have to get keys. You handle the guards," Sao-rin said quietly. He and Err-dio made their way through the rows of sky-bikes toward the building.

Anais watched and noted the Elorian who headed back for the guards at the entrance. No one seemed to care which way she went, but she figured it would be best to stick with the firepower. He was the reason they had escaped and not been stoned to death, after all.

A *shnk* sound came from the Elorian. Energy appeared, protruding from his hand like a sword of light. He rammed it through one of the Sekaran guards' backs before she could blink. The second Sekaran fumbled for a laser-repeater, but by the time he had it the Elorian had slashed his body in two. The laser repeater clanked on the ground by his feet.

Anais watched, stunned by the violence. Even after her abuse of the last several days, to stand in front of such elegant carnage disturbed her.

Unfazed, the Elorian bent down and picked up the laser-repeater. His light sword shimmered out of existence as if it had never been there. He turned it over to inspect it, and then offered it to

Anais. "If more come, you'll need a way to defend yourself. Do you know how to shoot?"

She shook her head, timidly reaching for the weapon. It was heavy in her hands. The thought of firing it made her stomach churn.

"Point at your target. Pull the trigger when the time comes," the Elorian said. It sounded like a joke, but his voice was so deep, so deadly serious. He walked past her, pointing toward the row of sky-bikes. "Our friends have our keys."

The two Skree ran toward them. Several of the other Skree slaves watched curiously. Sao-rin tossed the Elorian one of the keys and pointed to a bike. The Elorian straddled the vehicle. He motioned to Anais. "On back. Quickly."

Anais moved over, lifting her leg carefully over the vehicle. In her sheer coverings, she didn't intend to give the Skree slaves a free show. She wasn't sure how she should sit, but the Elorian moved as if she should hold onto him, so she wrapped her arms around his torso. It was rock-hard, which didn't quite surprise her, but it did make her eyes go wide.

The sky-bike engine fired up, rocking them back and forth, and soon they were hovering off the ground. The two Skree each flew their own vehicles. They lifted in the air behind Anais.

Laser-repeater fire shot right past her head. Anais looked to the entrance. Several of the city guard funneled in through the gate.

"We have to go, now!" the Elorian shouted.

The Skree took off ahead of them. They had to be the ones to lead the way. The Elorian slammed his hand down on the accelerator, and they moved away at a blinding speed.

ELEVEN

THE SKY-BIKES ASCENDED TOWARD THE CLOUDLESS SKY. THE wind in Drin's face felt good after a hot day of fighting. Drin still lingered with uneasiness despite the pleasant sensation. This was exactly the kind of scenario he came to this planet to avoid, but he'd had no choice in recent events. He leaned, banking the sky-bike to follow the two Skree slaves ahead of him.

Laser-repeater fire came from the town below. Most of the shots fell behind the sky-bikes. One came all too close to the left-hand side of Drin.

"Watch out!" shouted the girl riding behind him. Her grip tightened on his shirt, nails digging into Drin's skin.

He didn't complain, but it wasn't as if he could do much about the incoming blasts. The odds of them being blown out of the sky were small, despite the girl's fear. The city guards below wouldn't be able to fire accurate shots at this range. If a stray laser hit them, then it would be God's will.

The Skree pulled ahead. Drin hit the thrusters to match their acceleration. At least they were out of the crowded streets. They were lucky the Sekarans hadn't decided to riot and mob them, given

Drin's display of Templar power. Those people had been taught from a young age to fear and hate him, and despite how easily he had made his way through the guards, if they had all decided to pile on him, he wouldn't have been so lucky.

Best not to dwell on the past. Focus on the present. Yezuah's teachings were clear.

Drin brought the sky-bike to a stable altitude, parallel to the ground below, and tapped the controls to put it on autopilot. Piloting one of these crafts wasn't so different from his needler, though he did crash-land the fighter the last time he'd flown one.

The buzz of more speeders came from behind them. "They're coming after us!" the girl shouted.

Drin banked the sky-bike again and looked over his shoulder. Four sky-bikes with very official-looking men in guard armor were in pursuit. This time the laser-repeater fire came at them from a flat angle, which meant they'd be more likely to strike true. Evading them would take a lot of work. He hoped the girl would be able to hang on.

The two Skree slaves fanned their sky-bikes in different directions, breaking up the targets. Drin could only speculate as to their strategy in dealing with the guards, but they were out over the open desert now. They likely wouldn't want to lead the Sekarans to their base. Which meant they had to lose these guards here and still manage to follow one of the Skree for a chance of long-term survival. Drin decided to follow the leftmost sky-bike, which he thought was Sao-rin, but at these distances, he couldn't tell which Skree was which.

The Skree's identity didn't matter at the moment. Much more important were the Sekarans firing at them. Drin considered what to do. This craft didn't have any weaponry, and he didn't have any long-range weapons with him—the nanites had to stay within an area surrounding him or they would disconnect from the general field. With the girl behind him doing nothing but clinging, he regretted having given the laser-repeater to her. But then, he needed to pilot the sky-bike.

One of the Sekarans gained on Drin's sky-bike. The girl gripped Drin even more tightly. Drin tried to push her back without making her fall off, and then he dropped one arm from the handlebars to let his light sword form. With a quick reverse thrust, the vehicle came to a halt in the air.

Unprepared for the maneuver, the Sekaran sped by. In his attempt not to crash into Drin, the city guard dodged, running his sky-bike directly into Drin's light sword. Metal *screeched,* and sparks flew. It was followed by the distinct sound of an engine losing power. The Sekaran's sky-bike dropped from the sky.

The girl behind Drin screamed her lungs out.

"Stop that!" Drin shouted back at her.

"Stop trying to get us killed!"

"I'm trying to save us. Why don't you make yourself useful and do the same?" Drin said. He didn't mean to lose his patience with her, but he was fast getting sick of babysitting in the middle of battle. There were three more Sekarans left, all in close pursuit of Sao-rin and Err-dio.

"How?" the girl asked.

Drin hit the accelerator, causing a rush of force against them while he caught up with the others. "Use the laser-repeater."

"Oh." The girl sounded sheepish. She had both arms around him still, her entire body tense against him. With a careful movement, she pulled her gun-hand free, straightening it over Drin's shoulder. Her other hand gripped him to the point he thought he might be bleeding through his armor.

"Careful not to hit our allies," Drin said as he pressed forward. If only the girl could have done some of the flying, then he could fire at the Sekarans. There was auto-pilot, but this sky-bike's simple AIs wouldn't be able to keep up with the sharp turns needed for a combat situation.

They looped around and found themselves behind the Sekarans. The girl pulled on her laser-repeater trigger several times. One of the blasts connected with the Sekaran pilot's back. The enemy pilot fell to the side and then off the sky-bike, which kept going forward and down until it crashed in the sand below.

"I got him!" the girl cheered.

As she gloated over her lucky shot, one of the Sekarans returned fire, his blasts coming all too close to hitting Drin. The girl reflexively pulled her arm back and, in the process, dropped her weapon.

It took everything in Drin not to shout at her. He had to be patient. It wasn't her fault. This woman wasn't trained in combat. It was a blessing she'd done as well as she had.

And she knew she'd done wrong. She let out a single sob, pressing her face into Drin's back.

Drin turned their sky-bike again, trying to get out of laser-repeater range. He moved the bike erratically to make it more difficult for their enemy to make accurate shots.

One of the Skree had come about and joined the fray. The slave's sky-bike skittered across the air, drifting to its side before the engines reengaged and pushed forward. The Skree slave timed it just right. The sky-bike nose lifted, slamming into the Sekaran pilot. The piloting maneuver required so much precision, Drin couldn't help but be impressed. The Skree's vehicle spun out of control with the impact, but he succeeded in knocking the other pilot off the bike.

It left one remaining enemy, who was gaining on the Skree who flew ahead of them all.

Drin punched the accelerator again, trying to line his bike up with the remaining Sekaran. "You're going to have to keep this going. Don't crash," Drin said.

"What?" the girl asked, her voice panicked. "I don't know how to—"

Before she could finish her thought, Drin lifted himself to his knees on the center of the Sky-bike. The vehicle lost a little altitude as his trajectory took them beside the Sekaran's vehicle. Drin rose to his feet, balancing in the air with the assistance of his nanites.

The Sekaran had his laser-repeater pointed away from them,

toward the Skree slave, but he had the sense to look over at Drin. The Sekaran's eyes went wide with fear.

Drin jumped.

He landed on the Sekaran, who immediately fumbled with his laser-repeater and fired a shot into the air. The blast dissipated in the atmosphere, and the two men struggled, Drin trying to keep the gun away from the city guard pursuer. The Sekaran landed a blow on Drin's helmet, jarring his neck backward, and causing him to lose his balance. The sky-bike accelerated to the right, further jarring Drin.

There was nothing to grip onto. Drin fell. The nanites wouldn't save him now. But his quick reflexes did. He managed to grab onto the sky-bike's landing skis at the bottom of the craft. The vehicle rocked, swinging Drin as he hung on by a single hand.

The Sekaran glanced over the side and then twisted the handle-bars to try to shake Drin from the sky-bike. Drin swung wildly below, causing the craft to lose some of its balance. It proved enough of a weight imbalance that the Sekaran didn't attempt to shake him again.

Instead, the pilot shifted his laser-repeater to his other hand, pointing it at Drin. His glance fluctuated between Drin and facing forward in the act of piloting.

Drin tried to scan for the others' positions, but he couldn't see any sky-bike in his immediate view. The others couldn't be counted on for help. The girl was useless in battle as it was, and the Skree would prioritize assisting each other before an off-worlder. He didn't have much time before he would be shot.

The nanites swelled in power within him, giving his arm the extra strength he needed to pull himself upward. Both hands clasped upon the bottom skis, which gave Drin better balance. He pushed with all his strength and released, drawing the sky-bike downward from the force of his weight.

The Sekaran fired his shots, but too late. Drin had already moved.

The sky-bike continued at its tremendous speed. Drin scrambled to grip onto something. He barely managed to fall onto the rear of the seat, clawing at the pad to stay atop the vehicle. He righted himself as fast as he could.

His adversary pushed his own body back to try to force Drin to fall, but Drin had already gained a foothold. He had his legs up over the body of the sky-bike, and his thighs pressed together to keep him steady. From this position, the Sekaran couldn't point his laser-repeater at Drin, which gave a distinct advantage.

Drin pressed his hand against the Sekaran's back and summoned his light sword. As the blazing light formed, it drove the nanites' energy through the Sekaran's chest. The pilot screamed. When Drin drew his hand back, that was the end of his target. Drin pushed the corpse over the side of the craft.

He slid forward on the seat, gaining control of the sky-bike. The desert went on for as far as he could see, hills rising and falling in his vision, all made of sand. No landmarks anywhere to help orient him. Without a navmap, he wouldn't be able to find his way back to the city—or anywhere else.

The two Skree came into view. They'd circled their bikes back around to find him. Sao-rin waved a handless arm at him, bringing his sky-bike up along Drin's left side. Err-dio flanked his right.

"Where's the girl?" Drin shouted, hoping that Sao-rin was close enough to hear him. The Skree responded by scanning the horizon. She was nowhere in sight. Had she crashed?

Drin looked along the desert floor. He counted the sky-bikes. Four of them. Those had to have been the Sekarans. Where could the girl be?

"There!" Sao-rin pointed his stumps to the horizon. A small dot moved across the horizon ahead of them, barely visible to Drin.

With the assistance of his nanites, Drin focused, zooming his visor for an enhanced view of the sky in front of him. Sure enough, it was a sky-bike, ridden by a furred girl with very long ears. She held on for dear life.

Drin pushed on the accelerator bar, bringing his sky-bike to full thrust. This girl would be the death of him.

TWELVE

Anais screamed.

No, she wasn't screaming anymore. Her voice had given out on her several minutes ago. The wind rushed in her face, making her eyes teary and blurring her vision. It was much better being behind the hulking Elorian. She hadn't been able to see where she was going, and that had frightened her enough, but she couldn't control this craft. Turning required too much strength, and the blasted man hadn't told her how to speed up or slow down.

She was going to die. After all of this, her luck had run out.

What were her options? Should she try to crash? Jump off of this thing and hope for the best? She could wait until it ran out of fuel or the engine had a problem and forced her to sputter out of the sky. None of those options sounded appealing.

The sky-bike kept speeding along. Sand passed by in familiar hazy patterns beneath her. It would have been nice to have any different scenery in this world. Without the Skree guides, she was completely lost.

She tried to look behind her, but that caused the sky-bike to tilt.

Moving around wasn't an option, save for jumping. It seemed to be her only choice.

As she pontificated flinging herself to her imminent doom, another sky-bike pulled up beside her. The Elorian. He deftly banked his craft not to collide with hers but to run parallel. His mouth was open, and he shouted, but Anais couldn't make out what he was saying.

The Elorian stretched a hand toward her. Was she supposed to try to grab his hand at these speeds? She would risk ripping her arm clear off.

Anais shook her head. There was no way she was going to do as he asked.

He looked frustrated with her and frowned as if trying to come up with another plan. This time, he waved frantically at her.

What was that supposed to mean? She saw him clearly. She shrugged her shoulders and held her hands up for a moment to signal she didn't understand.

Before she had any more time to process, he was back on his feet, just like he had been when he jumped to the Sekaran's sky-bike in the first place. He meant to jump back onto her craft.

Anais scooted back as far as she could on her seat, clutching the bottom of the center bar as tightly as she could. This was crazy.

The Elorian jumped. As she saw his body flying toward her, time seemed to slow. If he misjudged, if he hit her, they'd both go spiraling to the ground at incredible speed.

He almost flew over the bike, flailing both his arms and using his upper body to grip the handlebars. The bike banked hard to the side, almost enough to make her fall off, but she had prepared. Her grip held tight on the seat below. She managed to stay on.

The Elorian gained control of the sky-bike, pushing it back to level equilibrium. He jammed on the controls, slowing their speed as he settled himself, swinging one leg over the other side. "You okay?" he asked, turning his head slightly toward her.

She was stunned but no worse for the wear. "I'm fine."

"We'll find the others," the Elorian said and decelerated the bike.

Hours later, they had settled and determined that the Sekarans had taken them too far off course to make it to the Skree hideaway in a single day. Instead, the Skree turned them to an area that actually had a little life to it, some robust trees and a small watering hole.

They all welcomed the water, no matter how dirty and stale it was. At least it was something. They'd had no time to gather supplies, which left them parched after a day in the hot sun. The water tasted terrible, but Anais found it refreshing enough.

"We'll stay here for the night, get some sleep, and make our way to my people tomorrow," Sao-rin told them. Err-dio and the Elorian seemed to agree with this, though Anais didn't relish the thought of sleeping on the sand and getting it in her fur.

The Elorian searched the area and found a pile of bark and wood, which he set into a small fire pit he dug out of the sand. He'd worked for hours finding the materials and setting up. He didn't appear to want any help, and she didn't know what use she could offer him.

Anais sat in the sand, bored, staring at the watering hole beyond. The others didn't talk to her much, and she wouldn't have known what to say if they had wanted to. She just wanted to be home.

Bright energy came from the Elorian's hand. Flames engulfed the pieces of wood he'd piled near her. The strange miracles didn't faze her this time. At this point, Anais wondered if there was anything he couldn't do. She brought her knees closer to her and wrapped her arms around herself. As the sun set, the desert chill filled the oasis. The fire felt good, warm, like home.

She missed the palaces of Deklyn, the comforts of what she had once perceived as her prison. The confines of studies and having to have bodyguards follow her around everywhere when she wanted to go out. It all seemed so tedious then, but what her mother and father had given her was a sense of safety. She didn't have to worry about living to see the next day, or so she'd thought then. In truth, even those protections hadn't been enough.

In the haze of the last few days, she hadn't had time to consider her friends from the other merchant-lord families. Lyssa. Elaym. She wondered how they were doing now, if these Sekaran invaders took more than just the palace. Were they alive, in similar slave confines to the one she had been a few hours earlier? Or had they disposed of them? And her family. They probably didn't make it out alive. The possibility of dead friends and family made her shiver.

The Elorian stared at her. She'd been focused on the fire, not considering her surroundings. The Skree were engaged in conversation down by the water, seemingly impervious to the cool, dry air.

"Are you cold?" the Elorian asked.

"A little," Anais said.

"Mm."

That was it? Wasn't he going to offer to warm her somehow? She canted her head at him, her long ears twitching. He was an odd one. She couldn't say she'd ever met anyone exactly like him before. He was so sure of himself, of his path. It must be nice to have a life like he did. A real sense of safety and security. Not having lost everything.

She shook her head. No. She couldn't let herself fall into a pit of despair. She'd been on a Sekaran ship, only moments from having so much more taken from her. The Sekarans had threatened to stone her to death over rejecting the sheikh's advances. She'd made it out the other side, and she owed this strange man for being able to draw breath. He was like a gift from...

"Who are you?" Anais found herself asking.

The Elorian turned his attention to the fire. He grabbed a stick and stoked the flame. "A great question. Something I've spent the last few days trying to figure out myself."

His answer was irritating. Anais found herself wanting to slap him. But she remembered these last several hours had to be as stressful for him as it had been for her, perhaps more so. She hadn't been the one performing death-defying jumps through the air on sky-bikes, after all. "I meant, what's your name?"

"I am called Drin."

"Well, nice to meet you. I'm Anais of the Fen merchant-lord family, Deklyn."

"Sounds important."

"It is," Anais said, her words coming out sounding defensive. She slid her legs closer to the fire, feeling the heat of the flame.

But it wasn't important now. No one on this world cared about her titles or who she was, and she had no way to confirm her world would be safe. She frowned.

"You should get some rest," Drin said. "We have more traveling to do tomorrow."

"Okay," Anais said. Now that he had mentioned it, her body felt like it was about to give out. She'd had too many days of no rest. She turned away from the fire and lay down on the sand, keeping her back to the warmth. It wasn't as bad as the cell floors she'd been sleeping on. She drifted to sleep to the sound of the crackling flames.

THIRTEEN

DRIN AND THE OTHERS RESUMED THEIR FLIGHTS ON THE SKY-
bikes once first light peeked above the horizon. The Skree kept to
themselves through the night, though Drin did not take much time to
rest himself. They hadn't shown more interest in Yezuah or the holy
book so far, but after the long day, Drin understood a lack of eager-
ness in philosophy.

The trip took them another several hours across the desert, until
they came to an area that looked like it might have had some greenery
in different seasons. At least there was life on the ground, brown
grasses, and shrubs, an occasional tree. Even some birds and rodents
crossed the plain on the hot day. The scenery changed further,
becoming hilly, and they approached an area with several rock formations of different colors. The sight was by far the most aesthetically
pleasing thing Drin had seen on this world.

The Skree landed their bikes in a circular dirt area beside the
rock formations and powered down their engines. Drin set his bike
down soon after and waited for Anais to slip off the back. Once she
was securely on the ground, he dismounted.

Several Skree seemed to come out of nowhere. They blended in with the rock formations, their skin, and clothing acting as camouflage. No wonder they had been able to hide here.

Sao-rin and Err-dio moved to greet their fellows and spoke to them in their native language for several minutes. The girl, Anais, looked up at Drin. "Do you know what they're saying?" she asked.

Drin shook his head but moved forward along with their Skree companions. "I've not had an opportunity to learn their language."

"My brothers greet us and welcome us to the hideaway," Sao-rin said, turning toward Drin. "You are welcome here as long as you would like. I told my brothers of what occurred in Altequine, and the miracles you showed in saving us. A true sign from God, don't you think?"

Drin hadn't thought of it in those terms. He had been praying for God to reveal his purpose. Could it be to act as a witness to these Skree? It wasn't what he was envisioning when he left the *Justicar*. He had wanted to stop the violence, get away from it and reflect. As a result, he'd only created more violence. But maybe he was looking at it wrong. "The ways of the Lord are mysterious," Drin said diplomatically. "Who leads here? Are you sure we're welcome?"

Sao-rin chuckled. "My people defer to me. As I told you, I am the descendent of King Sao-dei. Though I'd been enslaved a long time, my people have been awaiting my return." He motioned with his stump. "Come."

The Skree led them into a deep cave, lit by glo-rods along the path every three to four paces. It provided adequate lighting within the cavern, which twisted into a network of dug-out hallways and rooms. They had no doors, allowing a full view of everyone they passed. As they walked, Drin could see some of the sleeping arrangements the Skree had: bunk beds to allow four Skree to one room. They had to make efficient use of their space. It must have been difficult to dig into this rock, even with the hardworking Skree doing the tunneling.

They looped around to a larger room with several makeshift benches and tables. One of the Skree turned. "This is our feasting and gathering area. Please," he said, pointing with three arms from one side, "have a seat. You must be famished."

Drin had to admit that his stomach churned with hunger pangs. It grumbled at the thought of food. "Water as well, please." He sat on the bench as directed, happy to take any hospitality after the way he'd been treated by the Sekarans.

Anais kept close, sitting beside him. Err-dio and Sao-rin flanked them at either side. "Once you're rested and settled in, I told my friend Tre-sal you would be willing to tell the tale of Yezuah and the peace he brought to Eloria."

The man standing and offering food nodded. "We are eager to hear your words. You rescued the heir, and we are grateful." He then bowed his head and departed with some of the others, ordering them to retrieve food and drink.

"They keep calling you heir. Are you still in line?" Drin asked.

Sao-rin leaned against the table, resting his elbows on it. "I cannot rightfully take my place until we are returned to our home. Though our ancient throne room no longer exists, having been plundered and rebuilt by the occupiers, certain ceremonies must only be performed on the king's grounds. Until we can return to such a place, the heir I will be, or perhaps the next generation will take their rightful place if I am so fortunate to find a mate." He flashed a smile with his last words.

Drin looked up to the cave ceiling in reverence, an act Drin always found odd. But it was how he thought of God, up above him, ever watching, even through the hideaway's rock wall. As his path on this strange world unfolded, it seemed more and more that he was being guided for a purpose. Increasingly, that purpose appeared to be to liberate the Skree from the Sekarans. But he had come here to avoid violence.

Before he could think about it further, the others returned with food and drink. The plates had some form of cooked animal flesh on bone and some greens mixed into a stew. They also had pitchers of water and poured cups for the four of them.

The girl Anais must have been the most famished, as she didn't wait to even smell the food, or for the others to have their places set. She picked up the meat with her hands and bit into it.

The other Skree brought them utensils, and Anais flushed. "Sorry," she said, wiping her mouth. "I haven't eaten in a few days. I'm starved."

Err-dio laughed. "Don't worry about it. We've lived as slaves long enough to know that sometimes you have to eat scraps off the floor."

Several of the Skree laughed, though Drin didn't find the matter funny. They ate and talked for the next several minutes, and as they did, more of the Skree came into the room to view the visitors. Some pointed and whispered about them, many never having seen off-worlders other than the Sekarans who had enslaved them.

By the time Drin finished eating, the room had filled. Several whispered and soft conversations became a loud rumble within the echoing cavern. Tre-sal glanced around the room. "It looks like our people have heard of you. Perhaps you would introduce yourselves?"

Anais's nose twitched. She had a little bit of the stew on her face. "I don't think I want to talk in front of this many people."

"I'll do it," Drin said. Crowds didn't make him nervous, especially ones receptive to the holy book. The Skree seemed malleable. Yezuah had told his followers to go to the downtrodden for good reason.

He stood, surveying the room. More than a hundred faces stared back at him. What they had been told, Drin didn't know, but he could only imagine they were in awe of his green skin and two arms. He'd not summoned his armor to cover him since entering the cave but had taken some of the Skree's cast-off clothing to help blend in with them. It was little more than rough burlap, but it was functional enough. The differences between the species seemed pronounced here. It didn't bother Drin, who had been to several worlds in his duties. Most of the time he had been among other species in the past, he had been slaughtering them, paving the way for the fathers and bishops to come in and convert and rebuild. After that, it was difficult to fear anyone or anything.

"My name is Drin. I was a knight of the Holy Church in the high crusade declared by the pontiff against the Sekaran invasion of so many worlds. Our purpose is to retake these lands in the name of the Lord God on high and bring salvation to all who profess faith in Him," Drin said. And also one day to retake Eloria, but the Skree didn't need to know his homeworld had been captured by the Sekarans.

"Who is this God you serve?" one of the Skree asked.

"A great question." Drin paused to collect his thoughts. "The Lord God is the creator of all things. This world, mine, and every other in the known systems. All life is His design and His design alone. You'll note that, even though we have our differences, we are very similar, a sign that our creator had a hand in both your and my making.

"When God became Elorian, the world had been ravaged by what we call the Hundred Years wars. The tribe of Dawn and the tribe of Nazray fought each other relentlessly, bringing the other ten tribes of Eloria into their endless conflict. Many died over that period. Several philosophers thought this war was going to bring about the War to End All Wars, and that the dead would rise to experience the kingdom of Heaven.

"In its hundredth year, a warrior named Yezuah came from the Nazray tribe. He came from nowhere. None could recall him being among their ranks. He fought with honor and seemed impervious to the Nazray enemies. He also spoke truth, that even in battle, we should love our enemies. We should treat prisoners with kindness. The only way to end the war would be to ensure the young saw our compassion. Many of the Nazray leaders took exception to this, but Yezuah persisted with his message of divine love.

"It paid off in his battles. His units were energized and victorious, always. His disciples didn't take casualties, either. The Lord bestowed tangible blessings from on high, technology from the creator that, to this day, even though we are a copy of a copy of those who came before, grants us the gifts of the Kingdom of Heaven here in this universe."

Drin paused to survey the crowd. They were with him, hungry for more. God must have willed him here to bear witness to the Skree. This was his calling.

"Then what happened?" a younger Skree asked. "Did he destroy all of his enemies like you when you saved our heir?"

"Quite the opposite," Drin said, shaking his head. "A great battle approached. Both sides had amassed their most sizable armies to date. Yezuah led his disciples and a contingent of forces to a place we now call the Mount of Alms. He held his armies back and went forward with the flag of truce, offering parlay to the tribe of Dawn. He was betrayed, however, as the Dawn general came forward under the guise of speaking peace and ran a sword through Yezuah.

"This time, Yezuah did not resist the blow. He was showing a new way. Both armies looked on in horror as they saw what had occurred. The tribe of Dawn laid down their swords and refused to fight. The Nazray moved forward, but they remembered Yezuah's teachings and did not slay the enemy general. Instead, they took his weapon, treated him with dignity, and took him away. Both tribes went back to their homes without further blood being spilled.

Drin looked over the crowd to make sure they were still with him. The Skree appeared to be intently focused. "The disciples waited. The planet trembled with a violent quake, as it could not take the death of its creator. The ground opened up, and the disciples scurried backward. It swallowed Yezuah whole, and the crack in the ground closed over him, making the world His tomb.

"His disciples were devastated. They sat and fasted for days. The women shed many tears for who they had thought was going to be their messiah, a king to rule all of Eloria. It was not to be the case.

"However, in three days' time, Yezuah began to appear to the nobility of the tribes. Each king was given a private audience, and He called them to peace, to bring Eloria together as one so that they might venture forth to other worlds and tell them of the glory of the

Divine Creator. The kings—well aware of Yezuah's death at the battle—as the news traveled, all went to their knees in fear. They begged forgiveness for the Hundred Years War and all the bloodshed and vowed to work together.

"Thus the kings formed a council of twelve and elected a holy father—one of Yezuah's disciples—to show the way of the true God. Yezuah then appeared before his disciples, giving them hope, and telling them not to be afraid. They had been endowed with His gifts, but He must return to the heavens. He prophesied that peace would reign for a thousand years, and it did. His teachings were written down by the disciples to form the holy book in which we base our beliefs."

The Skree clapped for him when he finished.

Sao-rin stood. "When he told me this in the jail cell, I was interested. When I saw the way he miraculously saved Err-dio and me from the Sekarans, I came to the faith. It is simple. His God... our God, only requires faith in Him, and from that devotion, we will grow and have salvation."

Several mutters of, "I want this salvation," echoed through the chamber.

Drin looked to the girl, Anais. She was no longer sitting where she had been eating. In fact, he couldn't see her anywhere in the chamber. Where had she gone to?

Err-dio raised a hand. "If we all convert, perhaps our new friend will lead us to victory and rid us of the Sekarans?"

The room erupted into cheers.

Drin grimaced, but he did not address the crowd. The enthusiasm they had for battle was not his message. It wasn't Yezuah's message, either. The whole point of it had been that battle could end. It was the very thing that bothered him so much about the crusades his people had been waging. But now, seeing how the Sekarans treated the Skree, he saw that battle was necessary. It had been right to free Sao-rin and Err-dio. If he were honest with himself, these Skree, cowering in a cave system in the middle of the desert, needed a champion as much as those in the stoning pit had. It didn't make him feel comfortable, however. He'd come here to evade war.

"I should retire. It's been a long day, and I need to meditate and pray," Drin said to Sao-rin.

The Skree nodded. "Should I show you to your chambers?"

"Perhaps later. I'd like to be outside. I'll find you?"

"Ask for me when you're ready, my friend. Yezuah be with you."

"And with you," Drin said. Several of the Skree looked eager to speak with him, to meet him, as he departed the chamber, but he made his way through without a further word. He had far too much to reflect upon before he could answer any more of their questions.

FOURTEEN

ONE OF THE SKREE ATTENDANTS SET ANAIS UP IN A SMALL enclosure within a rock wall. It had a bed and even sheets. They were small luxuries she missed. Even though the sheets were much coarser and the bed much harder than hers back at the Deklyn palaces, the comforts weren't something she would complain about. She lay atop the bed, staring at the ceiling above. Glo-rods from the hallway outside lit her enclosure. There appeared to be no way to turn off the lighting, as well as no door to secure, or to give her privacy.

Finally having a moment to herself, Anais breathed deeply. What would she do from here? She had to find a way back to Deklyn, to her people. Or at least to find out what happened there. She tried to recall the night she'd been kidnapped. The Sekarans overwhelmed the palace, but did they secure the whole city? Did anyone else of her family make it out alive? She couldn't remember seeing a large army. It seemed more like a small strike force or a raiding party.

But they had knocked her out. She recalled seeing the palace, and then their transport ship. Anything could have happened. Her father and mother. Her friends. She worried about them. The uncertainty was almost worse than knowing they were dead.

She turned to her side and brought her knees to her chest. It had been a rough few days, with very little sleep. Despite her weariness, her mind spun too much to sleep. Plans of returning to her home ran through her head. Worst case scenarios where Sekarans captured her again. Those thoughts chilled her. She'd only narrowly avoided abuse and a painful death. Would she be able to be so lucky again?

The Skree seemed content to believe the Elorian's explanation of some almighty God looking over them in everything, protecting them. She couldn't believe a God would allow what had occurred to her. Or to Sao-rin. The Sekarans took three of his hands! How could he be so quick to believe in the Elorian's stories of some messiah from more than a thousand years ago?

"Hello," a voice said from the hallway.

Anais sat up to see who was there. No privacy. She wouldn't be able to handle this for long, being used to such solitude in her former palace.

Sao-rin stood at the entrance, leaning a couple of his stumps of arms on the enclosure wall. "I'm sorry to disturb you," he said.

"No, it's okay. I couldn't sleep anyway. What's going on?" Anais asked.

Sao-rin stepped into her small room. "It's Drin. I saw you left in the middle of his explanation of his theology. You didn't hear how it concluded."

Anais shook her head. "Go on."

"My brethren are filled with hope. Hope we haven't had in several generations. They believe with Drin's holy magic, we can retake our ancestral city, and remove the Sekaran scourge from our world."

Anais let out a laugh. "The Elorian is powerful, but one man is not an army."

"It's our hope he can train us."

"Well, good luck with that." What did this have to do with her? She was no fighter. In the city, she had been unable to hold her own.

She'd felt useless, slowing the whole group down. It was almost the same now.

"I was hoping you might be willing to help us. I know you have little attachment to the Skree or to this world, but we are here... and perhaps when we retake the city, we can help you return to wherever you belong?" His dark eyes shone at her, hopeful.

"I'm not sure how I can be a help, to be honest."

"The Elorian. He trusts you more than us. He sees you more as a companion. My brother and I noticed this when we stopped at the oasis. You were the one he turned to for solace."

For a strange reason, that made the hair on Anais's arms stand up and her ear twitch. She was his solace? She didn't get that impression from the conversation they'd had. "I don't think you're right about that. He saw me as someone to rescue but probably thinks I'm more a nuisance."

Sao-rin shook his head. "We Skree... we sense connections. It's hard to explain to off-worlders. You'll have to trust me. This is how we know his God is real, as well."

Anais frowned. She didn't have any better idea of the logistics on how she'd return to Deklyn, or even get word of what happened there. The truth was, she needed the technology of the city. And that meant returning there one way or another. It would be better with the Elorian's help. "I'll see what I can do, but I'm not sure I'll be helpful."

"Great!" Sao-rin said, excitement unmistakable in his voice. "He went outside. I don't think he much liked the prospect of leading us into battle, to warn you. Perhaps he'd best be eased into it. Or if he believes that it is his duty to his God?"

"I don't believe in his God, so I'm not going to lie to him," Anais said, pushing off the bed to her feet. She shook her hindquarters to let her tail fluff outward. "But I'll try to find him and talk to him."

Sao-rin motioned toward the hallway. "The exit is to the left. Continue down the burrowed corridor until you see the outside sparkle of the stars."

Anais passed him and followed his directions, guided by the glorods and the shadows they cast on the cavern floor. Eventually, she reached the outside.

The skyline was so beautiful. So many stars that lit the world like a million tiny fireworks. One of those was the star Deklyn revolved around. She wished she knew more about star charts so she could spot her home. It warmed her to some degree to think of her world being out there.

It was amazing to see what stars looked like without the lights of a city dimming them. She'd never experienced this kind of open space on Deklyn. It gave the universe a sense of grandness, stirring something inside of her she found hard to describe.

She looked around and spotted a silhouette on a large rock protruding from the hills a small distance away. Determined, Anais made her way over and saw the Elorian when she came closer. Tall, muscular, she'd noticed him before, but now that they were out of a panic mode, and he was sitting there, staring up at the stars as she had been a moment before, he seemed... beautiful.

"Hey," Anais said. She stopped at the bottom of the rock, not about to climb the thing and risk falling.

It took Drin a few moments before he seemed to notice her, but he turned his head. "Hello," he said, almost having a questioning tone to how he greeted her, as if asking why she was bothering him.

"I heard you stormed out of the cavern. I wanted to make sure you were okay," Anais said. It was mostly true.

Drin stood from his place on the rock. He turned toward her and, instead of cautiously heading down the gentler slope of it, he leapt. His legs and boots seemed to sparkle as he sailed over her.

Anais couldn't help but cringe as he came toward her. What if he misjudged and landed on her?

He didn't, coming down on the opposite side. He took a couple of steps to balance himself and then dusted off his pant legs.

"Show off," Anais said. He pulled these stunts when they were being chased by the Sekarans. There probably were easier ways for him to do things, but he had to give reminders that he had powers the others didn't. It unnerved her, in both a bad and a good way.

He turned toward her. "We have to take small pleasures in the gifts we have, and in the victories we can create for ourselves. Otherwise, our journeys will swallow us in darkness," Drin said.

"Is that something from your holy book or whatever?" Anais tried not to roll her eyes.

"No. Something I've discovered along my path." He stepped closer to her, as if trying to read her eyes in the darkness. "They told you I stormed off, hmm?" Drin sounded amused.

Anais nodded. He was so intense it left her speechless.

"Not exactly. I wanted to go think, and to be alone. I don't make decisions lightly or without consulting the Lord in prayer."

"You really believe in that stuff, huh?"

Silence fell again. Awkward. It let her know it was a stupid question.

Anais shifted her weight onto her heels and rocked to her toes. "So, what did you figure out? How to get us out of here?"

"I'm still not certain," Drin said, frowning.

"Back on my world, I had every comfort. These last few days have made me understand I shouldn't take anything for granted. How stupid I was," Anais said. She glanced at the dirt in front of her feet. "I've hated it. More than anything. This isn't the life I was supposed to lead, and I want to be back. I'll pay more attention to my father's teachings so I can handle the family's estates. I don't know. I wasn't even first in line to inherit, but I saw the look in his eye when I was bored. I hated it. Now I understand why he was so insistent. It's so easy to lose it all. And I wouldn't even have had any hope of getting my old life back if it weren't for you..." She trailed off.

A hand fell upon on her shoulder. It was strong, masculine. His skin was a bit rough, even through the loose clothing the Skree had provided her. Even if it didn't fit quite right, it was better than walking around in the Sekaran's sheer garb. Anais lifted her eyes to

Drin again. He met her gaze. His eyes were so tender, so truthful, she found herself lost in them.

"It's okay. There is a plan for all of us, but we have to seek and find the truth in our callings," Drin said.

She wasn't sure what he meant, but she did sense in his voice, and through his touch, that he intended to be reassuring. It did more than that. She felt that shiver going through her as she did earlier, something she hadn't wanted to think about at all. He was so close to her. His musk filled the air, and it was pleasant. If he wanted to kiss her, she would let him. She found herself moving to her toes to facilitate that. His hot breath fell upon her face. It felt good, like he was always supposed to be this close. She wanted him closer.

Suddenly, he turned his face away.

Anais's ears twitched, and she slumped off her toes. "Seriously?"

Drin didn't turn back to her but inclined his head upward toward the sky instead. "You are dangerous," he said.

"What's that supposed to mean?"

"I took a number of vows when I joined the Templars. Some I... may have broken, but only in my attempts to better serve God."

"I don't understand what that has to do with me."

He turned back to her, sidestepping so he wouldn't be so close to her this time. Anais found his action made her heart hurt more than it should. "One of those vows is of chastity. I must ask your forgiveness in that I may have stumbled. My thoughts toward you just now were not pure."

Anais blinked. It made more sense now, but she didn't find any more solace in it. If anything, it made her more annoyed. In all of her time on Deklyn, she hadn't let herself become close to any of the boys in her schooling. Several had been interested in her. Who wouldn't, with her father being the most powerful of the merchant lords? Now that she found someone who stilled the beat of her heart, she couldn't have him? Because of some dumb vow?

It wasn't dumb. She had to respect it. He was honest. *More* than honest. That was part of what attracted her to him. Or perhaps she had some strange psychological reaction to him having saved her. Either way, the mood was killed. She wouldn't have to think about it anymore. At least until next time. She shook her head, her ears flopping to the side. "It doesn't matter. What matters is you're my only hope of getting off this world. And you're the Skree's only hope of not having to live in fear, hiding in this rodent hole of a hideaway." She motioned to the cave entrance behind them. "Or worse, as slaves to those monsters back in the city."

"You're right," Drin said.

"I am?"

He paced toward the rock. "You are, but I need to consider what to do about it. God delivered me here, I know this. But he hasn't answered me as to what comes next."

Anais watched him for a long moment, and then stifled a yawn. "I should get back inside. I hope you figure out what to do, and soon. I don't think the Sekarans are going to take our escape from the city lightly."

"I don't think they will, either."

She found herself waving at him even though he faced away from her. Her feet dragged, everything in her body begging to stay with him. She had to will herself away from him. No good would come of staying. He'd made his intentions—or lack thereof—clear. Hopefully, her talk with him would at least have some impact toward what the Skree needed. They deserved help, even if she didn't.

FIFTEEN

IN THE MORNING, THE SKREE GATHERED FOR BREAKFAST IN their large chamber. One of them had asked Drin if he'd be willing to speak before the assembled group over their meal. Though Drin was no priest, he agreed. He told a tale of Yezuah healing the wounds of a thousand soldiers after one of the bloodiest battles of the Twelve Tribes. "The next day, none were weary. Yezuah's healed men fought in battle, and won a great victory, more united than ever before. One day, God willing, your people around this world may be united under the Lord as well."

The race of six-armed men proved very receptive to Drin's message, if their applause and nods of agreement meant anything. "Will you pray over our meal?" one asked from across the room.

Drin obliged with the Lord's Prayer, something they'd learn anyway in their journey in the faith. "Lord God on high, Your name is sacred forever. This kingdom is Yours now, as You have gifted us, and will hold us until You return. Forgive us our sins, as we forgive the sins of our enemies. Never let Your flock go astray, but keep us apart from evil, that we may grow in our faithfulness. Power and glory to Yezuah," Drin said.

Unlike when he had been with his people on the *Justicar*, the Skree did not repeat the end line. Of course not. They hadn't been taught to as he had from a young age. "There is a response, where you say 'power and glory to Yezuah' as well."

The Skree repeated the phrase enthusiastically.

Despite the reception, it disturbed Drin how quickly they followed him. What if he had been some false prophet, would they have done the same? No, the Skree had not followed the Sekaran false prophet's words. They understood truth when they saw it. These people starved for truth and good news. He shouldn't worry. Their faith should be refreshing to him.

He sat to partake in the meal, with Sao-rin at his side.

"You've done much for the spirits of our people. I've never seen them with so much energy," Sao-rin said.

Drin mumbled something noncommittal while bringing food to his lips. This all was out of his comfort zone. He was a soldier, not someone to be looked to for spiritual advice. This was why E.C.S. ships carried a full contingent of clergy and nuns. It allowed the Elorians to follow through with the local populations and provide wisdom after the Templars cleared the dangers aside.

"Our people want to work to reclaim this planet from the Sekarans. We're all in agreement. You heard the early ideas last night, but with your help, I think we may be able to make progress toward the goals." Sao-rin produced a scroll from a satchel next to him. He unfolded it on the table and swiped across the thin screen to reveal a glowing map. He pointed to a city. "This is Altequine, where we were most recently held. As you observed, the city is located in the middle of a desert. It does have an underground water system that supplies some of its needs, but the city is dependent on trade from the more temperate farm zones. They have large shipments that come from here," Sao-rin drew his finger across the map to an area with a river. "Twice a week, the trade is brought to both them and the space-port, of which they use the supplies and garner a profit on the sale to other worlds. My people have been able to procure supplies from private merchants, but we haven't dared attack the main Sekaran transports."

"You wish to disrupt their supply line," Drin said, following with what Sao-rin proposed. He couldn't help but let out a small sigh.

Sao-rin looked up from the map and scrutinized him. "You do not like the plan."

"No, it's not that. It's what I would look at were I in your situation. You can't know this, but I came to this world to avoid war and conflict. I wanted to seek Yezuah through peace and find peace of mind."

"From what you said, your God does not find war to be something against His will. Sometimes it was necessary. Didn't your Yezuah first bring these powers you display to us?" Sao-rin motioned his stump over Drin, signifying his armor.

"That He did."

"And wasn't His will to protect the weak, and ensure that they were treated with dignity in order to end such wars righteously? Look how the Sekarans treat us as their slaves for generations. Do you think that would be of His will?"

Drin frowned. "No. It wouldn't be."

"We need you, Drin. From what you have told us of the true God, it sounds to me as if you were guided here by His hand. Your purpose is clear. Your will may be otherwise. You may wish to avoid conflict, but that is not the path set before you."

Those words struck Drin. He could feel they were true. He didn't want to admit it, but all his prayers had pointed him to this same path. The Sekarans were brutal. They did not respect life. Souls were in danger because of the way they abused others. It was exactly the sort of thing Yezuah came to put an end to.

Was his own pride standing in the way of helping people? His own unwillingness to fight, and to use the gifts that were given to him by the holy church? It was his imagination, but Drin could swear that he felt the nanites stirring within him, as if they were energized by his thoughts.

"You know the land," Drin said finally. "You can be a help to me. Can your people fight?"

Sao-rin glanced around the chamber. "They are hearty people. Some have done what they could in the streets and desert to survive. Others can learn. And we are all willing. We want our world back."

Drin nodded. He scrutinized the map. The path Sao-rin had laid out of their supply lines glowed in a green color atop the image. The details were clear. Most of the trek would be across dunes and sand as they had traveled themselves a day before. But there was one area with a canyon and giant boulders they could use as cover. He pointed to it. "This is where we start. We do reconnaissance here with a small team and see what kind of guards the Sekarans use for these transports."

"We're one step ahead of you," Sao-rin said. He flicked the image on the scroll which became a moving picture of a large transport. The vehicle was sand-colored and hovered not far off the ground. It was box-shaped except the contours that reduced its drag. From a distance, it would barely stand out from the scenery. It didn't seem to have any weapons on the outside, but it was well-armored. Drin could easily cut through the transport with his light sword.

"They send no guard ships with them?"

"None," Sao-rin said.

"Foolish."

"They've grown complacent in recent years. It's not as if we had the means to oppose them." Sao-rin laughed. "None of us would even be able to break through into the transport. Its plated hull absorbs laser-repeater fire. This is why we need you."

Drin nodded again, focusing on the transport. There was no telling what kind of resistance would be inside. He recalled how easy it had been to get out of the city. None of the Sekaran guards were able to stand against him. The only risk would be if he came up against a battlemage, but such a one would be unlikely to be used as a guard for a standard supply transport. Especially if the transports had made safe runs for generations.

He took a deep breath and exhaled again. This was what he wanted to avoid, fighting foes who were unable to fight back. It couldn't help but bring him a sense of dishonor. The Sekaran actions, however, justified a response. Glancing around the room, he saw the Skree, how poor they were. Sao-rin's stumps, whether intentionally or not, hung prominently in his vision as well. Those had once been full arms with hands. He could only imagine the tortures the Sekarans put him through. Finally, he looked the Skree heir in the eye.

"You'll have my help. I'll need a small team. We'll use the same point I mentioned for reconnaissance. I assume you know the supply schedules?"

Sao-rin's eyes shone bright, and he smiled. "We do. I already have a team of volunteers ready. We'll leave tomorrow."

SIXTEEN

Anais made her way through the underground caverns, orienting herself to her new home. Home was the wrong word. Hopefully, she wouldn't be in this place much longer than she had to. She had to get back to Deklyn, no matter what it took.

The Skree were economical with their space. With expansion meaning they had to dig out underground caverns in rock, it made sense. The low corridors gave a feeling of walls closing in around her. It was disorienting. She had been used to the sprawling palace back on Deklyn, where tall hallways led to grand rooms, a great place for holding parties and state functions.

There were only a few larger corridors along the main entrance. The smaller ones led to storage rooms or Skree living areas. Most of the Skree gathered in the main room where they took their meals and discussed their society's plans, but there were a few small study and work areas some of the Skree used for reading, writing, or general study. Anais came upon one of these studies, one with a tower of books and scrolls stacked along the back. Some were of the real paper variety. Those would have sold for good money back on Deklyn.

As she stared at the books, she failed to notice Err-dio seated at a desk in the corner. "Awe-inspiring, isn't it? These are the works my people have been able to collect over the years in our hideaway. Sometimes slaves sneak a book from off world. Others come from the ancient Skree when we ruled our planet. Did you know Altequine used to have gardens that sprung from the rooftops and flowed over the tops of the buildings? I learned that from one of these books. You can learn many things from books."

Anais stepped to the books and scrolls, grabbing one with a pink frilly string hanging from it. She stopped herself and looked to Err-dio. "Can I?"

He nodded.

She took the book out and flipped through it, but it was in a language she didn't understand.

"Ahh, that one is famous. It's called *The Sword's Flower*. A romance about an ancient king who gave up his throne for a peasant girl. The high cleric was angered by his abdicating his throne and set a demon upon them. The king had to take up the sword to save the flower. Such lovely imagery." Err-dio smiled.

Anais carefully set the book back down. "On Deklyn, I had a tablet with all of the planet's collected works on a library. We were a trade hub so we would have art, history, philosophy from all the major systems. I never wanted to read. I never even considered losing all of that information or not having access to it."

"It's humbling, isn't it? Perhaps this is why the true God set my people upon this course of toil and slavery. We require humility," Err-dio said, his voice somewhat pained.

"I don't know about that," Anais said, unable to help but have her lips fall into a frown. Slaves for generations. That's what the Sekarans created when they invaded worlds. It reminded her of Deklyn. "I actually have something to ask you."

"Go ahead."

"I need to get back to my world, or at least find a way to get word to my world that I'm alive. Do you have any space-worthy ships here?"

Err-dio shook his head. "The Sekarans tightly control space traffic. They keep us here to work for them by cutting off our communication and ability to leave." He motioned toward the ceiling. "Up there, they patrol with their warships. Any unauthorized exit..." Err-dio clapped multiple hands together. The sound echoed through the study and down the corridor, "boom."

Anais found herself with her jaw clenched. She forcibly relaxed. It wasn't fair. How could the Sekarans dominate everything on this world? Was that what they would do to Deklyn over the next few generations? She had to know what happened to her world, to her family. "What about a communications device to try to contact other planets?"

"We don't have one of those with a subspace range, I'm sorry," Err-dio said. "If we had a way to help you, we would."

Her heart sank. She couldn't lose hope just because they didn't have the tools necessary for her to get out of here. Things were getting better for her. Every experience she'd had on this planet so far had been far worse than her current situation. At least she had food, a place to sleep, and no worry that an ugly slob of a Sekaran was going to force himself on her. Even without that, though, this hideaway was little more than another cell. A place she couldn't escape from without dire consequences. Desert surrounded them, and it wasn't as if she could show herself in Altequine without someone noticing her. She didn't exactly blend in with Sekarans. "I have to find some way to contact my people," she said.

"I'll tell the others. Perhaps they know of a slave who can sneak one from their master? If any of their masters have them. The Sekaran overlords don't share knowledge of such devices with us lowly types. At least in my experience," Err-dio said.

Anais headed back for the room entrance. "Let me know if you hear anything," she said.

"Of course."

She returned to her room, trying not to let despair overcome her as it had so often since she'd come to this desert world. In some ways, she had less hope of returning to a normal life than ever before.

SEVENTEEN

DRIN AND THE OTHERS SECURED THE SKY-BIKES IN AN AREA OF the rock formation where they couldn't be seen either from the sky or from oncoming traffic. The desert had been quiet since pre-dawn, but they had to remain vigilant for when the transport came. He'd taken Sao-rin, who insisted on coming despite his important position as heir of the Skree. "A king who leads from behind is no king at all," he told Drin in their pre-flight preparations. He had no argument.

Sao-rin brought three other Skree with him, his most trusted men. One had powered binoculars, an excellent scout. The other two were burly and muscular individuals, who Drin had at first assumed were guards or soldiers. It turned out they were farmers who had worked hard in Sekaran fields. Now they harvested smaller crops in the Skree hideaway. Their strength would make for useful soldiering skills if the Sekarans gave Drin proper time to train them.

In the past few days, Drin learned the Skree subsidized the production of their hideaway with raids on Altequine and other nearby cities with markets. "With your presence," Sao-rin had told him, "we can take on larger targets and supply our people for a longer time with less effort."

After they'd discussed some of the logistics of their plan, Drin led the Skree in prayer, a much more personal prayer than the one he had taught them the evening before. This prayer asked for God's blessing directly on their endeavors. He told them they should ask for the Lord's assistance in all things, and they would find many blessings because of it. The Skree agreed to implement the practice of prayer before all of their future missions.

"Many of the brethren are asking to find a copy of the holy book you keep talking about," Sao-rin told Drin while they waited for their mark to arrive.

Drin frowned, turning his head toward the skyline. The large red sun rose in the distance. Soon, its oppressive heat would beat upon the desert. The Skree didn't seem to mind, and the nanites helped him repulse most of the heat. The Sekarans would not be so fortunate. "It would be good for your people to have the holy book to read. From what I've seen of this world, though, I doubt we would find any the Sekarans hadn't already destroyed."

"I believe you are right about that," Sao-rin said. "They destroy everything they touch."

Those words lingered in the dry air. Drin knew that to be true not just from his experiences here, but from what he'd seen of other planets he had gone to and conquered in the name of the holy church. The Sekarans did terrible things. Why had he been so adamant against fighting them? God sent him on this journey to open his eyes, he was certain of that now more than ever.

"They're coming," one of the Skree scouts said. He lowered his powered binoculars.

"Everyone to their positions. We're going to have one shot at this," Drin said. He hurried over to his sky-bike and mounted it.

The sky-bike rumbled when he turned the engine on. Dust flew up around him. His nanites shielded most of it from his body and face. The Skree didn't seem to have a problem with the dust either, despite not having protective gear.

Drin had watched them over the last couple of days, and they appeared to have an inner-eyelid that protected them from the relentless sand and dust of this planet. Their skin was thicker and heartier than his as well. It made sense, since this was where God placed them. His designs granted His peoples what they needed for survival.

Another cloud of dust rose in the atmosphere in front of them. It had to be their target. The transport wasn't quite visible yet in the morning sky, but only a large vehicle would kick that much debris into the air.

Within moments, the hulking box of the transport became visible in the distance. It approached at a rapid speed. They would have to slow it down before it came within the range in which Altequine would assist it.

Drin took off. The sky-bike zoomed at speeds that made the scenery blur. His life had been a similar blur since coming to Altequine. Even though it had only been a couple of days, it felt like so much time had passed. So much had changed within him. He had new resolve. God stirred his spirit. It was something he hadn't felt since...

One of the Skree shouted something and pointed ahead. Drin couldn't make out what he said, but something agitated him.

Drin focused on the transport. The vessel wasn't alone. A swarm of sky-bikes surrounded it, hovering in a protective formation. Nanites enhanced Drin's vision, zooming in on the target ahead. He counted four sky-bikes. Not too difficult to deal with, but they would have to make quick work of the guards on the bikes. If those Sekarans escaped, they could bring the entire planet's defenses down on them.

The Skree weren't prepared for anything but a quick boarding mission. They weren't organized, didn't move together as a unit. Even with so few of them, they were located haphazardly. If Drin had a few more days to train them, they could have been formidable. But that was hindsight. He could only hope they could adapt to the situation quickly.

Drin sped forward, accelerating to the sky-bike's top speeds. If the Sekarans weren't alert, perhaps they could gain a quick advantage.

Laser-repeater fire blasted past him. So much for that idea. He'd been spotted.

From behind him, the Skree fired their own laser-repeaters back at the Sekarans. One connected with a sky-bike, causing the Sekaran to spin out of control and crash to the sands below.

Drin closed in with his sky-bike to point-blank range, perfect for him to be able to use his light sword. The Sekarans fired at him, but he maneuvered too quickly and erratically for them to train their laser-repeaters on him. Drin pitied his enemies. As with most of his encounters on Sekaran-controlled worlds, the guards had never faced anything like him in combat before.

A cry of pain came from behind him. Drin turned back to see one of his Skree companions hit by the oncoming fire. The others couldn't pilot with nearly the skill he had. With more enemies ahead, there was no time to mourn the man. "God rest his soul," Drin said under his breath.

Finally within range of the other Sekarans, Drin willed his nanites to form into a light sword. The bug-eyed creature shrieked, unable to move out of the way of the impending doom thrust upon him.

Drin lowered the light sword like a lance, speeding his sky-bike forward. The light sword cut right through the screaming Sekaran's neck. Body and sky-bike continued forward while the guard's head rolled off his neck and fell backward. Dark blood splattered on the white sand. Two sky-bike guards left.

These Sekarans weren't stupid. Unwilling to fight a superior force, they abandoned the transport and sped ahead. "Don't let them escape!" Drin shouted as loudly as he could, letting his light sword dissipate.

It didn't appear as if the Skree heard him at first. They swarmed around the transport, implementing their original plan. But Sao-rin led his men to circle around the transport. They pushed hard on their accelerators, moving to intercept the fleeing Skree.

The transport loomed in front of Drin, taller than him by three body-lengths and much longer than he'd expected. This vehicle must have carried quite a number of supplies, hopefully including some food and water for the Sekarans. Regardless, it would provide them something they could trade for their necessities.

He had to trust in his team to handle the Skree speeding away. It left him to handle the transport alone. His sky-bike matched speed with the transport, and Drin pulled the bike just above the top of it. At these speeds, he didn't want to risk a tumble to the ground below, even with his armor.

The two vehicles lined up about perfectly when Drin made the jump. The transport kept pressing forward. Drin skidded across the top of it. He landed farther back on it than he would have hoped when his movement slowed. The metal was smooth, leaving him nothing to grip onto. A gust of wind pushed him back even farther. His eyes went wide: he had miscalculated. As the transport sped along, he would fall off of it soon enough.

He had one last hope. He reformed a light sword in his hand and let its laser-edge cut into the metal below. It cut along the back and dragged, but slowed him to where he could reach his hand around and find a grip in the molten metal. The jagged opening ripped into his armored glove. The hot, sharp edge pressed into his skin. Pain shot through him, but the maneuver stopped his regression and gave him a moment to breathe. Drin left a long, smoldering line of ripped metal in front of him. About a quarter of his work of opening the transport was already done for him.

But it also alerted the Sekarans inside. Their voices rang out, alarmed.

Drin had to act quickly. He pulled his light sword around and carved a square into the top of the transport. The metal sagged by its own weight and bent inward before he finished his cut. On the last line of the square, it dropped down to the floor below.

Three Sekaran guards stood inside the transport. It was well-defended after all. Drin considered the implications of their presence, along with the escort sky-bikes. It meant the Sekarans had some information as to the Skree activity. With the slaves swapping places in the city, Sao-rin had too many leaks. When he had a moment, Drin would have to suggest putting a stop to the practice, even if it meant some of the Skree suffered more.

Those thoughts had to be pushed back until later. Drin focused on the task ahead of him, and the three laser-repeater barrels pointed directly at him.

The Sekarans fired their weapons. Drin dropped into the transport compartment. Two of shots missed, but one pelted into Drin's armor. The nanites dissipated the blast with ease.

Drin landed on the floor below, bending his knees to absorb some of the shock. He spun, waving his light sword in an arc to cut through the closest Sekaran.

The other two Sekarans stumbled backward, stunned. One dropped his gun, trying to flee, but thudding into the side of the transport. The second stood slack-jawed, unable to fire. Drin charged forward, letting his light sword drag alongside him. He cut through both of them with one stroke. Too easy. Just as it had been when he'd faced hordes of these infidels with the *Justicar's* Templar units.

The three Sekarans bled out on the floor beside him. In many ways, this battle felt no better to him than any other he'd experienced in recent months, but at now least he had seen firsthand how the Sekarans mistreated others. Being here on Konsin II was God's plan, he had to keep reminding himself. He was saving slaves from both a torturous existence and eternal damnation from not knowing the true God.

A deep sigh escaped him as he stepped over the pools of blood at his feet. Crates lined the transport walls, piled all the way to the ceiling. Aside from the walkway where he'd descended, it was completely full of supplies. Some were labeled as food, some as cloth goods and furniture, and some water: all useful items the Skree desperately needed in their hideaway.

The transport still hummed as it barreled forward. Drin couldn't take the time to survey the spoils of this battle. He had to shut its engine down.

As he made his way down the pathway in front of the goods to the front of the craft, he scanned carefully to make sure there were no more Sekarans waiting in ambush. None came.

Drin slid into the cockpit. The transport moved via a simple display screen, slaved to an outside control. As he was sitting down, Drin turned off the program controlling the vessel from the city. The transport stuttered, continuing on a forward trajectory. A small slit in the front of the craft gave him a view of the desert ahead. There was no danger of him crashing into anything. He just had to slow down before it came close enough to Altequine for Sekaran reinforcements to arrive.

The controls were in the Sekaran language. While he knew how to operate most craft, he'd never spent time reading their crude symbology before. The nanites produced a filter over his eyes. He accessed their memory banks with a thought and a flick of his eyes to the side. Translations for the symbols appeared as translucent light in this visor.

The accelerator control and the air-brakes were easy to find from there. Drin tapped the marker on the screen, and the transport came to a hard halt. He nearly lost his balance, jolting forward, but he managed to brace himself against the front windshield.

The transport's engines powered down with a rumble, sand littering the air in front of it. Drin found a control to pop the side hatch. It opened into the hot desert, the sand now radiating heat as the sun beat upon the landscape. He stepped out of the pilot's compartment, toward the ramp.

Three sky-bikes appeared along the skyline. They pulled alongside the transport and slowed. As they came close, Drin could see the Skree, with Sao-rin in the lead. The heir slid off his vehicle and made his way over to Drin. "A one-man army. You didn't even need the rest of us," he said.

"The Sekaran guards would have found reinforcements if you had not been here to assist."

The other two Skree moved past them into the transport. One of them whistled. "Good find, heir," one called from inside. "There are enough supplies here to keep the hideaway stocked for the next couple of weeks. Now that it's safe, we'll inform the others to bring the wagons to help bring the goods back to hideaway."

"Hey, come to the cockpit. The lady with the long ears was looking for a transmitter. I think we can take the one out of here," the other said.

Drin waited outside while the two Skree surveyed their spoils of battle. Sao-rin stood with him, a pleased smile plastered on his face. "I can feel things are changing for us. Your God has blessed us."

"Your God, too," Drin said.

"Of course."

"I don't think this is a complete victory, however," Drin said. He looked back at the transport.

"Why not?"

"Before the mission started, you said the transport would have no guards."

"So? There were only a couple to deal with. It was simple."

"Some is more than none. It means they at least tried to prepare for you." Drin leaned against the transport's side wall. "If you didn't have me fighting with you, would this have been so easy? You lost one of your own as it was."

Sao-rin shaded his face from the sun. "I see what you mean. I feared this day would come. We've been too loose with our people."

"I don't mean to tell you how to lead," Drin said, "but I believe the practice of swapping out with slaves will have to stop. It provides too many opportunities for leaks, which we can't have in the days to come."

"Days to come? You sound as if you're planning something bigger than a supply raid," Sao-rin said.

Drin shook his head. "Now isn't the time to talk about the future. The Lord told His disciples to cherish victory. Tomorrow's worries will come upon a new dawn."

"Sensible advice." Sao-rin nodded. "As far as changing my people's ways, it's something I'll have to think about. You don't know how hard the Sekarans work us Skree. The breaks our system provides for rest and recovery are necessary for our survival." The heir's face grew long, and he moved toward the ramp. "Let's hurry up and get this back to hideaway to unload," he said to his people inside.

EIGHTEEN

Anais stood watching Err-dio while he worked on the transmitter device the others had ripped from the Sekaran transport during their raid.

He'd spent hours on it already. Anais could only stand and watch, never having worked on any mechanical devices. On Deklyn, she would have servants for such things, people like Err-dio whom she would have taken for granted. Her whole experience had opened her eyes to other people's lives, especially among those who worked in physical capacities. She would never be able to look at a number of things the same way again.

Err-dio sat on the floor, legs crossed. He leaned in toward the device, which he had plugged into a local power supply. All six of his hands adjusted components or held tools. One of the contactors sparked, and he drew a hand back. "Damn," he said.

"Are you okay?" Anais's ear twitched in sympathy to his pain.

"Just a little shock. This thing was meant to be a component on a vessel, not tied into our emergency battery systems. Voltages are different," he said.

"Does that mean it's not going to work?"

"No, I can make it work. I just have to be a little more careful what I plug into where," Err-dio said and went back to work.

Minutes went by. Anais waited as patiently as she could. She perused the bookshelf on the back wall, but she didn't much feel like reading. She was much too antsy. Err-dio's tinkering made for her best chance of contacting her family, even if it would only be an audio signal.

Drin came into the room with a long and somber expression, as usual. Anais began to wonder if he ever smiled.

He watched for a moment, then turned to her. "How are you doing?" he asked, his voice clinical. It wasn't as if he sounded unconcerned, but it still came across as impersonal.

His tone irked her. It served as an unwelcome reminder of how they'd come so close the night prior. How she could ever have let herself become lost in whatever it was that made the others follow him? She wouldn't be making that mistake again. "I'm doing okay. Hoping I can contact my people and see if they're safe."

"We should be careful to ensure signals aren't intercepted. We wouldn't want to bring down the Sekaran forces on this hideaway," Drin said.

"We have a scrambler," Err-dio said. "But we can bring the comm device out into the desert to send the signal if it makes you more comfortable. Once I get this running."

Drin nodded and shifted his attention to the Skree and his work. The display powered on and shone in several colors. The text on it was in a language she didn't understand.

"We're almost done here," Err-dio said. He tapped a couple of the controls, apparently having no problem understanding what the symbols meant. "I'm afraid I've got some bad news, though."

Anais's heart sank. "What?" she asked, her voice coming out meek.

"This transmitter doesn't have an off-world option. It's meant for local only. Sorry," Err-dio said.

"Couldn't you have figured that out before?" Anais asked. She sounded like she was scolding him, and she wished it didn't come across that way.

Err-dio shrugged. "Communications devices aren't my specialty. I performed maintenance on sky-bikes before. Some have small devices embedded, but I look at the screens to see their functionality. It's still very useful. We have full access to the Sekaran guard frequencies." He tapped on the display a few times. "This can provide valuable intelligence."

A crackling sound came from the unit, and then several voices.

"We've got one just like the Sheikh wanted."

"The one who escaped?"

"No, same species, though. Long ears, the tail. He liked that look."

"Bring her to Watcher Tellah for inspection. Hopefully this one will have a little less of an attitude than the other. The sheikh will not tolerate any more rebellion from his slaves."

"On our way."

The device made another crackling sound. Err-dio turned the sound down. "Huh," he said.

Anais's knees went weak. Her stomach turned over. Another girl from her planet? She couldn't help but mentally put herself in the other girl's place. The sheikh's foul breath on her neck, on her face, pressing his fat body against her. What if the Sekarans had broken this other girl? Anais had barely escaped a terrible situation herself because of several fortuitous circumstances. She couldn't help but glance at Drin.

He stood, stoic as ever as he considered the situation. "These Sekarans are relentless in their lust. How they bring shame to their false god."

"That's all you're going to say?" Anais said. She felt the urge to slap him.

"What?" The Elorian blinked.

"How can you be so cold? There's a real person who was just captured by those... those monsters. Do you know what they'll do to her? What they tried to do to me?" Anais found herself approaching him. She pounded her fists against his chest. He didn't move. His muscular form was hard rock against her hands. Anais fought tears.

This time, he didn't move his hands to console her. He was much stiffer than he had been the other night, here with Err-dio watching.

"This planet runs on slaves, Anais," Err-dio said. "It has been the way of things for generations."

Anais jerked her head toward him. "Yeah? Well, it's time to put an end to that. And Mr. No-Emotion here has the means to do it!"

"It's not that simple," Drin said.

"And why not?" Anais asked, looking up at him. His square chin was so close to her eyes, almost begging for a slap to wake him up from whatever religious trance kept him from real feeling. What good was his God and all of his religion if he couldn't help a poor girl in a precarious situation?

"Because we don't know anything about the city. Or about their defenses. We were lucky in our escape. God was with us. If they have battlemages, or electromagnetic pulse weaponry, my nanites won't be much help. It's tragic what is occurring to your compatriot, but to mount an offensive on Altequine will take planning. A lot of planning."

"Just break in, break out like you did before. No one would be expecting it. We can't just allow this sheikh to have his way with her!"

Drin shook his head. "No. It's not a good idea."

Anais slapped him on his cheek. He didn't budge, didn't raise a hand to her, despite her reflexive cringe. He stood there and took it. Err-dio watched, gasping when her hand struck.

She didn't have to deal with this at all. They couldn't stand by in complacency while someone else from her world suffered. Before allowing the shock to wear off and the men to respond, Anais ran away from them, down the corridor, and past several other Skree, who moved out of the way. She was on a rampage, and they appeared to sense it.

But what would she honestly do next? Was there anything she could do?

She could hide herself in a cloak, keep her ears concealed. If she moved around at night, she might be able to get a glimpse of what was going on in Altequine and help her friend.

That was the answer. The Elorian said he wanted information, well, she would gather it. But she wasn't going to sit around and wait for this other woman's life to be ruined in the process. One person could make a difference, and she was tired of sitting around being useless.

Anais ran down the hallway to the alcove where she'd been sleeping. There, she grabbed a hooded cloak the Skree used to keep covered from the blistering sun. It wasn't the most beautiful thing she'd ever worn, but it would have to do.

She jogged out of her alcove and through the main entrance to the hideaway. Err-dio and Drin hadn't followed, probably figuring it best to let her emotions fade. The evening had already begun to cool with the sun below the horizon. She glanced around, getting her bearings before heading toward the flat sky-bike landing pad. How did these vehicles work again? She had watched Drin use it after nearly flying to her doom. She wouldn't make that mistake again. The accelerator was on the left side of the bike, which meant the start button was directly in the middle. She smiled, proud at how well she recalled the details. It might be difficult to fly one of these things, but she would try, not for herself, but for the girl in captivity.

With the push of the button, the sky-bike hummed on. A couple of Skree followed out of the hideaway to see what the commotion was. They flailed their multiple arms, running toward her.

"Wait, stop! What are you doing?" one of the Skree shouted at her.

But they were already too late. Anais slid her fingers up the accelerator, and the sky-bike began to move.

She didn't know exactly where the city was, a flaw in her plan she wished she had thought of before she took off. The sky streaked in front of her, cool breeze on her face, causing her ears to flop behind her.

When they'd arrived at hideaway originally, they'd come in at an angle. Anais set her sky-bike to travel in the direction she recalled coming from. The journey had taken hours, compounded by the fact that they had to fight, throwing them off course.

Anais glanced behind her. No one came after her. She flew alone. After a while, the flying itself became boring. She swerved the sky-bike back and forth, banking it to the point where she almost would tip over just for the fun of it. The sand dunes had been monotonous during the daytime, but at night it was worse—she could hardly see anything.

Time passed slowly. She had no real means by which to measure how long she'd been riding. The controls of the bike were in the Skree language, which didn't help her. How many hours would she have to ride through the middle of the night?

The sky-bike kept moving, and she tried to keep her focus. She thought about back home but drifted to thoughts about the Elorian, something she quickly purged from her mind. But more, she ran over scenarios of what she would do when she reached Altequine. She vaguely remembered the sheikh's palace. Would she be able to get inside? She hoped she could sneak in and look like one of the other slaves. The more she thought about it, Drin had been right in saying they shouldn't foolishly rush in.

But how many hours was she out into the desert? If she tried to turn back now would she even be able to find hideaway? Probably not in the dark, at least.

She could scope out the situation. That would be her best plan. Then she could head back and report her findings.

But there was a flaw even in that plan. She had no way to report back to anyone. The sky-bike might have had a comm unit, but she didn't know how to operate it. Even if she did, how would she keep her signals from getting intercepted by the Sekarans?

Stupid, stupid, stupid. She'd reacted out of pure emotion, a desire to rescue one of her own still lingering deep inside of her. Despite all of the challenges, that care for one of her own didn't diminish. She'd never prepared for this sort of thing in her life, but what she did have was smarts, and perhaps some ingrained ability to negotiate and trade. That had to help somehow.

The wind silently ripped by her as she tried to figure out how to utilize her skills. Nothing came to her. She didn't have anything worth trading for. If she tried to bargain, the sheikh would probably just return her to some slave role like he had been going to do the first time they met.

Dejected, Anais found herself becoming tired. It had to be late in the night, since she'd left after darkness had already fallen. When she wore herself out, she tended to think negative thoughts. It reminded her of being alone, in bed back in her palace, staring at the ceiling and attempting to sleep until the wee hours of the morning. She'd worry about all sorts of things she'd seen on the nets. Natural disasters, wars, dying. Mostly dying. Those fears seemed so distant now. Having come so close to death, she would almost have found that to be a relief compared to what the Sekarans wanted to do to her.

Which was why she had to push forward and at least come up with a plan for the sheikh's new Deklyn slave. She couldn't allow someone else to go through that mental anguish, let alone have it become a reality.

Several minutes later, she shook herself awake. The sky-bike tilted forward, nearly making her lose her balance. She must have drifted off to sleep. Another dangerous and foolish problem she'd brought upon herself. Her eyes adjusted to the dark, and she noticed a brightness in the distance. The lights of a city!

Anais was careful to divert herself so she wouldn't fly right over Altequine. The city guards would capture her if she drew their attention. She ran her hand along the accelerator, pulling the bar downward to slow the sky-bike.

The vehicle responded with a natural descent pattern and soon approached the ground. A button on the top right switched the craft to landing mode. The sky-bike's nose lifted, sand flying everywhere as its bottom thrusters engaged, setting her down softly on a dune a reasonable walk from the city.

She swung her leg over the sky-bike and dismounted. Sand swirled around her, still lingering in the air. Anais covered her face with some of the cloth from her robes so she wouldn't breathe it in. Her feet slipped in the sand, still warm despite the cool night air. Each step burned in her weary thighs as she trudged toward the city. Her lack of sleep was overcoming her, and she found it difficult to remain standing, let alone to keep walking. Still, she willed herself forward.

Sometime later, Anais found herself near one of the city walls. There was no gate in view, no guards looking down upon her. She circled around until she found an open entrance where a sandstone road jutted out from the city and continued onward as far as she could see. The streets were fairly empty, but some people traveled along freely, with no city guards in sight. A transport vehicle sped by her. Anais kept to the side of the road to make sure she wouldn't be run over.

She kept her head down, not wanting to draw any attention to herself. Her hood concealed most of her features, which should keep her safe, at least while it was still dark out. After that, she would have to find somewhere to hide.

The empty streets made her fur stand on end across her body. It was uncomfortable. Perhaps it was paranoia, but something gave her the impression she was being watched the whole way through the city. She had no idea where she was going. For most of her time here, she'd been on the run, or in line as a prisoner, not exactly taking in her surroundings.

The streets wound, buildings haphazardly placed through the city over time, rather than planned in an orderly fashion. Many domed buildings loomed above her, casting shadows onto the already dark street, glo-lamps doing little good to give much of a sense of comfort. Anais pulled the robe more tightly around herself.

Soon she passed through the market bazaar square, where she remembered running through. The place was so open and empty without all the people crowding it. Once past the bazaar, she traveled down to the square where the Sekarans had their stoning pit. She tried her best not to look in its direction and recall the horrors of that day. She hadn't been injured, but she did watch a Skree die and several Sekarans get slaughtered by the Elorian with his strange technology. She'd never seen death before, and hadn't had time to consider it. Scrunching her nose, she cast those thoughts aside. There was certainly no time to consider it now.

The top of the palace peeked through several buildings. She recognized its bulbous design. The glimmering golden color of its dome shimmered in the dim light of the glo-lamps.

Anais had been continuing along and not paying attention, her eyes drawn to the palace. She bumped into someone and let out a small yelp. During the collision, her hood fell off her head, her ears perking up into the air.

With so few people in the street at this hour, she hadn't been worried about running into anyone. Another mistake. It was starting to feel like she couldn't do anything right. Drawing her arms up quickly, she pushed her hood over her head to conceal her Deklyn features, and then turned to the side.

The person she'd bumped into remained still, focused on her as if she owed him some kind of reparation. It was a man, who wore flowing dark robes. When she saw his eyes, they gave her chills. They were dark all the way through, and some metallic patch glimmered over where his brow should have been.

"I-I'm sorry," she said, backing away from him.

The man grabbed her by the wrist. "You're not from around here. I've seen one of your kind before. One of the new slaves brought from the *elzitti* world."

Anais didn't know what that word meant, but her instincts told her she needed to get away. Fast. She tried to rip her arm away from him, but he was too strong. He didn't falter in in his grip.

"Where's your owner?" the man asked.

"I don't have one. Let me go."

"Such spirit," the man said. His teeth came out as he flashed a grin. "No, I don't think so. If you don't have one, you surely should." He gave her a hard tug, forcing her off balance and toward him. "Come with me and don't make a sound, infidel."

The rest of the street was quiet. No witnesses around. He had her. She wanted to scream, but it would only draw more attention to herself. If she tried to resist, the Sekarans would probably frame her for some fake crime as they had the last time.

The man didn't wait for any answer, but instead, kept moving in the direction he had been going. She could barely keep up with him without stumbling. Anais cursed herself silently as she was forced along. She hadn't even been able to get near the palace. She was right back where she started when she came to this godforsaken planet.

NINETEEN

Drin stood on the flat landing area where he'd originally landed at the hideaway. In front of him were twenty Skree, standing in lines of five, orderly as if they were Templars in training. The group had just completed Yezuah's prayer, the first part of the morning, and Drin had led them in a more specific prayer for safety and peace. Now they followed his lead in stretches.

Sao-rin had asked Drin for advice on turning some of his men into a fighting force so they could be more effective against the Sekarans. It would take time, and perhaps more insight than Drin could offer. He had never been a teacher or instructor, but only a soldier as they were now.

One thing they didn't need was strength conditioning. Their work as slaves in agriculture or other capacities made them some of the strongest people Drin had seen in the galaxy without nanite assistance. Because many were used to walking in the hot sands, they had several other qualities that could be honed into an excellent fighting force, as well. Their stamina was incredible, as was their ability to work together.

What they needed were weapons and tactics training. Drin could provide some of that, but most of what he did at this point was instinct and reflex. His instructors had drilled fighting into his very being. He rarely took the time to think about the details of what he did.

It would be different with them, as well. They didn't have nanite assistance. They had to fight as regular ground units. Given their relative stamina, and that this was their homeland, Drin wanted them to be more like a light infantry unit than his Templars were. More mobile, flexible. At the same time, they needed the lockstep discipline. They couldn't be forced to scatter in fear as the slaves had been in the past. Watching their eyes, Drin saw clearly that he brought them a confidence they didn't have before.

"Each of you take a sparring partner for hand-to-hand training. Let's spread out a good distance and give some room. We're going to run through drills that will help you react to specific enemy attacks," Drin said.

The Skree followed his orders and spread out. Drin paced through them until he came to the head of the group. He motioned for Sao-rin, who had been watching from the shade of a rock overhang, to join him. The Skree heir stepped forward and moved to the position Drin told him. "We're going to work on someone charging from the front, what to look for, and how to react. Gaining advantage in confrontations is all about keeping your own balance and forcing your opponent off theirs. Here's what you look for..."

Drin went through several scenarios over the next hour, the Skree following along with his slow-motion demonstrations and then applying them against their partners. They were eager and worked hard in the morning sun before it became too hot to do too many physical exercises in the afternoon.

All in all, it was a successful first day. "We'll do this every day for a couple of weeks, and in the evening work on laser-repeaters. It'll be easier to see those when the sun goes down, which will make for better targeting. Are there any questions?"

The Skree students shook their heads.

"Dismissed," Drin said.

The area cleared, leaving Drin with Sao-rin. Drin let out a deep breath. "I've never taught before. It's energy-consuming work."

"Never?" Sao-rin smiled and patted Drin on the arm. "You've been teaching us much since you arrived here. We are grateful to you, Templar Drin."

Drin shifted at the use of a formal title. "Just Drin. Whether for noble reasons or not, I had vows to the Templars and I reneged on those to be here."

"This is your calling from God. In many ways, you are upholding your vows to a greater degree." Sao-rin canted his head and narrowed his eyes at Drin's expression. "But the matter is not something to fight over. If you wish to be simply Drin, then simply Drin you shall be. We are ever thankful for your presence here."

Drin nodded to that. "To God be the glory, not me."

Sao-rin chuckled. "Yes." He glanced toward the hideaway entrance. "Some are a bit too keen for their own glory. Such is the way of the world, hmm?"

"Anyone specific?"

"For one, Anais, the woman you came here with. She has a kind heart and a stubborn determination both."

"Ah, yes." Drin unconsciously rubbed his chin where she had slapped him last evening. Had that been about her own glory? She had a number of reasons to be frustrated with him, reasons out of his control, but he understood it nonetheless. "She was not happy when Err-dio and I told her we would have to wait before rescuing another woman from her world who had been captured by the Sekarans. Your people aren't ready for a full assault of the city just yet, I think."

"I'm aware of what transpired. You hadn't heard?" Sao-rin moved toward the hideaway entrance and motioned for Drin to follow with his stump arms.

"Hadn't heard what?"

"The woman. She ran off in the middle of the night—took a sky-bike. We don't know if she was able to get to the city or not, but with the way she flew before, I'd doubt she went too far."

Drin stopped in his tracks, dragging his feet and kicking up a little bit of sand in the process. "She what?"

Sao-rin turned. "She's gone. I'm sorry. Were you two—"

"No." Drin cut him off. A little anger swelled within him at the very question, but he repressed it. These people couldn't have known about his vows of chastity. They would assume that a man and woman in their positions would be intimate. The ways of the world were not the ways of the Templar. He took a breath to calm himself. "But it is distressing she is gone. Have you sent out search parties?"

Sao-rin shook his head. "We wouldn't know where to search."

"Does anyone know what way she went?"

"One of the men saw her leave, he could probably point you to her."

"Fetch him for me," Drin said.

Sao-rin nodded. "I will." He headed into the hideaway and returned a few minutes later with another Skree.

The second Skree bowed his head to Drin. "She was too quick for me. I'm sorry I failed you, Shepherd."

Shepherd. That was a new one. In some ways he was, and this was certainly his flock. It was a metaphor that Yezuah and his disciples used at length. That was a title Drin wouldn't fight. One of his flock had gone astray. He shielded his eyes from the rising sun. "Which way did she go?"

The Skree pointed in a direction.

"I'll need a sky-bike."

"And some guards?" Sao-rin asked.

Drin shook his head. "Too risky. I'll cloak myself. It'll be easier for me to move alone. If something goes wrong, I have the protection of my armor. I'd hate to risk any Skree right now. We'll need every man when the time comes. Just give me a sky-bike with a good nav so I can find my way around." He turned back toward Sao-rin. "And have a few of your other people patrol the area to make sure she didn't crash. I'll check in via comm when I get to Altequine."

"Are you sure about this?" Sao-rin asked. It was clear from his expression the heir didn't want Drin to leave.

"This is something I must do."

"I'll get your sky-bike ready," the other Skree said and moved off.

TWENTY

Much like the sheikh's palace, the home of the person who brought her here had a large open room for entertainment. Over the course of the day, several of the man's servants readied the place for visitors, preparing food, drink, and decorations. Several large hookah pipes were placed in different seating areas, and a stage was set for musical entertainment.

The master-servant, a man by the name of Jeddah, oversaw the day's preparations. He immediately put Anais to work scrubbing the floor and dusting. At least here she hadn't been put to use as some kind of pleasure slave, at least not yet. While she worked, she surveyed the area for exits. Though it was a large mansion, it wasn't as secure as the sheikh's palace. There were a number of exits, but the back courtyard and adjoining buildings were enclosed by walls. Right now, it seemed too many eyes were on her, but eventually, she might be able to escape. She needed to find the right moment.

"You missed a spot," Jeddah said. He pointed to a section of the floor she hadn't been to yet.

Anais wiped her brow. "I was just taking a small break. I'm tired." It was true. Other than the brief moment when she'd passed out on the sky-bike, Anais had been up for more than a full day. The whole world felt like she was watching some sort of holofilm through her own eyes. Her body so weary that it made her reactions sluggish. Or maybe it was her mind that was sluggish. Either way, the prospect of sleeping sounded wonderful.

"Once we're ready, there will be time to rest. We'll need you fresh for the party this evening. Do you dance?" Jeddah asked.

She went back to work, scrubbing the remaining dirty floor section. "Not professionally," Anais said.

Jeddah chuckled. "It won't matter with how drunk and stoned Master Trydeh's guests will be. Your figure will be all that matters to them. And your exotic alien features. Where did you say you were from again?"

"Deklyn," Anais said, grunting as she had to scrub with her full arm-strength to remove some caked dirt. "There aren't many of us here, then?" She tried to sound more like she was engaging in passive conversation than fishing for information.

"You're the only I've seen, though typically slaves are not allowed to flaunt their feminine features in public as you did. Most wear full coverings with only their eyes revealed. Those fortunate enough to own such slaves wouldn't wish to be forced to execute you for causing impure thoughts."

Anais shivered, suddenly feeling very cold in the sheer gown she'd been forced to wear. It was different than the one the sheikh had, not quite as short, but equally revealing. This crazy backward culture blamed women for a man's indiscretions, even though all the women she'd seen were forced into whatever behaviors the men wanted. And then they had the gall to blame the women for being too alluring! The Sekarans were beyond sick in the head. "We wouldn't want that," Anais said, sarcasm dripping from her voice.

Jedah nodded approvingly. "Good work."

"I have another question for you," Anais said, standing upright and letting out a tired breath. "What did Master Trydeh do to get to a place where he has all this?" She motioned around them.

"He is of the blood, of course," Jeddah said, smiling. "But much of what you see around you is because of the spoils of victory in his battles against infidels. Or at least the gold he used to purchase this finery with came from that."

"Looting and stealing," Anais muttered under her breath.

"Hmm?" Jeddah said, so wrapped up in his pride of the home he maintained he didn't seem to hear her.

"Nothing. Does he still go to battle?"

"Whenever ordered. Master Trydeh is away nearly half of the year. Such is the life of a battlemage. It must be quite an adventuresome time. I am honored to have been chosen as a master-servant for such a household."

Battlemage. The word resonated with her. Drin had mentioned even he might not be able to defeat a battlemage. It was good she hadn't tried to fight him when he grabbed her. She'd had a feeling it would have been a bad idea to do so, but now she understood it would have been the end of her life. She gulped. "You're Sekaran too, aren't you?"

"Not all of us are born of the noble blood. I'm in a very fortunate position. Master Trydeh treats his slaves very well." He took the mop and rags from her hands. "And you've shown yourself to do a good job today. I'll make sure to recommend you for reward when I speak to Master Trydeh next. Why don't you find your way to our baths and freshen up? You'll want to be at your best tonight. If you do well, you'll *really* impress Master Trydeh."

"Great," Anais said. Impressing Trydeh would be the last thing she wanted to do. She needed to avoid attention if she were going to escape here.

She followed Jeddah. The slave-master led her to another slave, who escorted her out of the main building and through an open courtyard. Their path took them through a beautiful garden filled with strange plants with jagged leaves. The slave told her it was a standard layout for the nobility's residences, as they liked to impress others with their gardens. Anais passed the servant quarters and came to another smaller structure. She pushed through arched doors. Inside, it was humid.

The slave let Anais know where she could find a towel and various fragrances to add to the baths and left her there alone. It was uncomfortable to slip out of even her small covering, not knowing who might enter or be around the corner, but while she was in the bath, Anais was left alone. There was a marking clearly designating this as a place only females could go. At least they had some sense of propriety.

She soaked in the warm, almost pool-sized tub. The water and the heat felt good upon her tired body, loosening her muscles and relaxing her. She leaned against the back wall of the tub and couldn't help but doze off.

"New slave," a voice said, stirring her from her slumber.

Her short fur became soft, and her skin shriveled. How long had she been asleep? Remembering she was naked, Anais crossed her arms over her breasts. "Huh?" She looked over to see the other slave girl who had escorted her here in the first place.

"You've been in here much longer than I anticipated. I would have come sooner, but there are so many duties with the party approaching. You have to get out and ready. Master Trydeh will be demanding your presence soon."

The other woman had a fresh change of clothes and held the towel out for her. Anais carefully made her way up the steps and out of the water, letting the towel fall over her shoulders before wrapping it around herself.

She dressed and was hurried from the baths to the servants' quarters. Several girls from various species were there, applying make-up and getting themselves ready. They jockeyed for space in front of a long mirror, across from a long row of bunk beds.

"Ah, a new girl," one of them said. "Here." She shoved a bag full of cosmetics into Anais's arms. Some were useful, but others wouldn't be applicable for her fur-covered Deklyn features. In some ways, it was nice to make herself pretty. Before the slavers took her, Anais had spent hours a day on her appearance, much as she was doing now. It was another luxury she wouldn't take for granted if she ever made her way off this sand-pit of a planet.

The other girls chatted, and Anais learned what she could expect to come. The nobles of Altequine had parties once a week. A big social gathering that rotated from the residences of different nobles, all posturing and trying to show how wonderfully they ran their estates, in hopes that the sheikh would look kindly on them and give them more power and responsibility. It wasn't unlike the company parties the merchant lords had for clients on Deklyn. The names were different, but no matter the people, the galaxy had a way of making things run the same. The difference was, Deklyn didn't take people as slaves.

Instead of her usual place as a guest, here she would be an entertainer. When she'd had to look pretty for clients, it was a way to get business. This... this would be putting her on display in a way that one of them might find her all too compelling. She would have no recourse if they decided to lay hands on her. These Sekarans were disgusting, she couldn't forget that, even if this Trydeh treated his slaves better than the sheikh had.

The sheikh. Anais stifled a breath. If the nobles of this city had a party, it meant the sheikh might be in attendance. He would recognize her as a Deklyn, and it wouldn't go well. Her fur stood on edge.

Before she could figure out what to do about her precarious situation, Jeddah came in and surveyed all the women in the servants' quarters. He clapped his hands together. "Good, good. You all look ravishing. I'm sure I don't have to tell you that. Are you ready to put on the best entertainment in Altequine?"

The women responded in a rousing chorus of agreement. It made Anais's skin crawl. These women actually *liked* being meat on display for these awful men. Was it because they enjoyed some luxuries that weren't afforded to the Skree? They all had their limbs, which several of the Skree she had seen, including Sao-rin were not afforded. The nobles seemed to treat these dancing girls somewhat better than the rest of their slaves, but only somewhat. It tugged at her heart to think how some of these women must have been slaves so long they'd forgotten what freedom was like.

That couldn't happen to her—it *wouldn't* happen to her. She nodded to herself to strengthen her resolve.

Jeddah made a windmill motion with his hand to try to get the women to line up. "Single file, everyone. We're going to introduce you one by one as you enter. Musicians will already be playing. Dance your hearts out. Socialize with the guests. If they require assistance, you assist them. You know what to do."

They filed into the courtyard garden and made their way to the main building. Anais stood on the tips of her toes, ears perked as she tried to hear what was going on. It was loud inside, busy. Night had fallen over the desert city, and while it was cooler outside, she felt the heat from all the bodies radiating from the door. Smoke wafted from the room.

Anais was too frightened to show her distaste. She had to hope these men were too out of their minds, drunk or otherwise. More, she had to hope the sheikh wouldn't be here. Maybe he had other things to do? Something in her doubted it.

Either way, she had to blend in, be an average dancer and hope no one took undue notice of her. When Trydeh left for his next assignment, she would make her escape, and if she was lucky, she'd have time to liberate the other Deklyn girl from the sheikh's palace.

She tried not to get her hopes up too high, but it gave her something to fight for.

While she'd been thinking about her future plans, the other girls ahead of her had entered. They performed for the men inside. Anais was up next. She took a breath, nervous at having never done this before. She didn't want to dance, but she understood better than to act out in a public setting. She'd seen the results firsthand.

"We have a rare specimen here, a long-eared girl with a perky tail!" an announcer said, his voice amplified by Trydeh's sound system.

The men hooted at the end of the sentence.

"She calls herself Anais... and she is certainly alluring!"

A push came from behind her, causing her to stumble forward into the room. She looked back and saw Jeddah standing there, holding the next girl in wait for her turn. Standing on her tip toes, she peeked into the room. It was hazy with smoke, and she was unable to get a good look into the gathered crowd. At least she hadn't spotted the sheikh.

The music was sultry, strange dissonant tones mixed with some sort of reed instrument. The men leered at her, and Anais suddenly felt very naked in her sheer slave's garb. She couldn't cover herself now, though, and there was nowhere for her to hide. So she moved. The music was slow and fluid enough that she could move her arms and legs like waves of the ocean. How she'd missed seeing the ocean, something she'd visited with her family on retreats. She thought of that while she danced instead of these men with their hungry eyes and panting mouths.

Anais danced. Though she'd only had cursory dance classes for physical education in school, she managed not to look foolish. Most of the other slave girls seemed to enjoy the dancing, and she didn't want to stand out. Not that the quality of her performance mattered anyway. Seeing how hazy some of these Sekarans' eyes were, they would be unlikely to remember many specifics. Except for Trydeh. His full, black pupils honed in on her. His stare was something different than the others. Those eyes were hard, as if communicating she was already his, and there was nothing she could do about it. Like so many things these last few days, it made her hair stand on edge.

Anais made sure to look to the other side of the room so she wouldn't have to see Trydeh. She kept dancing until the song stopped. Once the music died down, she tried to catch her breath. A number of claps came from the room. Someone blew a puff of smoke in her direction.

Another person stood, or at least attempted to. It was a rather large man, and with his own weight and whatever intoxicants he'd consumed, he couldn't quite manage the feat. A couple other Sekarans beside him darted up, grabbing him by the arms and assisting him.

In the dim light of the room, Anais couldn't make out his features at first, but when she focused on him, his body type and his gaudy jewelry was unmistakable. A commotion started in the room as others noticed him standing. This wasn't just any drunk lout. He was here just as she had feared—the sheikh.

His face contained a blood rage, whose like Anais had never seen before.

"Harlot!" the sheikh shouted at her, the word coming out in a slur.

Anais backpedaled, but there wasn't room to get away from the sheikh, with all of the people crowded into the room. While dancing, she'd had to navigate very carefully. Now, she found herself bumping into someone. The person shoved her forward, and she fell flat on her face right at the sheikh's feet.

The sheikh grabbed her by the ears and pulled her upward, forcing her to look upon him. She could barely see his face with his round belly in the way. "This... temptress was supposed to be my wife. She was also supposed to have been stoned to death."

Murmurs of shock fell across the room.

He gripped her ears so hard it felt like they were going to be ripped off her head. Anais couldn't help but cry. Though she wanted to remain strong, she let out a whimper from sheer pain.

"Sheikh," Trydeh said from across the room. "I am not sure of what your issue is in the past, but she has been brought into this household and is one of my own. If you harm her, I am bound by honor to take from yours what you take from mine. It is in the code Eltu put forth to us through his holy prophet."

The sheikh didn't let go of her ears, but his attention shifted from her to Trydeh. He frowned. "Battlemage Trydeh, this slave was my property first. You would do well to stay out of this."

"I cannot do that," Trydeh said, his voice cool. "This is my home.

If you are to do violence in my abode, it calls for other rectifications of honor."

The whole room went quiet. The rest of the party guests stared in disbelief. These were two very powerful men, Anais understood that much. All she wanted now was to have her ears released.

The sheikh's grip only tightened. "I am not an enemy you want to make, Battlemage," he said, staring down Trydeh for a moment that felt like an eternity as he squeezed on Anais's ears. Finally, he released her.

Anais gasped, realizing she'd been holding her breath. Her ears throbbed, but no bones had been broken. She dropped to her hands and knees while she recovered her breath.

"You have made a wise choice," Trydeh said.

The sheikh huffed. "I am leaving," he announced. An entourage of servants and other nobles stood around him, having received their cue to follow. Ten people left the room. Anais remained in place.

Her tears dripped to the floor. All of her hope, all of her attempts to fix things, they'd failed so badly. Would her life be one disaster after another from this point forward?

A gentle hand touched her shoulder and then wrapped around her arm, tugging to lift her. "There, there. I see how he grabbed you, child. That must have been painful," Jeddah's soft voice said. "We'll get you to the quarters. You've done your work for the night."

Anais let him pick her up. Conversation continued in the room. No one else seemed to care about a slave, regardless of what happened. The music started a moment later, another sultry song. As Anais was escorted toward the back exit, she saw another woman beginning her dance for these people.

Jeddah hurried her out the back. "You've certainly caused some trouble, haven't you?"

"I just want to go home," Anais said, choking back more tears.

"This is your home now. Master Trydeh will protect you as long as you perform your duties," he said, ushering her to the slaves' quarters.

As long as she performed her duties. And at what point would this Trydeh demand more from her than a simple dance? She'd had firsthand experience as to what these slave women were expected to do. Jeddah didn't elaborate. He returned to the party, leaving her alone. She had to escape, or die trying. There was no other choice.

TWENTY-ONE

Drin didn't approach the city proper but found his way back to the farm where the young boy had given him shelter when he first arrived on this planet. Returning to the farm was unexpected, but as he had told the girl before she left, there had to be more strategizing before assaulting Altequine again. He would certainly heed his own advice, even though he had taken off quickly from the hideaway out of worry for Anais.

The mere act of running off in haste worried him. In some ways, this marked the second time he'd fled his duties to pursue something else. This time, he hadn't even taken the time to deliberate in prayer or to ask God for advice on a situation. There had been one too many crises these last several days, with no one but him able to handle them. It was getting to him, or perhaps worse—*she* was getting to him.

During the flight, Drin prayed several times. First, for forgiveness in not considering God before he acted. Second, to ask God to guide him in this path. So far, there hadn't been a clear answer on what he should do about the woman. Part of his reactionary issue went deeper than he wanted to think about. Drin tried to ignore some of the more basic implications, even in his initial prayers on the situation. With all the time he had to reflect alone, however, he couldn't avoid thinking about the subject entirely.

His lust.

It went back to that one night they had spent together under the stars. Drin had come too close to her. He'd touched her, and he liked it. He still liked it, and that was dangerous. In many ways, it disqualified him from being the one to go and rescue her. It meant he had personal, selfish reasons for wanting to help. It wasn't solely for her good or the good of the community. Would God still want him to be doing this?

The silence in the cool morning desert air was deafening.

That made it all the more important for him to take some time, assess the situation, and make sure he had the right strategies and objectives before bounding into the city.

The farm was much as he remembered it from several days earlier. A pasture, a fence, and a nice place by the barn where he could park the sky-bike. He flew up to the place and disembarked, seeing no sign of the family who had taken him in before.

He turned the corner behind the broadside of the barn, and when he did, he found Mohiel, the farmer, with a laser-repeater pointed directly at Drin's chest. "Elorian," Mohiel said, sneering, "what do you want? You shouldn't be here."

Drin put his hands up in surrender. "I mean you no harm. I just want to talk."

Mohiel kept the weapon trained on him for another several moments. Yiv, his boy, came running around the corner, stopping in his tracks when he saw Drin and his father. "Da?" he asked.

The presence of the boy made Mohiel lower the gun. "Come inside," he said to Drin.

"Our friend is back?" Yiv asked. "Where have you been?"

"Run along," Mohiel said. "This isn't for young ears, and you have eggs to gather."

The boy kicked dirt. "Aw," he said, but he didn't fight the request further, scurrying away soon after.

Drin followed Mohiel into the house. They made their way into a kitchen, where Mohiel motioned for him to sit. Drin obliged, sliding into the chair.

"Would you like some water?" Mohiel asked.

"That would be nice," Drin said. The man's hospitality impressed him despite the fact he had pointed a weapon at him a moment earlier. These were good people. Not the same Sekarans he'd been used to fighting. These were the type of people to convert.

Mohiel moved to a pitcher, poured him a cup, and set it on the table. He moved to a seat opposite him. "Why did you come here? Your very presence brings danger to my house."

What had brought him here? His thoughts. He had recalled this place and how they had been so kind to him. Even in admonishing him, in stating his anger toward Drin and his people, Mohiel had provided him food and means to escape the Sekarans searching for him. "God brought me here," Drin said, taking the glass into his hands.

"Your God. Not Eltu," Mohiel said with a frown.

Drin met the man's eyes. "The true God," Drin said.

Another awkward silence fell between the two men. "Your people killed my brother in the name of your God. I've told you this. I should cut your throat for your audacity."

"I don't believe you would do that," Drin said.

Mohiel threw his head back, laughing, and then shook his head. "No, I wouldn't. I'm a farmer, not a fighter. I thought my brother was foolish to go join with the legions. I told him so."

"I am sorry about his death. While I was imprisoned in the city, I said a prayer for his soul," Drin said.

"Now how am I supposed to hate you when you talk like that?"

"I believe that is why I've been sent here. You're not supposed to hate me. And perhaps more importantly, I'm not supposed to hate you. Can I tell you a little of how I came to this planet?"

Mohiel nodded.

Drin told the story of his recent past, starting with the last several battles he'd fought with his fellow Templars aboard the *Justicar*, and how he found no honor in tearing through Sekaran troops who couldn't stand up to him. He felt God was calling him for something different, a life outside of endless battle. Then he came to Altequine, but since he'd arrived, he'd only found more endless battle.

"You are made for war, as I am made for farming, Elorian," Mohiel said.

"I didn't want to accept that, but we do have our callings. Our gifts, as Yezuah told his disciples."

"From what it sounds like, you are being protected. That much is clear. What man without divine providence could have survived in your situation?" Mohiel's forehead creased. He shook his head. "I didn't want to believe our creator could favor an Elorian."

"The creator favors all who serve Him," Drin said.

Mohiel turned his head and gazed out the window. He was silent for several minutes. "Eloria—no, " he said, shaking his head. "What is your name?"

"Drin."

"Drin," Mohiel continued. "Despite my telling you I can't forgive you, you've treated me with respect. It's made me curious about your God. He sounds merciful."

"He is."

"My life has been in constant fear of Eltu and those who serve him. Doing things right, not offending anyone in power. We're taught from birth that we must respect the order of our society. Even when wrong is done. The way you're treated, and how you say slaves are treated, they are similar to how I've seen others treated in my time. I cannot believe God would approve of such things."

Drin held silent this time. He wanted to say, "Because he doesn't," but at some point, it was better to leave a man with his thoughts to work things out on his own.

Mohiel met Drin's eyes once more. "How would one go about dedicating themselves to your God?"

This was the first Sekaran Drin had ever seen so open. Drin worked hard for him on the farm when he'd first arrived here, and he was glad it left an impression. After working with the Skree and answering their similar questions, it was much easier for Drin to communicate the message. "It's simple. My God requires no oath, no rigorous following of creed. How you honor Him or don't is between you and God. All He requires is that you understand you are an imperfect being, a sinner, and that you accept in your heart that you will earnestly join in the fight against evil in this world. Yezuah became flesh and came to us and brought peace to the tribes of Eloria, dying and rising again in the process. His word will now bring what we know in peace to all of the other planets. His commandments are simple, treat your enemies and others with respect, and consider God in all you do," Drin said. "I have no copy of the holy book to present you or I would. Perhaps soon."

"I'll consider it," Mohiel said, shifting in his seat. He appeared uncomfortable.

"Your open-mindedness is admirable."

Mohiel nodded.

"If I may be so bold, would you pray with me?"

"I'm not sure I should." Mohiel's eyes darted away from him again.

"It can't hurt," Drin said.

The farmer considered for a long moment and then sighed. "Very well."

Drin closed his eyes and folded his hands on the table, bowing his head in a reverent position. "Lord, bless Mohiel and his family. He has only shown kindness to one of your servants. I pray a place awaits him in your heavenly kingdom. Forgive our sins and bless us until the end of our days." He reopened his eyes.

"That was a nice prayer," Mohiel said.

"Thank you."

"I'll consider your words. When you are able, I would like to see your holy book."

"I'll bring a copy as soon as possible. Though it may be some time. For now, perhaps you can help me in this cause?"

"I'll do what I can," Mohiel said, "but I'm not sure what I can provide you other than a night's stay and some food."

Drin took a sip of his water. "What do you know about Altequine's defenses?"

Mohiel considered. "There's a gate guard, a city guard and watch, and many of the nobles have their personal armies, as well. They have their arms, but there hasn't been much of a need for a formal military in generations. Not since the Skree were subdued."

"Just guards? What about battlemages?"

"We have two battlemages who call the city their home. But they aren't always on planet. They're often called to duty."

Two was more than enough. Even one battlemage could cause difficulties for a Templar, as Drin had seen before, but two could be overwhelming. The worst part of having a battlemage present was they might have weapons they could disburse to the regular guards to disable Drin's nanites. Without them, he would be little more than a naked warrior with his fists. He didn't relish the thought. "I'll have to be careful. Best not to engage in an open fight."

"That I would agree with, though you haven't had trouble so far, hmm?"

"I wouldn't wish to test God by asking for too many miracles," Drin said.

Yiv, the young boy, peeked his head up through the window. Drin couldn't help but laugh at the boy's curiosity. Mohiel turned around to shoo the boy off. "They never listen, kids."

"Don't be too hard on him. He has a kind heart. I might not be alive if he hadn't helped that day when I first landed here," Drin said.

The farmer made a sound half like a grunt and half like a laugh. "I took you in because of him. He is a kind boy," Mohiel said, staring out the window. Yiv ran along the yard, paying no more mind to the two men inside.

"The best way to thank him is to provide a faith as steadfast as bedrock." Drin stroked his chin. "Is there anything else about the city's defenses I should find notable? And have you perhaps heard any rumors about recent aliens coming to the city? One of my companions has a tail and long ears. A woman."

Mohiel raised a brow. "Ah, so that's what brings you back to the city."

"Not like that," Drin said sternly.

"I don't judge. The market actually had quite a bit of gossip this morning when I dropped off my crops. The merchants were rather excited. Apparently, there had been some scuffle last evening at Battlemage Trydeh's estate. The nobles have these parties and bring in slave girls as entertainment. Merchants like to talk about the girls, a little manly humor, you know?"

"I don't know."

Mohiel shrugged. "I'm happy with my wife as it is. But others... Well, they like the more exotic offerings that the sheikh and the other nobles put on display. Some even are invited. Rumor has it, there were some words exchanged between the sheikh and the battlemage, and none-too-friendly ones at that. Some people said it came to blows, and over a girl with long ears and a tail like you said. Must be quite a beauty."

Reflexively, Drin stood. He wanted to head to the city as soon as he could. If Anais were in these men's clutches, who knew what they could be doing to her? "Did you know if she was with the battlemage or with the sheikh?" Drin asked.

"Anxious to find her?"

"She is in great danger."

"It was Battlemage Trydeh's residence where the party was held. I would start searching—"

The pitter patter of small feet sounded in the rear of the house, and Yiv came running into the room. "Who're we trying to find? I love to hide and seek," Yiv said.

"You shouldn't eavesdrop, Yiv," Mohiel said in a scolding tone.

The boy frowned.

"It's fine, this isn't sensitive information. Where do I find this Battlemage Trydeh? Can you show me to him?" Drin asked. "I have to locate the girl before there is trouble."

"I still have crops to tend to today. I wouldn't be able to escort you into the city until I go to the bazaar again tomorrow to meet with my merchant," Mohiel said.

"I can take him! I know where it is. I want to see the battlemage." Yiv brought his hands together as if he were holding a sword of air, swinging it in a manner he must have imagined a battlemage fought in.

Drin laughed. "It would probably be best for you not to be near me."

"As long as you keep your hood on, Yiv can lead you. He knows his way through the city and back. He helps me most mornings."

"Can I really?" Yiv's eyes light up brightly.

"You'll have to be careful," Mohiel said. "No talking to Drin here while you lead. He'll have to stay behind so you aren't seen with him." His eyes searched Drin questioningly.

Drin nodded. "I can do that. It would be a big help. Any delay could put my friend in more danger."

"Then let's go!" The boy hurried out the door.

Mohiel slid out of his seat. "Ah, youthful energy."

"Are you sure about this? I don't want to put your family in danger," Drin said.

"I'm sure. This is what little I can do for God. I pray it is enough," the farmer said. He offered his hand to Drin.

Drin took it, giving a firm shake. This had been a resounding success and provided more evidence that God had sent him on this path. He followed after Yiv and made his way outside, forming a cloak from the nanites and slipping a hood over his head to conceal his face.

Yiv led him down the road where he'd been carried on a cart the first time he'd entered the city. Guards stood at the gate, lazily watching the traffic flow in and out its main road. The boy skipped along ahead of Drin. They looked no different from the many other travelers, merchants, and workers busily heading through the city's thoroughfares. They weaved through streets, with no one noticing them, until they reached an estate with high stone walls.

Yiv leaned against the wall. "Didn't get to see the battlemage." He snapped his fingers and looked at Drin. Following his father's commands, he didn't speak to Drin but motioned his head to the wall. He then went running back toward the gates of the city.

Drin thought a silent prayer for the boy, thanking God for the help provided. The wall stood tall, but it wasn't too high for a Templar. With the assistance of his nanites, he would be able to leap over it without a problem.

His more immediate issues came from the street. People walked by at a near constant rate. He positioned himself under an overhang of a nearby building as he watched people go by. He would have to wait for a lull in the traffic to ensure no one saw his feat. The last thing he wanted was to alert the battlemage while he still had an element of surprise.

After some time waiting and watching, the street cleared. Drin didn't hesitate. He ran toward the wall, increasing his speed with each step. With a focused thought, he called upon his nanites and leapt.

Nothing could compare to the feeling of jumping through the air. It gave him a sense of freedom, a loss of control where he totally surrendered himself to faith in his God-given technology. His move through the air was graceful. He could feel the wind on his face.

The other side of the wall gave him a view of a few buildings in a square configuration. Drin's trajectory took him to the roof of one. When he reached it, his feet slid across red shingles. A couple cracked beneath his feet, not able to withstand his weight through the force of his jump.

Drin quickly bent his knees to give himself some leverage and pushed himself into another jump off of the roof. The crumbling shingles didn't give him the best balance, but his arc allowed him to get his feet more solidly under him when he landed on the ground. He braced himself in a crouch, safely behind some bushes to give him cover.

A couple of servants moved by, seeming not to notice his presence as they chatted with one another. Drin didn't know where to begin looking for Anais in this compound. It wouldn't take too long to go through all the buildings, but the more he snooped around, the more likely someone would see him and raise an alarm.

He crept around the bushes in the battlemage's garden. When the servants passed, he hustled to one of the back buildings, concealing himself in the shade of one of the overhangs. Each of the buildings had small windows, which allowed him a look inside.

The first room he saw appeared to be living quarters. Several bunks lined one room but no sign of any slaves. Drin kept himself close to the wall, scooting along the edge of it. He checked a couple more windows, seeing servants this time, but no Anais.

At the next window, he stopped in surprise. The familiar long ears and lithe figure of Anais stood inside. She folded a blanket and didn't notice him. Most importantly, she appeared to be alone. Drin tapped on the window.

Anais jumped, dropping the blanket. She turned to the window, her eyes going wide. Then she put a hand on her chest, saying something Drin couldn't hear. She moved over to the window and slid it open. "You scared me," she said softly.

"Come on. Let's get you out of here before someone spots me," Drin said, offering his hand through the window.

She glanced behind her and then squeezed through the window. Her ears went flat against her head as she shimmied through the small opening, finally taking Drin's hand when she dropped through to the outside. He helped pull her out of the window and then placed both hands on her sides to help her safely down.

It brought her body close to him, just as the night he had sinned.

Drin took a step back. "I think I can jump the wall with you on me, but you'll have to hold on tightly."

Anais looked up at the wall beside them. "That's crazy. I can't—"

"What have we here?" came a deep voice.

Drin spun around to see where the voice came from. A man stood with fists clenched. He had purple robes, a shaved head, and the metallic plate above his eye, a protrusion marking his implants. A battlemage. This was about to get ugly.

TWENTY-TWO

Trydeh seemed to come out of nowhere. Despite herself, Anais yelped when he spoke, the second time in as many minutes she'd been so startled. Her heart pounded in her chest. Adrenaline coursed through her.

The Elorian pushed her to the side. She barely managed not to smash her head against the wall. "Hey!" she protested, but he took steps to put himself between her and Trydeh. In the course of his maneuver, he'd activated armor, shining and reflecting off the sun. His tech made a shimmering shield of energy in front of him as it had when they were in the pits. A light sword formed in his hand.

A ball of blue energy formed in Trydeh's hands. He worked the energy like it was dough, eyes focused on his adversary. Drin charged, raising his light sword to chop downward at Trydeh. The attack illuminated a translucent shield just above Trydeh's head as it connected with a *fizzle*. He extended his hands outward toward Drin. The ball of energy blasted at him.

Drin's energy shield fluttered and dissipated. The force of the blast sent him flying past Anais. She pressed herself against the wall of the servants' quarters, trying not to scream. Drin landed against the back wall of the complex, his body *thudding* hard against concrete.

A large crack formed in the wall. Trydeh moved forward casually, confidence in each step. More energy formed in his hands. He threw bolts forward with sidearm throws, one after another. The energy pelted the poor Elorian.

Before Trydeh could finish Drin off, he rolled out of the way. The next bolts of energy missed, their full force hitting the wall behind him. It blew a hole in the bottom of the wall, dust filling the air. The top of the wall collapsed.

In the confusion, Drin scrambled to his feet and moved out of Anais's view. Trydeh followed him around the corner, seeming to forget about her. Several servants heard the commotion, as they moved toward the battle between their master and the Elorian to see what was going on. One of the gardeners came from behind Anais, a large metal shovel in his hand.

Anais reached out and grabbed it. "Give me that for a moment," she said.

The gardener looked none too happy to have his tool taken, but he didn't say anything. He held his hands up and let her have it.

Determined, Anais trudged forward to the corner where Trydeh and Drin had gone. Sounds of electrical clashes came from the garden. One of the buildings was hit by an energy blast, its tile roof crumbling to the ground below. The building wall had scorch marks on it when Anais passed it.

The two men came into view again. Drin used his light sword defensively, absorbing the energy from Trydeh's repeated blasts, but he couldn't get close enough to do any damage to the Sekaran. It was only a matter of time before Trydeh took him down. The battlemage stood his ground, throwing bolt after bolt of energy. The blasts came closer with each one. Drin struggled to block or dodge them. Trydeh was in control of this battle, and if something didn't even the odds, Drin wouldn't last much longer.

Sweat dripped down the Elorian's face, and it looked like blood stained his armor. Some of the blasts must have breached it.

Several of the servants stood around, watching. Jeddah was among them. None appeared as if they would interfere with the battle. Anais couldn't blame them. Getting between these two men would be like getting between two stars about to collide and go nova.

But she had to do something. Another energy bolt flew, this one pelting Drin in the shoulder. He stumbled backward and then dropped to a knee. The attacks were overwhelming him.

She weighed her options. If she stayed now, she probably would be blamed for this rescue attempt, and that could cause all sorts of problems, probably resulting in a judgment for her stoning as her last capture had. If she got involved and Trydeh won, she would face the same fate. None of her options sounded appealing. It meant Drin was her only hope to get out of here.

Anais charged forward, lifting the shovel above her head. She grunted at the weight of it but tried to keep quiet the rest of the way so Trydeh wouldn't notice her approaching.

Trydeh kept his focus on Drin. "Time to finish you off, Elorian scum," he said, readying the most sizable balls of energy he'd summoned yet. The glow of the energy made Drin's face turn a strange muddy color. The Elorian held his light sword in front of his face to defend himself, but this blast would be big enough to ram through Drin's defenses if the last several were any indication.

Jeddah scrambled to follow Anais as she approached Trydeh. He wouldn't have been able to reach her in time. Instead, he yelled, "Master!"

The battlemage turned his head, but the warning came too late. Anais used all of her strength to bring the shovel down hard into Trydeh's face. It landed with a *crack*. Trydeh stumbled backward and brought his hand to his face, gripping the implant along his forehead. "You witch! What have you—?"

He convulsed and fell to the ground. His light sword flickered out of existence. Anais couldn't believe her attack had been that effective.

But she couldn't rest now. She swung the shovel around her to keep the other servants from coming near her or Drin. Jeddah was closest to her wild swing, having to jump back to avoid getting slammed in the stomach.

Jeddah stayed out of range. "Anais! What are you doing? This is our master!"

"*Your* master. I didn't choose this life," she said, hovering over Drin. She kept her eyes on Trydeh, but he didn't move. He was still breathing. She hadn't killed him, but he looked to be out cold.

Drin pushed himself to his feet, moving much more slowly than she'd seen him before. He stumbled as if off balance. He must have been badly injured.

Anais prodded her shovel toward some aggressive servants to keep them at bay, but none came close to her. The other slaves backpedaled.

Drin stumbled, his eyes glassy and disoriented.

Anais moved to brace him. She moved one arm around him, keeping the shovel forward with one arm.

Drin leaned and whispered in her ear. "My nanites are depleted. We must leave this place."

His words were disconcerting, but Anais tried to keep her face from showing any fear. "Leave us be, or you will suffer a worse fate than your master!" Anais said to the other slaves. She hoped her bluff would work.

Jeddah's eyes looked like they were going to pop out of the back of his skull. "Don't align yourself with this heretic, Anais!" Horror dripped down slave-master Jeddah's face. Now wasn't the time for words, it was the time for leaving before the servants decided they could overpower them.

"Jeddah. Let us go," Anais said. She had to maintain her bluff. "There's no more good you can do here. Consider this later, it was I who made the Elorian spare you."

Jeddah moved out of the way, allowing Drin and Anais room to move for the caved-in section of the estate wall. Drin moved slowly, his face hard as stone. He must have been trying not to show his wounds. Anais kept close to him as they made their way past the stunned slaves.

As they moved, Anais slipped but managed to stay standing. The ground was moist beneath her. When she looked, she saw blood, which dripped from Drin's body at an alarming rate.

"Are you going to make it?" she asked under her breath.

"I have no choice." Drin clenched his teeth.

They made their way over the rubble and into the street. Several of Altequine's citizens slowed to rubberneck and see what caused the damage. Some whispered in horror, recognizing the Elorian. "We need to get off the main streets," Anais said.

Up ahead, a small boy peeked his head from an alley. He waved and motioned them over.

At first, Anais thought the boy must have been pointing past them. She turned her head, but no one behind her paid the boy any heed. She turned back to him and with her free arm pointed to herself. "Me?" she mouthed.

The boy nodded.

"He's here to help," Drin said weakly. He stumbled into her as he spoke.

Anais grunted, struggling to keep him upright. "Okay," she said, trusting him. She headed for the Sekaran boy, and they turned into the alley. Despite all of the people watching them escape from the battlemage, no one followed.

The boy led them through the alley, into an area blocked by an aged fence, rusted and broken from years of neglect. The place smelled like rotten meat, or worse. Anais could barely breathe. Several jugs of oil were on the ground, some spilled. The building to their left blocked the hot sun from reaching them. Boxes and trash were stashed here, and bugs swarmed everywhere. Anais had to flick them away from her face several times.

"Wait here," the boy said. "I'm going to get my Da and horses to carry you. When I'm playing hide and seek with my friends, I come here. No one ever comes during the day. It's safe."

No one comes here because of how disgusting it is, Anais thought. But she had little choice. If Drin trusted this boy, she would have to, as well. Anything would be better than facing the battlemage or a magistrate.

The boy scurried down the alley, leaving the two of them alone.

Drin fell back to lean on one of the walls. He slipped and sat in the filth on the ground. His face was tight with pain. He clutched at the place on his side where Trydeh's energy had pierced him.

"Are you going to survive?" Anais asked.

"Have faith," Drin said before his head drooped and he fell unconscious.

TWENTY-THREE

DRIN WOKE TO ANAIS SHAKING HIM.

"Hey," she whispered.

The last thing he remembered was passing out in the alley. His whole body ached, and his side throbbed from pain. The world spun before he could orient himself. He must have lost a lot of blood.

"You need to be alert, it's important." Anais's face was filled with concern.

"How long has it been?" Drin asked in a low voice.

"You've been out for hours, but it doesn't matter. Your friend, the boy, he brought you back here. His mother tried to clean your wound the best she could, but your energy field came back and stopped her from getting too close. But listen to me. We have worse problems now."

If the energy field returned, it meant the nanites were at work repairing his wounds. No wonder it stung so badly. Their healing came with a cost when there was no anesthetic. It would take days for them to heal what would have been a mortal wound if he hadn't been a Templar. "What could be worse?" Drin asked.

"The city guard is here, interrogating your farmer friends. They're on the hunt for us. I think with the battlemage injured, they've mobilized everyone," Anais said. "I was able to get a look at them coming down the road, but they stashed us here in this hayloft. I don't think it's safe to stay here."

"It's probably not," Drin said, recalling the last time he'd been hunted.

"Shh, they're coming. Footsteps."

"How do you know?"

She wiggled her long ears.

The barn door opened with a loud *creak*, which would have been the first of Drin hearing anything. He heard voices. "There were numerous witnesses who reported seeing your boy being followed by the Elorian. Assisting a heretic is punishable by death, you understand that, Mohiel," said a deep voice with the Altequine accent. Drin couldn't see from behind all of the haystack.

"He's a little boy. He wouldn't be assisting a heretic. This is an insult to my family," Mohiel said.

"Search the barn," the Sekaran city guard said.

There was a rustling down below.

"Careful with my things! I'm going to tell the sheikh."

"We're searching on his orders. Now stop obstructing us if you have nothing to hide!"

More shuffling came from down below. Anais turned even paler than she usually was, shaking with fear. Drin held still, measuring his breathing. Any noise could alert them, and though he might be able to take down this complement of the city guard, even in his weakened state, it would bring trouble to Mohiel and his family. They didn't deserve to become martyrs on his account. He had a responsibility to them as his converts as much as he did the Skree.

"I don't see anything," said one of the Sekarans from below them.

"Is this everywhere?" the first city guard asked.

"You've searched my home, my barn, and rummaged through my

things. What else do you want from me? Leave my poor family alone," Mohiel said.

The guard grunted. "All right. Let's clear out of here. The sheikh isn't going to be happy. This is the second time we've failed on a search for the heretic. He's becoming quite a thorn in his Excellency's side."

More sounds of feet shuffling before the door made the creaking noise for a second time.

Anais exhaled deeply from beside him.

"Were you holding your breath?" Drin whispered.

She nodded.

"That's not good for your health." He relaxed his shoulders and leaned back into the hay. The nanites sent a fresh flare of pain through him, making him wince.

A few moments passed in silence while Anais stared toward a crack in the wooden flooring of the loft, focused, her ears erect. The tips of her ears drooped, and she nodded to herself. "I don't think it's a good idea to stay here. Every minute we're here is one where we risk them coming back, or a neighbor seeing us. These poor people helped us," Anais said.

"I agree," Drin said. "I parked my sky-bike not too far from here. I should be able to walk the distance, though I may need your help. They may have sky patrols as well, though. We will have to be careful."

Some hours passed before the barn door made its opening *creak* once more. Drin sat up straight.

"It's just us," Mohiel said from below.

Something clanged against the loft. Drin stood to look over the hay and saw a ladder had been placed there.

"I moved it in hopes they wouldn't think to go up there without easy means to climb. It worked," Mohiel said.

Drin motioned for Anais to go ahead of him.

"Are you sure you don't need help?" she asked.

"I can manage," Drin said, standing. The stretch of his torso hurt worse than the wound had originally. He clenched his jaw tightly so he wouldn't scream.

"It was rather difficult to get you up there in the first place," Mohiel said. "You weren't coherent."

"Mm," Drin said non-committedly, following Anais down the ladder rungs. He took very careful steps. Reaching the bottom proved time-consuming, but it was a relief when he did. He turned to face the others. "It's not safe for us to be here," he said. "We will depart. Brother Mohiel, your hospitality has been unparalleled. I will pray for blessings upon you and your family."

Mohiel nodded. "Thank you. And thank you for opening my eyes to the truth."

Anais had a skeptical brow raised. "We should get going. I haven't met you before but, uh, thank you."

"Our pleasure," Mohiel said.

Yiv scurried up behind him along with his mother. They said their goodbyes as well and gave cautious hugs to Drin. The woman brought Anais and him fresh cloaks to conceal themselves. Drin's didn't fit quite right, it being a garment the smaller Mohiel used to wear before it faded and stained, but he was grateful for it none-theless.

Drin and Anais left, traversing the farmer's fields. Night settled on the land around them, giving them more cover within the crops than they would have had during the day. As Drin had assumed, sky-bike patrols flew overhead at regular intervals. Some had glo-lights shining down on the fields, but Anais's hearing gave them ample time to duck and hide within the crops when any came close.

The walk took most of the night, even though Drin hadn't parked all that far from the farm originally. His wound slowed him down too much. He would need more time to heal and recover.

"Do you remember the way?" Anais asked when they reached his sky-bike at last.

"My nanites will assist me to retrace my path," Drin said.

Anais stared at him and bit her lip. "I'm sorry. I made a mistake. I won't do it again."

"We all learn," Drin said, mounting the sky-bike so they could return to the hideaway.

TWENTY-FOUR

WHEN THEY RETURNED TO HIDEAWAY, THE SKREE CELEBRATED. They brought Anais and Drin inside and honored them as if they were heroes. She was no hero but had put herself at incredible risk—all for nothing. The sheikh still had another girl enslaved in his palace. She hadn't even been able to get close enough to let the girl know there was hope out there.

Regardless of the outcome of her foolish errand, the Skree gave her a feast and allowed her to bathe. After soaking through to her bones, Anais finally let her weary muscles relax. Once she dried herself and returned to her cot, she curled up on her bed and dozed off.

She awoke to the loudest *bang* she'd ever heard in her life.

Several of the Skree shouted in their own language. The cave walls seemed to sway, dust and debris falling from the ceilings and side walls. In the hallway just outside her hole of a room, half a dozen Skree ran by with urgency.

Anais pushed herself to her feet and made her way to the entrance.

Err-dio stopped near her. "Part of the cave's collapsed. We're not sure why. We think—"

Another *bang*.

This one broke part of the cave wall above them. Err-dio grabbed her and tackled her to the ground. A large piece of rock crashed where they had been a moment prior. It would have crushed her head if he hadn't helped her.

His six arms pushed off her before she could even consider what was going on. He helped her to her feet. "This isn't natural," Err-dio said. "We're under attack. I have to find Sao-rin."

Anais nodded, barely able to orient herself upon standing.

Err-dio took off running down the corridor. He knew his way around this cavern much better than she did. It would be safest to stay with him. She ran along behind.

The Skree were in disarray. People looked confused wherever she turned. Several tried to stop Err-dio for questioning, but he kept going until they reached the great room where they took their meals.

Several of the Skree were there, guards Anais was beginning to recognize, along with Sao-rin and Drin. The latter two men were deep in conversation. Whatever they said, they'd agreed upon, with Sao-rin turning to break the conversation.

Sao-rin inclined his head to Err-dio when they arrived.

"We're under attack," Err-dio said.

"I know," Sao-rin said. "I've just conferred with Drin, and we believe the best course of action would be to evacuate."

"Our home?" Err-dio's face flashed with horror.

"There's no choice," Drin said. "The Sekarans likely discovered us when we came back from Altequine. They know you're here now, and they'll keep bombarding your hideaway until there's nothing left. We need to gather all we can and leave now."

"We'll head toward the Tiltah Oasis. Can you help lead some of the others if we get separated?"

Err-dio nodded.

Sao-rin looked to Anais. "We'll need help to tell the others. Are you up for this task? You move quickly from what I've seen."

Anais wanted to laugh and ask why he'd want her help. All she'd done since arriving was make matters worse, but she found herself nodding. Even if she could do a little for them, it made her feel better about all the hospitality she'd taken from them.

Sao-rin dismissed her with a motion from his stumped arms. She jogged down the corridor, making sure to stop in each room and look for people. When she found them, she told them to evacuate, and once she had an acknowledgment, she moved on. There were a lot more branches of the main cave corridor than Anais could have imagined. Even with her speed, it would take her a good amount of time to check every room. The Skree had to have spent generations building this hideaway.

Dozens of people were holed up in their rooms, some hiding under furniture when she found them. Another *bang* resounded when she reached the end of one corridor. She had to steady herself not to lose her footing. A Skree family came from the room just as the cave wall cracked. The room collapsed, and rubble fell behind them.

"Our home..." the woman said, clutching onto one of her children.

The children cried and hollered.

"There's no time. We have to get out of here to keep your family safe. The heir ordered all to evacuate," Anais said for what felt like the hundredth time. At first, she'd said Sao-rin's proper name, but the Skree looked at her like she was crazy. She'd remembered several called him *heir*, and they seemed to take to her using his title far more easily. "Can you lead me out to the surface?" Anais asked, not sure it would be wise to try to travel these corridors any longer. She'd done what she could. Now it was time to get out.

The woman nodded and motioned her to follow. Her husband picked up one of the children and two more followed after them. They found their way through the winding cavern together.

When the group came to familiar surroundings, or at least

familiar openings, as none had discernable markings as far as Anais could tell, they bottlenecked with other Skree. Everyone rushed to get out of one entrance. "You don't have multiple exits?" Anais asked.

"There's never been need," the woman said with a shrug.

There was certainly a need now. It took them far too long for the crowd of all of the Skree to evacuate. Worse, she was at the back of the line. When she did get near to the opening, she saw laser-repeater fire ahead. It was dark, but they flashed brightly in the evening sky. Some of the bolts hit the rock face above her, causing some pebbles and dirt to fall. The children screamed.

The Skree fanned out, running for cover once away from the cave entrance. Anais slipped to the side and kept to the rock face wall. She darted for a pile of boulders so she could find cover rather than heading out into the open like many of the others.

Dozens of Sekarans wearing city guard armor had taken up position in front of the caves. They shot down the fleeing Skree as fast as they could run out of the caves.

Some of the Skree fought back, holding weapons of their own, but not in nearly in the numbers or in an orderly enough fashion to hold off the invading force. Sky-bikes zoomed overhead, along with unmanned drones. One drone dropped something that made a whistling noise.

It exploded behind Anais.

She ducked, covering her neck and head the best she could. The blast shot rock and dirt up through the air, and when she looked up again, she saw the cave entrance had collapsed. Skree screamed as rocks fell atop them. Anais clenched her teeth, hating to hear the screams, but also grateful she couldn't see the people being crushed by falling rocks.

Where was the Elorian? He was the one who could turn the tide here.

As if in answer to her question, a figure moved in the night sky above her, leaping over the running Skree. His familiar light sword glowed like a lightning bolt.

It brought fear to the Sekarans.

The ones who had been holding their ranks and firing backpedaled. Some turned their attention to fire at Drin, but most dropped their weapons and ran. Drin cut through the front line with his light sword, slicing through the Sekaran armor with ease. The amount of bloodshed he caused was unimaginable and even frightened her to some degree.

Drin's movements allowed for some of the Skree to pick up weapons and move into better positions to fire. They formed a line, much like the drills Drin had been teaching them since he'd arrived at their hideaway. They shot at the fleeing Sekarans. Drones still continued to blast the Skree defenders, which forced them to turn their attention skyward. The drones managed to connect with several Skree, but when one fell, another came to take his place. It was amazing to watch their discipline, their willingness to sacrifice for the chance to save their people. Anais hoped Deklyn had fought off the Sekaran invaders the same way. She worried about her people, even in the midst of this battle.

Instead of continuing the melee fight, Drin leapt again, flying through the air toward the drones. He struck one mid-air on the descent of his jump. It split in two and collapsed to the ground. The drones switched to a defensive posture, pulling back to evade Drin, which allowed the Skree defenders freedom from the pressure that had been on them.

"My people, follow me!" a voice shouted.

Anais turned to see Sao-rin ahead of her. He held a laser-repeater, which he shot into the air. The bolts formed a beacon for the others to find him.

The civilians and some of the soldiers scrambled toward their leader, and Sao-rin took off running through a small canyon.

Anais wasn't going to wait around to see the result of the firefight. Whether they won or not, the Skree who fired upon the Sekarans were buying their people time. Drin didn't worry her. He could handle himself in a fight like this in his sleep.

Everyone ran as hard as they could through the canyon. A small stream opened from groundwater, and the Skree took to one side of it. Anais followed, assuming they knew the terrain far better than she did.

After what seemed like several hours of traveling through the rocky terrain, they descended a slope. It was still night, difficult to see ahead, but the Skree appeared to have a purpose to their direction. They continued onward. The slopes began to flatten out. The dirt beneath her feet became sand, making it harder to move with speed or precision.

The large group continued along in the darkness of the desert for a long time. Anais's mouth dried from the constant exertion. She hoped they would arrive at their destination soon.

After a time, with the sun's light peeking over the horizon, they reached a place with water and trees. It looked a lot like the resting place where they had stopped when fleeing from the Sekarans the first time, but much bigger.

Sao-rin surveyed his people with Err-dio at his side. They talked in their own language, and maintained stoic faces, but Anais could sense the tension and panic from them. They led these people, and their homes had been destroyed under their watch. What would they do next?

The sound of motors echoed in the distance, which didn't bode well, especially with Drin still back at the cave entrance. If the Sekarans attacked now, they would be helpless, with little cover. Oddly enough, none of the Skree seemed to notice. Then it struck her.

Her hearing.

They might not have noticed what she did. Anais rushed ahead of some of the other Skree to catch up with Sao-rin. "Heir," she said.

Sao-rin turned.

"Sky-bikes. They're coming." She pointed back in the direction of the sound.

"Marksmen, set up a perimeter and get ready to fire!" Sao-rin shouted.

Several of the Skree scrambled to battle positions. Some dropped to their knees, others flanked around the edges of the crowd. All pointed their weapons in the same direction.

Anais was determined not to be useless anymore. She asked the Skree for a laser-repeater pistol and pointed it in the direction of the noise. If these last several days had taught her anything, it was that running and cowering accomplished nothing. It wasn't good to go off half-cocked either, but she could fight with the Skree if need be.

The sky-bikes came, and at their head, the leader of the pack held a blazing light sword in the sky. A calling card.

"Don't shoot. It's Brother Drin!" Sao-rin commanded his people. He trudged forward through the sands to the point where the sky-bikes landed.

Anais lowered her weapon.

Drin let his light sword dissipate and dismounted. Several Skree on sky-bikes did the same behind him. The Elorian moved to greet the Skree heir.

Most of the Skree were engaged in their own conversations. They were frightened, removed from their homes, with their futures uncertain. Though she didn't understand the language, their tones varied from frantic to dejected. Exactly like Anais was. But one conversation that could shape their future was far more important than the others. She didn't want to bother them, but curiosity got the best of her. Anais maneuvered herself toward Drin and Sao-rin.

"The Sekarans must have spotted us when we flew back to hideaway and followed the girl and me back there," Drin said.

Something about the way he said *the girl* made Anais's skin prickle. So soon after she had made the determination to be better, to fight, it made her feel small again. She held her tongue, listening from a place where they might think her out of earshot, but still gave her the benefit of her keen hearing. She glanced to the side so she wouldn't appear to be eavesdropping.

"Which means they will know where we are now. We're in the open," Sao-rin said. "But if you hadn't been here, we wouldn't have survived."

"We'll need some kind of plan or you still may not," Drin said.

"Won't God protect us?" Sao-rin said.

"God protects those who protect themselves. We are exposed, as you said."

"If only there were a way to get more of your armors, hmm?" Sao-rin said. "Imagine what we could do with an army of those."

Drin paused. Anais caught him looking at her, even as she side-glanced to peer at him.

"The nanites can replicate when a Templar wills it, but they are reserved for holy knights of the church alone. It has been ordained that way for generations. I can help you, but without the training from the church and the Holy Father's blessing, I cannot bestow such upon you in good conscience," Drin said.

"I see," Sao-rin said, but he sounded disappointed.

Drin paced toward Anais. "Regardless. We'll need to counter-attack soon. We can't just sit here and wait for them to destroy your people. They know where we are, and what our capabilities are. They have superiority in numbers and in supplies. If we wait too long, we will have nothing to fight for."

"Then we attack soon?" Sao-rin asked.

Drin frowned. "Would that God gave me any other way, but I don't see one. The Sekarans won't anticipate such an action, and perhaps if I can get through to kill their sheikh, they will be at a loss for leadership. I'll have to think on it."

Anais worked up some courage and crossed the distance to the men. If they were going to discuss the future of the city, she wanted to help. This was her moment. Even if she'd made mistakes before, she could work with Drin this time. "What about the slaves? They can't all be satisfied to be there. It's hell," she said. Perhaps there was hope she could rescue the Deklyn girl in the sheikh's palace. If the

Elorian planned to assault the city, she might have another chance to save her.

Sao-rin's brow furrowed. "That's not a half-bad thought. Several of my people interchange with some of the slaves to keep ourselves from working to death. The Sekarans don't notice, or turn a blind eye as long as the work gets done. Many of the slaves want the sacred city to be returned to us. Brother Drin, what do you think? A revolt?"

Drin frowned. "It could work. But we have to be ready to take the whole city. The Sekarans won't be planning for it, that's for sure. I'm just not sure we have the numbers."

"With the slaves, we just might," Anais said. She bit her lip before mustering up more courage. "I want to train with the Skree. Teach me how to fight."

"I'll pray on it," Drin said. He walked away from them, off into the desert alone.

TWENTY-FIVE

Several days passed while Drin and Sao-rin planned the assault on Altequine. The Skree scouts saw no sign of the Sekarans, which was good, but they couldn't hope for peace forever. The time to fight would come sooner than Drin would have liked.

Counting the number of able-bodied men among the Skree who fled with them, they had nearly a thousand. Of those, about a third were trained in combat. Drin increased the frequency of drills, spending entire days teaching and working. Err-dio led some of the classes to allow Drin to plan with Sao-rin.

In the hot desert, making men work all day proved difficult, but they had no choice. The Skree proved incredibly resilient in the elements. It helped to have a water source nearby to keep everyone hydrated. Some still collapsed from exhaustion in the heat.

The girl Anais pestered him those first days to be allowed to train along with the soldiers. Drin wasn't sure about having her involved, but she was determined. Her will had grown stronger since being captured by the battlemage. In the end, Drin relented. It would be better to have more able bodies helping than less, and having someone with such a strong will to fight was always good for morale. She was not nearly as conditioned as the Skree slaves had been, but she gave her best effort, and her nimble physique proved more adept at some of the callisthenic training activities than the rock-solid Skree were. Given time, she would make for a decent light infantry soldier. Her lack of skill in some areas didn't get her down. It only made her more determined. Drin found himself impressed with her.

"Good work," he told her at the end of the third day, when she sat beside him at their campfire, looking too weary to move.

The words sparked excitement in her twinkling eyes. "Thanks," she said.

Every day that passed was one more in which the Sekarans might bring a whole fleet of drones to bomb and make waste of them. Drin could only speculate as to why they hadn't done so already. He would have, in their position. But then, these were a backward people, lost in their luxuries and sins. They weren't tacticians. Hopefully, the Sekarans' hubris would continue when his Skree force faced them.

Sao-rin coordinated with many of the Skree. There was a buzzing energy about them, as if they'd been waiting a long time for this very moment. They seemed eager to fight, and more eager to reclaim their prior heritage, something Drin appreciated, reminding him of the childhood tales the nuns told him of prophecies where the Templars would retake Eloria. It was easy to teach a man discipline, or how to use a weapon. The will to fight, one either had it or didn't. All too often, it made for the difference in battles, even against a superior foe.

"Several of our scouts went ahead on sky-bikes and spread the word to our people in Altequine. The slaves on the inside are in position. They're ready. Several of the women will be disbursing throughout the city when the time comes to give the signal for revolt. Everyone is excited, but I'm not sure how long that excitement will hold. We are eager for freedom, and I to return to my familial crown," Sao-rin said.

"I cannot guarantee a victory," Drin said.

"I have faith," Sao-rin said.

Drin nodded. "God will be with us, whether His plan be for us to take the city or to become martyrs in His name."

The words proved a sobering reminder of their mortalities, causing a pause of silence between them before Drin and Sao-rin began planning the assault. The main group of Skree would slowly enter the main gates of the city as if they were traders, over the course of several hours, or perhaps even a day, preferably during busy bazaar hours when the amount of traffic wouldn't appear unusual. Drin would then take a small team with him via sky-bike to rush the inner city and the sheikh's palace. With the Skree in place to do battle against the city guard, some would be drawn from the palace, and Drin would have clear access to the sheikh. Easy enough plan. Most of the women and children would remain here at the oasis, and he hoped the Sekarans wouldn't get wind and retaliate.

The only problem would be the battlemages. Drin wasn't able to face one alone last time they met. Would the Skree prove enough to handle the city and assist him when the battlemages arrived? Mohiel had told him they often were off planet in their duties, but Drin was all too aware one was present. He had to trust in God to provide a means to defeat the powerful Sekaran, and a means to keep the second battlemage away. Either way, this would be the Skree's best opportunity to act. If they couldn't mount an offense, the Skree would be continually on the run until the sheikh tracked them down and killed them all. Drin couldn't allow that to happen.

Once they agreed where the main forces would be deployed for maximum impact, it was a matter of waiting for the right time. No one had any news from the city. The Sekarans had followed and attacked the one evening Drin and Anais had returned, but there was no sign of pursuit or even investigations. Were the Sekarans content to leave the Skree alone if it weren't for him? He would hate to be responsible for deaths.

But he couldn't worry about hypotheticals. He had prayed on the situations, and the Lord pointed him toward conquest. But further piety couldn't hurt, especially while they spent so much time waiting. Drin took several of the most faithful of the Skree and led them in a group prayer.

As the sun dawned on the next day, the time felt ripe for battle. They could wait no longer. They had water, but not much food to last beyond the week, and the longer they waited, the more likely the Sekarans would find their new encampment and wipe them out. Moreover, Drin could feel the call of God urging him to battle. It was in his soul.

The Skree trickled out of their makeshift encampment a few at a time, just as planned. Drin waited, along with several of the others.

Anais approached him while he watched one of the Skree teams depart the encampment. "Are you nervous?" she asked him.

"If God wills victory, we will have it. If he does not, we will not," Drin said.

"Such a joy to be around," Anais said with a small laugh. "Listen, I've never rightfully thanked you for all the times you've rescued me. I haven't always been the most helpful to you, or to these people, and I wanted to let you know I appreciate it."

"You are part of God's plan as sure as anyone else here."

"Maybe." Her ears twitched. "If we do pull this off, you know what, I'll give you another listen about this Yezuah guy you say came to your planet. Deal?"

Drin couldn't help but laugh at the way she phrased it. So flippant. As if matters of the eternal soul were a triviality. He met her eyes. They were earnest. Could that be why she was here? Her positive attitude and joy came through even in the darkest of times. She was stubborn, and had no training in much that could be useful in these situations–excepting the last few days—but she did have a good morale impact, not just on him, but on the Skree. Perhaps her purpose in all of this was to show him the joy and peace Yezuah brought to Eloria. It was an important component to the faith. He shook his head. "It is I who should thank you," Drin said.

"Huh?" She blinked, confusion on her face.

"Don't fret," Drin said. He placed a hand on her shoulder. Perhaps that was too much. Some of his lust for her was still present, but on the other hand, it was God's will that she be here. "You have a deal."

"Another thing, I want to come with you to the sheikh's palace," Anais said. She didn't move, letting his hand rest on her.

"No," Drin said.

"You have to let me. There's another woman from my world there. I have to find her."

"It's too dangerous. You shouldn't even be fighting with the Skree. You stand out too much on this world."

"Please," she said. Her eyes pleaded with him. She stepped closer to him, not allowing him space to even turn his head away.

She was serious. These last couple of days of training wouldn't be enough for her to handle a fully-armed force, though the city guard acted more as police than as a military. On the other hand, it would be good to have someone he trusted by his side, someone who kept him grounded in the joy and truth of God. It might not be the best tactical plan, but he was also no commander. In his gut, he sensed this was God's will. "Fine. You can join the team rushing the sheikh with me."

Her eyes lit with joy.

Before she could speak, Drin raised a finger in front of her face, which caused her to step back and give him some space. "You'll follow my every order, and it'd be best if you'd stay in cover. Watch what the other Skree do in our team and mimic their movements."

"I plan on slipping past the battle and finding the other Deklyn," she said. "I should be able to blend with the other slaves. They might not even know I'm different than her if I'm careful."

"You're overestimating what you're capable of."

"Please. I have to try. It's one of my people."

Drin considered for a long while. It wasn't the best of plans, but she had tenacity, and he suspected even if he told her no, she would try anyway. He had to work with the team present, and this included her. "If you find a way through that's not too dangerous. But be careful. Remember how it went when you ran to the city alone unprepared. We don't want to repeat the same mistakes. Now we should get ready."

He slipped to the side and away from her, where he met with some of the others on his team. They appeared to be ready, weapons checked, supply packs loaded, and eager to fight.

Over the next several hours, the encampment's population dwindled to the barest of bones. Most of the Skree left for Altequine, and if they weren't in their positions already, they would be soon. The heat of battle was very nearly upon them, and Drin felt the familiar thrilling rush run through him. It had been too long since he had fought hard for a worthy cause.

His own ability to handle this situation wasn't in question. Even if he didn't have the Skree, he could inflict a lot of damage on the Sekarans alone. The threat of the battlemages still loomed in the back of his mind, but he couldn't allow himself to consider defeat an option. He glanced back to Anais. She was practicing her aim with a pulse-repeater. She had a good heart and work ethic.

He couldn't worry about the battlemage. It was as he had said, if God willed his victory, he would have it.

Finally, the time came. One of the Skree from his team came over to let Drin know they had to depart soon if they were to time everything right with the diversions of the Skree attacking and the slaves revolting. His party gathered around him—five Skree and Anais, all armed with pulse-repeaters and long, curved knives should they need to get into melee combat.

"In a moment, we head into battle. I wish I would have had more time to train with you, and more resources to impart Yezuah's wisdom, but God has given us this chance in this time. We must do what we can."

The others nodded their assent.

"Let us head to our destiny, but first, we pray as our Lord once did," Drin said. He bowed his head. The others followed his lead. "Lord God on high, Your name is sacred forever. This kingdom is Yours now, as You have gifted us, and will hold us until You return. Forgive us our sins, as we forgive the sins of our enemies. Never let Your flock go astray, but keep us apart from evil, that we may grow in our faithfulness. Power and glory to Yezuah!"

"Power and glory to Yezuah!" about half of the Skree said. A couple others muttered as if they knew the words, and Anais didn't repeat the phrase. Though part of Drin was disappointed she hadn't joined, at least she had heard the words.

The group mounted their sky-bikes, individually, save for Anais who hopped on behind Drin.

"I'm going to be jumping from my bike to draw fire and give the others time to get settled," Drin said.

"I'll take over driving when you get ready to make the jump," Anais said. "I'd rather you drive through the city, though. Who knows what they'll be firing at us?"

"Fair," Drin said before starting the engine. They ascended into the air, leaving the oasis behind them. The small attack force traversed the desert toward Altequine.

After a couple of hours flying, the city appeared in the distance. The sun was setting in the late-afternoon sky, directly in front of them, which made it hard to see. The timing wasn't good for the assault, but Drin hoped it wouldn't matter too much. His nanites could shield most of the sun's ultraviolet light from his eyes, and if all went as planned, the city guard would be too pre-occupied with two fronts of Skree problems to be looking for them in the air.

They sped toward the walls and over them. So far so good. The streets were filled with people: Skree, Sekaran, and others. It looked like chaos below.

Drin curved his sky-bike around a tall building. Laser-repeaters fired haphazardly below, some toward the air. He would have to be mindful of his surroundings to not run into a stray blast. He kept focused on driving, weaving through the sky above the city streets.

Some of the tower watch guard caught sight of his party. They shouted something Drin couldn't hear as he flew by. He couldn't stop now, they were almost to the sheikh's palace.

"They're coordinating fire on us!" Anais said from behind him. He'd forgotten about her superior hearing.

It made no difference. They had to proceed as planned. They flew past the bazaar, now a crowded jumble of fighting merchants, slaves, and city guard.

Laser fire erupted from the tower.

It proved much more difficult to dodge the blasts directed at them. Drin banked his sky-bike to the left, some of the others followed, but one of the Skree's bikes couldn't evade in time. His motor sputtered upon the direct hit, and he crashed into the crowd below. The sky-bike exploded when it hit the ground. Drin looked away. Anais dug her face into his back. With so many people packed together in the confined area, the explosion might have killed dozens.

A brief prayer for the deliverance of their souls was all Drin had time to offer. He had to stay focused on his target. He dropped his sky-bike's altitude, hoping that the buildings would block some of the tower guards' fire. It worked. The sheikh's palace walls were directly ahead.

"I'm going to jump," Drin shouted for Anais's benefit. "Get this out of the sky as quickly as possible so you're not a target."

He didn't wait for her to respond but pushed himself to his feet. Her arms released him, and he stood to balance on the center. The nanites helped him keep level while the sky-bike pushed forward. It approached the big, domed structure atop the palace. Anais would have to turn the craft quickly. There was nothing he could do for her now.

Drin jumped.

While midair, he summoned his light sword. It glowed brightly, even during the day. The shadows dissipated on the wall below. Drin hit the ground. Tile cracked beneath his feet when he landed.

It would be a few minutes before the others joined him. He had to make quick work of his enemies. The palace guard was reinforced with extra bodies, the sheikh apparently smart enough not to take any risks with the slave revolt going on outside his walls. It was just like so many in Sekaran authority to concern themselves with their own safety before that of their people.

Several of the palace guards charged him with spear tips pointed straight for his chest. Others fired laser-repeaters at him. His armor shielding repelled the blasts, leaving Drin to deal with the melee opponents. With the armor, he wasn't too worried about getting pierced. It let him be free with his light sword. He moved and whirled his blade as if it were a great dance. In some ways, it was like the bodily art in which he could give glory to God.

His first cut sliced through two spears. He spun and cut another weapon away. It left one guard with a weapon intact to try to pierce him. The Sekaran pushed the spear forward but was met with the clank of the armor the nanites formed. Drin cut the tip off the spear and then drove his light sword directly through the heart of the Sekaran holding it.

The others backpedaled, but Drin didn't slow. He cut two more guards down who stood too close to each other. They weren't used to fighting against a Templar. Even those who kept their distance by firing their laser-repeaters seemed afraid. They ducked behind the fountain at the entry or the decorative archways on the internal walls. Cowards. But rightfully so. They had no means to stop him.

Drin charged forward, felling another Sekaran in the process. His melee attackers were all dead on the ground, bloody and lifeless.

Finally, some of his Skree companions blasted through the main gate. The gate collapsed from an explosive one of them used, and they fanned out to take cover in some of the garden features. When they did, the Sekarans increased their fire.

Anais snuck through with the rest of them, which meant she

successfully landed the craft. Drin had been worried about her capabilities in doing so. Now he was more worried about her running through the guarded palace gardens.

She took cover like the rest of the Skree with her and seemed no worse for the wear. She even managed to fire a couple of shots off, and Drin heard the familiar gurgle of someone getting hit by a laser-repeater blast. He didn't need to worry. God was with her. God was with all of them.

"Sekarans," Drin said loudly enough to fill the palace courtyard with his deep voice, "my quarrel is not with you, but with the sheikh. Know the true God is here and with me, and He will lead me to victory. If you repent and cease your attacks, He is merciful. I will not fire on anyone who lays down their arms and approaches with their hands up. I will let you leave in peace."

It was good to give them this last chance. These guards didn't do anything wrong, they were just following orders to protect the sheikh. This was a similar mercy to the one Yezuah showed to the Dawn Tribe at the battle of Puku. He tried to follow Yezuah's lead in his mercy when possible.

As typical with the Sekarans, none came forward. The brief ceasefire didn't hold, and they increased their fire. Drin didn't bother to take cover but moved forward with slow, wide strides. They would watch the uselessness of their attacks and it would break their morale.

When Drin approached their line, hidden behind different garden features and wall arches, the Sekarans fled. The Skree moved on the fleeing enemy, opening fire as if in complete understanding of Drin's tactics. The Sekarans fell like game being hunted for slaughter.

Drin rushed forward himself, his nanite-enhanced speed making it easy to overwhelm one of the Sekarans. He lopped off the guard's head before the man could turn.

The courtyard was clear. The Skree and Anais carefully fell in behind Drin, covering him and each other in case more Sekarans came from the back. None did.

The big golden palace doors stood in front of them. Such a display of wealth and power in the midst of such poverty of the Skree slaves disgusted Drin. But they did not have God. They never knew how to act with charity.

Drin stepped forward and kicked the double doors open. The hinge broke and it swung inward, scraping on the tile floor. Several Sekarans stood in the entryway, waiting for the intruders. Raising his light sword, Drin pushed forward into the palace.

TWENTY-SIX

ANAIS PRESSED HERSELF AGAINST THE WALL OUTSIDE THE MAIN doors of the palace. Laser-repeater fire blew past Drin, who had gone to work cutting down Sekaran soldiers inside. She was glad he was on her team. It would be unimaginable to be facing him as an enemy. The Elorian was a one-man killing machine. If she hadn't been the direct recipient of a rescue, she would have been deathly afraid of him.

Despite the way he could kill so fluidly, he was on the side of good. Nothing he did was out of selfishness, but a desire to help others who were oppressed. That attitude had inspired her own earlier rescue attempt, even if it had been a foolish idea.

She didn't have time to consider anymore. With a laser-repeater in her hand, and Drin and the others occupying the Sekarans, this would be her shot to find the other Deklyn woman in the palace. When Anais had been confined here, she'd never been to the slave quarters, but if this palace were anything like the battlemage's estate, he would have a separate building away from the main residence. Unless he'd done similar with this girl as he had with her and brought her up to his own private room in some farce of an engagement.

Hopefully, the girl had more luck than she'd had. Anais slipped away from the fighting at the doorway, carefully keeping her back to the palace wall. She sidestepped around the main building and through a small opening between the palace and the side wall. Someone without a lithe form such as hers would have gotten stuck, the opening was so thin. At points, it was tight enough to scrape her body between the two sheer planes of stucco, but she managed to make it through relatively unscathed. Her heart pounded from both her exerting herself and the intense nervousness from being in this vile place again.

The back of the palace opened into a courtyard similar to the battlemage's estate, but several times larger in size, with several buildings lining the lushest display of gardening Anais had ever seen. She wished she had more time to admire it.

"You," someone said.

Anais hurriedly stuffed her laser-repeater into her cloak. Her ears flipped toward the voice, leading the rest of her body to turn. A Sekaran stood just outside the back of the house. Now that she had a chance to look around, she spied several guards lining the tops of the walls in the back. She'd been lucky one hadn't shot her down. "Yes?" Anais asked, blinking at the Sekaran who spoke to her. If she tried to hide, he'd know something was wrong. She had to stay cool.

"You're supposed to be in the slave quarters with the others." The Sekaran held up a hand that held a glo-light. He blinked it several times in a pattern. "I've signaled the others not to fire while you head in."

"Um, I'm new, which one is it again?" Anais asked in her sweetest tone.

The Sekaran let out such a deep sigh of irritation that she could hear the rolling of his eyes in the breath. He pointed to one of the buildings toward the back of the compound.

"Thanks," Anais said. She kept one arm pressed against her so it would hold the laser-repeater in place. If it fell out, she would have a much worse day than she planned on having.

A loud *crash* resounded in the front of the palace. The Sekaran turned without word, paying her no more mind. Anais kept her head down and hurried straight for the building he'd pointed her to. Two other Sekaran guards stood outside the entrance. The Skree hadn't organized a slave revolt at the palace, at the very least. The sheikh probably kept tighter control over his people than the rest of the city did.

The guards allowed her to pass. Anais stepped inside. Though the building itself was spacious, bunkbeds lined it as far as she could see. The slaves were all on their beds, some looking around the posts to see who had entered. About three rows of bunks down, on the bottom bunk, Anais saw familiar white-pink fur with a more familiar ear shape.

Before she could run to the other girl, another Sekaran stepped in front of her. She recognized the man—Watcher Tellah. The one who had first gathered her and brought her before the sheikh. Watcher Tellah's eyes went wide. He recognized her, too. "You!" he shouted, the word having a much different ring to it than had been spoken by the Sekaran outside.

"Is that all you people can say?" Anais asked with an incredulous laugh. She didn't hesitate but produced her laser-repeater from her cloak, pointing it directly at Watcher Tellah's chest.

He narrowed his eyes at her. "You've been trouble since the first moment you arrived. You should be burned at the stake, not simply stoned. It'd serve as an example." He turned his head. "Guards!" he shouted.

Anais didn't hesitate. She pulled the trigger, holding it down for repeat blasts. Several shots hit Watcher Tellah square in the chest. His flesh sizzled as he stumbled backward, finally falling to the floor, twitching.

She stepped over his body, keeping her weapon pointed straight ahead. It wasn't likely the slaves would have much fight in them, not after the way they were treated by these disgusting people. Sure enough, they watched but didn't move. Those eyes peered into her as if wondering what her purpose was.

The other Deklyn woman stood. "Anais?" she asked, her eyes almost in tears.

"Lyssa," Anais said and embraced the other woman. It wasn't just any Deklyn woman. One of her best friends from back home was here! She almost couldn't believe it. "I wasn't sure I'd ever see you again." Her voice came out in no more of a whisper, emotion overcoming her to the point where she found it hard to speak.

Before they could catch up or share in another moment, the guards burst into the room. Anais had forgotten about them when her best friend suddenly stood before her. She couldn't believe it was Lyssa. Now if she didn't do something, they might die together.

Anais pushed her friend back onto the bed before sliding around the post for some cover. Lyssa fell over with a small yelp.

Several laser-repeater blasts came her direction. There was too much furniture in between them, and the shots ricocheted off metal. Some blasted mattresses into feathers, which filled the air of the room like a dust cloud.

The shots stirred the slaves, who amazingly had little reaction to Anais gunning down Watcher Tellah. There must have been no love lost for him, which wasn't terribly unexpected given the way he had treated her as nothing more than cattle when bringing her before the sheikh. Now, the slaves panicked. The weapons fire was more haphazard, and it could hit anyone. The guards didn't seem to discriminate.

Anais used the confusion to drop to her knees, letting the lower bed in front of her act as a shield. It also gave her a way to steady her laser-repeater and aim better, a trick she had learned from Drin's training sessions.

With her weapon pointed, Anais let all of the air out of her chest. *Fire on the exhale*, another adage from his training. She wasn't sure how much of a difference it made, but this time, when she pulled the trigger, even from several beds away from the door, she connected with one of the guards.

The guard crashed back against the wall, knocking a hole in it before he slid to the floor, dead.

That left one more, and he met her eyes, focused on the one person in the room returning his fire. The barrel of his laser-repeater pointed directly at her. Anais ducked, hitting the ground hard, having no time to brace herself. It was good she did, as several blasts pummeled the mattress and the bedpost behind where her face had been.

The weapon's fire kept coming. Anais could see through to the end of the room, where the Sekaran's feet were planted. His boots stood out. She pointed her weapon toward the boots and shot.

The Sekaran cursed as his foot was blasted from under him. He stumbled to the side, and his fire ceased.

Anais pushed herself back up as quickly as she could, leveling her weapon across the bed once more. Despite his injuries, the Sekaran managed to point his own weapon at her. She had the choice to duck or to take the fire, but this might be her best opportunity to get him.

She hesitated. The worst possible thing she could have done, and she knew it. She braced herself for the shot she knew would kill her.

Before the Sekaran could fire, one of the slaves jumped on him. He shot, but the blast flew wildly to the ceiling, crumbling some of the material. The slave woman wrestled him to the floor. Several other women hopped from their bunks and started mobbing him. He couldn't get another shot off before he dropped the gun.

Anais stood but couldn't quite see the battle in front of her. Women kicked and stomped on the Sekaran. A *crack* resounded across his skull. He screamed in pain. The brutality made Anais wince and turn away. How did others handle this amount of violence? It was disturbing, to say the least. She'd had to shoot someone, which was hard enough, but this sort of mobbing gave her chills.

By the time she found herself brave enough to look again, it was over. The women who'd done the violence disbursed away from the dead Sekaran. The first woman who had tackled him turned to Anais. Another woman she recognized—Tarryh, from when she first arrived in Altequine. This woman who had comforted her when she'd felt so alone. Now she'd saved her life.

"Thank you," Anais barely managed to spit out, fighting back tears of both relief and joy. She'd found her best friend in the whole galaxy and the one person who was kind to her when the Sekarans had brought her here. Now she would have to get them to safety. Anais took a deep breath to compose herself and stepped to the aisle between the bunk beds. "Listen up, everyone," she said, trying to sound as confident as Drin did when he spoke to the Skree soldiers, "there's a revolution going on out there. Slaves are revolting all across the city. The Skree are attacking and reclaiming Altequine."

"But what about the sheikh?" Tarryh asked. Others echoed that sentiment, fear radiating from them.

Anais looked her right in the eyes. "There's an Elorian Templar in the palace right now. He's taking the sheikh down."

A couple of cheers came from those words. Relief fell across Tarryh's face. "Thank God."

Anais nodded. "Anyway. We need to get out of here. I'm not sure how much longer it'll be safe. There are guards on the walls outside, though. Can anyone shoot?"

"I can," came a soft voice. Anais pointed her toward a laser-repeater on the ground. The woman took it. Another woman stepped toward one of the downed Sekarans and grabbed his weapon. Three of them had taken weapons from the Sekarans who had come in. Better than one.

"Great. I'm not sure it'll be safe. I recommend running as quickly as possible and storming through the back of the palace. Our people should have it contained by now," Anais said. "Everyone good with that?"

Some sounded agreement, others nodded. None wanted to stay any longer. Not with the way the sheikh treated them. Anais could only imagine the things done to them. Some had scars or whip marks.

One even had an eye missing. Most of them looked like they had been beautiful once. It was clear to see which ones had been here the least amount of time. The sight broke her heart.

But she had to keep them going. "All right," she said. "Let's head out." She marched toward the door, readying for a battle that would occur when the guards saw the slaves escaping *en masse*.

Lyssa blinked as she watched Anais pass. "You've changed. I almost can't believe it's you," she said, following close to Anais's side.

"I know," Anais said. There would be time for them to reminisce later. These women needed to get to Drin and the others. She pushed the door open and steadied her laser-repeater in her arms.

The door swung open in front of her as one of the women held it. Anais pushed through. The two women with laser-repeaters followed soon after. The other slaves filed into line. Despite nerves creeping up and giving her flutters in her stomach, Anais willed herself to press forward.

The guards stood careful watch on the walls surrounding the complex. Anais tried to march forward and look like she was someone official at first. She'd learned early from her father that if you looked like you knew what you were doing, people tended to respect you as if you had every right to be there. It worked great for bypassing lines at the theatre back home, but this was the first time Anais had tried the tactic in a real situation.

Her ears twitched. The non-Deklyn women would have missed it, but one of the guards spoke into his comm. "Was it authorized for the slaves to be leaving their quarters?"

Another voice came through that comm, muffled and yelling. "No, you idiot. We have a revolt going on. Stop them!"

An explosion sounded in the distance. A plume of smoke rose in that direction. While it was a good sign for their fledgling resistance, this couldn't be good for Anais's particular situation. "Uh oh," she said to herself, picking up her pace.

The guards turned their attention—and more importantly, their laser-repeaters—toward the women.

"Run!" Anais said. She hustled as hard as she could. They had to get into that back door where the Sekaran had talked to her a few minutes ago.

The women behind her raised their weapons and fired on the guards. She should have done so herself. Fumbling with the laser-repeater, she fired it haphazardly toward the walls, not bothering to look to see if she hit her target. She had to keep moving.

More sounds of laser-repeaters went off behind her. Some bolts hit the ground. One ran into a long-stemmed flower plant, which caught fire. It would take her just a few more seconds to get to that back door. She pushed herself to run harder.

A shot fired from the walls. Her whole body felt like it was on fire.

Anais stumbled a few steps forward and found she couldn't keep herself upright. Her legs gave out, and she collapsed face-first onto the gravel path.

"She's been hit!" one of the women shouted from behind her. Several of the slaves gathered around her, acting as a shield. One picked up Anais's laser-repeater, which she hadn't been able to hold onto through the pain. The woman turned and fired at the guards.

Lyssa and Tarryh crouched down beside her. "It's pretty bad," Tarryh said. "They got her square in the back. The radiation will eat through to her chest soon if we don't get her help."

The pain was unbearable. Lyssa found herself crying, unable to concentrate on anything around her. It was chaos. Shouts. More sounds of weapons fire. Blasts in the distance. All she wanted was peace and quiet. Though her back burned, the rest of her felt so cold.

She lost consciousness for a moment and came back to reality. When she did, she found her arms draped around Lyssa and Tarryh. They carried her toward the back door of the palace. Her toes dragged across the ground, but she couldn't find the strength to lift them.

More blasts sounded. A woman screamed behind her. The guards must have hit her. Anais couldn't look back.

They reached the door. Tarryh shrugged Anais off her, leaving her to fall limply onto Lyssa.

"I know with how the sheikh feeds his slaves you haven't gained weight while you're here, but ugh!" Lyssa grunted, shifting Anais to balance her weight.

Tarryh managed to open the door. The world spun around Anais. Through her dizziness, she glimpsed the garden area behind her. Several women lay dead on the ground, but many of the slaves went on, following them toward the palace. This was her fault. She was responsible for those deaths. Without her, the women would still be back in the slave house.

What was their alternative, though? Wait there and hope the Skree won the day? Odds were against them, even with Drin and his magical armor. The women couldn't have relied on a victory. This was their best chance for freedom. They understood, or they wouldn't have followed her, would they?

Lyssa pulled Anais into the palace's back room as another blast nearly pummeled her. The bolt hit the siding of the palace walls, sending cracked stucco flying through the air. She was finally inside, safe. They were in a large room, one for receptions. This was where Anais had been lined up with the other women for the sheikh to ogle and pick who he wanted as if it were a buffet. The thought made her stomach clench.

Or maybe it was the pain in her back flaring up that made her want to vomit. She felt very sick and found herself gasping for air.

"It's getting worse. We need to find a doctor, now!" Tarryh shouted.

Lyssa let her down to the floor gently. Anais couldn't even manage to sit up straight. She fell against the wall, and then to the ground. The pain kept getting worse, so bad she found herself unable to see. She tried to scream, but nothing came out.

Darkness overcame her for the second time in as many minutes. This time, she didn't wake up.

TWENTY-SEVEN

ANOTHER SEKARAN CAME FROM THE TOP OF THE STAIRWELL, immediately meeting with blasts from four laser-repeaters. The Skree had taken up positions at the bottom of the stairs, poised to strike either at the door or at anyone who came from the second floor.

Several bodies piled at the top of the stairs, which was where Drin assumed the sheikh hid with his personal guard. The Skree around him had fought well so far, with no losses among his team. They cleared out the bottom floor of the residence in record time. If there were any Sekarans left inside, they were cowering in fear. Drin and his team took a moment to regroup and breathe.

The sheikh had to be there somewhere. Drin meant to end the Sekaran's life as soon as possible. He trudged up the stairs, light sword in hand, stepping over the dead bodies as he moved. Explosions sounded outside. The battle was reaching its apex in the entire city. He muttered a prayer in hopes Sao-rin and the others were doing well.

When he reached the upper floor, Drin was surprised to find no Sekarans waiting for him in ambush. The main hallway was empty.

Some of the doors were shut. The sheikh and his goons could be hiding behind any one of them. Drin was confident, but he still had to be careful in case someone had an armor-piercing EMP device, or if he came across a battlemage, or worse, two battlemages. Drin had already faced one. He prayed the other was off fighting another battle on another planet or was otherwise indisposed. One person with such power could make all the difference in this gambit.

He kicked the door to the first room open. It was empty. A bedroom with lavish decorations of silk, gold, finely-carved wood. The decadence he would expect from the sheikh, but no one there.

The next room proved equally empty. These rooms looked like guest quarters. When Drin kicked down two more doors, he found the same style of decor, but each room devoid of Sekarans. It left the one set of double doors at the end of the hall to check. It must have been the sheikh's quarters.

Drin took a deep breath, readying himself for intense combat. The nanites stirred within him, and though it caused no tangible sensation, he swore he could almost feel it. At most, the tiny machines provided him a heightened awareness. He moved forward and rammed his shoulder into the doors, bursting them open.

The doors swung inward, revealing the gaudiest room in the residence. Paintings, statues, and rugs adorned the room. Large windows provided a decadent view of the city outside, though the view was filled with smoke and flaming buildings. The battle must be raging with ferocious intensity outside if the damage were any evidence. Drin returned his focus to the room in front of him. The large, round bed was empty, with no space for anyone to be hiding under the mattress. The curtains were empty as well. The room didn't hide anyone. The sheikh must have fled.

Drin didn't curse. It would have done no good, and such language was an affront to God. But it was frustrating to have gone through the entire house only to come up empty-handed. If the sheikh made it out of the palace, or out of the city, it meant the battle would not end today. The sheikh would be able to mobilize forces and reinforce-ments from other Sekaran cities to quell this rebellion. His team had to move quickly to secure what they could.

After hustling down the stairs, he found his men out of position. They were down the hall, toward the entertainment room he had first explored upon entering. With the Skree were several women, one of them an Elorian.

Drin froze, not expecting to see one of his people here. She wore sheer silk that barely covered her feminine features, the same attire Anais had worn the first time he saw her. The woman spoke to the Skree in a frantic demeanor.

"We need to find a doctor quickly or she's not going to make it," she said.

"What's the situation?" Drin asked, moving closer. He inclined his head toward the Elorian woman.

Her eyes went wide in surprise, but she immediately bowed her head to him. "Templar," she said in a tone of reverence. All the panic in her voice disappeared. "My name is Tarryh. I'm here to help."

One of the Skree motioned to Drin. "Anais has been hit. She's on the back floor. The women have tried to make her comfortable..." He shook his head.

"The women? Anais?" The blood drained from Drin's face. More than a dozen women occupied the room beyond, all in the same slave garb. Anais had rescued them. She'd made it. But at what cost? "Let me through," Drin said, pushing past a couple of the Skree. The women parted ways for him.

One of the women was also a Deklyn, who must have been the girl Anais spent so much time and energy trying to save. At least her efforts had not been in vain. The Deklyn woman was out of her wits, crying profusely, pulling at her long ears with her hands.

Drin ignored her, seeing Anais on the ground. She was on her stomach, and Drin could see why. A laser-repeater blast had burned directly into her back. Her skin was singed in a big black ring that covered most of her shoulder blades. It was a miracle the bolt hadn't blown a hole straight through her. The wound smelled like burned meat, and in the areas the bolt hadn't cauterized, blood oozed and bubbled. "Yezuah," Drin breathed.

He didn't like saying the Lord's name in a profane manner, but it came out regardless of his ideals. His knees suddenly felt weak. He dropped to them. "Please, Lord, don't take her. Whatever ailment You place upon her, let me bear it instead," Drin said aloud.

Some of the others gathered around him. There was no doctor present. He didn't know of one among the Skree. Even if they had one, could they deal with a wound this severe? The Skree appeared to be limited in their technological capacities.

"Is there nothing you can do?" Tarryh asked.

Drin shook his head. "Only prayer."

One of the Skree pushed through the crowd of women. "Didn't you say something about nanites before? That they healed you? And you could transfer them somehow?"

It was true, he could will some of his nanites into another to begin a replication process. But to do so here, the very idea was sacrilege. Only a priest had the right to bestow nanites upon another, which meant an induction into the Templar order. It required years of training, of seminary, and of devotion to God. Anais had none of that, and moreover, she was a woman. It was forbidden for women to become Templars, as Yezuah himself had only conferred his blessings upon his twelve male disciples.

Anais convulsed on the ground. She moaned but remained unconscious.

"She's not going to last much longer. Do something!" shouted the other Deklyn girl.

Drin frowned. What would Yezuah do in this position? He performed a number of miracles, healing wounded soldiers and the sick. There was the miracle of the many rations, where his entire unit would have starved had he not produced enough for all of them out of nothing. Those stories didn't help now.

Drin closed his eyes and muttered a prayer. The others asked what he was doing, but Drin refused to be distracted. He needed God's voice, and God's voice alone. A feeling of peace overcame him. Yezuah's spirit was with him, in the room. The spirit provided him with an overwhelming sense of comfort, of peace. It was a sensation Drin tried to attain every day. It provided him clarity. The right thing to do would be to save the girl. Forgiveness for breaking the rules of the church would come later.

"Give me a knife," Drin said, reopening his eyes. Someone amongst them had to have one.

One of the Skree produced a long, curved blade, flipping it in his hand with precision and offering the hilt to Drin.

Drin took the blade, nodding to the Skree to relay his thanks. He held his own hand in front of the blade and sliced. It opened a deep cut, but one the nanites would repair in moments. The wound stung, causing Drin to clench his teeth. Blood flowed down his hand, dripping onto the floor.

The ceremony when he had been a youth went much like this. The priest held a Templar's hand up in the air, cut it, and did the same with Drin. The two hands were clasped together, joining blood with blood. Even though such ceremonies were rare, Drin still recalled the words the priest said vividly. "As Yezuah bound his disciples to him through the blood He spilled, you now are bound together as the body of the Church. Go forth and make disciples in His name," Drin found himself repeating aloud as he had heard all those years before.

He pressed his bleeding hand into the wound in Anais's back.

She twitched, her body reacting to the pain even in her unconscious state. Drin held his hand there for several moments to make sure the nanites had a chance to spread. He concentrated on a task he'd never done before, willing the nanites to replicate. Sweat beaded on his forehead from his intense focus. The process required a certain amount of nanites to activate their regenerative properties and to reproduce. The blood dripped over Anais's wound. It had to be enough.

"Now what?" Tarryh asked from behind him.

"Now, we wait and pray for her health."

TWENTY-EIGHT

ANAIS HAD THE STRANGEST DREAM. IT WAS AS IF SHE LOOKED AT reality through someone else's eyes. Where had she been? It was hard to remember. A battle. She stood in the middle of a battle. Her hands gripped onto a sword, but not of the typical variety. It was a sword of light.

Something must have knocked her in the head, a volley from her enemy. Anais focused her eyes.

A battlefield surrounded her. Thousands of Elorians like herself. No, that wasn't right. She wasn't an Elorian. Looking down at herself, not much could be seen other than the armor. She did have green hands, the color of skin typical to Elorians. All of these thoughts were so fuzzy in her head. This couldn't be right.

Over the hillside in front of her, Sekarans charged. She'd never seen such a big army, nor had any of her compatriots.

"We've got to fall back!" her commander shouted.

Looking around, several around her wore the same armor and held similar light swords. But at the front of the horde of Sekarans, there were at least a dozen of their battlemages, foes who could pierce through their armor, turn off the nanites that fueled it. If they didn't run, they would never survive.

But this was the Holy Land of Eloria. The very place where Yezuah and his disciples changed the course of Eloria's history and brought about world peace. Just over the hill was the large stone where the commanders of the tribes met the final time, where the peace was secured. Yezuah himself was betrayed there, by one of his own disciples, but though he had been struck down from behind, he rose again to bring the tribes together into one Elorian people. His final act before he ascended into Heaven.

There was still time for her and the others to get to the transport. They would ascend into the sky, as well, and perhaps never return to Eloria.

The Sekarans came closer. The battlemages had fire in their hands and shot it toward them. She had no choice but to run.

"SHE'S COMING TO," a familiar voice said.

"Good, we're spending too much time here. We need to find the sheikh," another said.

Everything hurt. Her body protested every movement, and her head pounded as if someone were driving a nail into it. What she needed to do was sleep for days, but with everyone talking and someone trying to get her to sit up, sleep would be impossible. She shrugged the hand off her and grumbled.

"I think it worked, whatever you did," the first voice said again. Lyssa?

Anais recalled her dream. It was strange. She'd remembered her name, but she was a completely different person. How had that been possible? Was this one of those strange signs from God that Drin kept rambling about?

She let her eyes open slowly. Her vision was hazy at first, but it settled into normalcy after a few moments. She rested on her stomach, but why? Her memory returned in a flood. The Sekarans had shot her in the back when she rescued the slaves. They'd made it into the house, but she couldn't stand any longer.

The firm hand gripped her arm tightly, assisting her in sitting upright. When she managed to right herself, she saw Drin beside her.

"What happened?" Anais asked.

"You nearly died," Drin said. "You're lucky I was near. I... bestowed the nanites unto you. They're repairing your wounds. Do you feel any different?"

Nanites? She had his strange machines in her, the ones that gave him enormous power? She'd recalled their conversation on how they could only be bestowed by a priest. She brought her hand to her temple, pressing against her forehead with her fingertips. "I feel a little light-headed, maybe."

"That's normal." Drin offered her a hand up, and she took it. Tarryh also stepped toward her and helped her to her feet. Amazingly, she was able to stand. The place she had been shot throbbed a little, like an old wound taking time to heal, but it wasn't debilitating as it had been a moment before.

Anais turned to Drin, meeting his eyes. Those dark eyes had a profound deepness to them, deeper than any ocean or perhaps even the vastness of space. Was it his focus on matters so much bigger than himself that created his depth? In many ways, she longed for it. The depth to his soul, for lack of any better term, was what attracted her to him. "Thank you," she said after a long moment.

Drin merely nodded. "We'll need to get the women to a safe point," he said, "and we still must find the sheikh."

"There's an underground safe room," one of the women said. "The entrance is hidden beneath a rug in his wine storeroom."

"Good. We'll find him and bring him to justice." Drin motioned to the Skree he had with him.

The Skree talked to the woman, and she offered to show them the store room. Before they could depart, however, the sound of several boots falling across the tile flooring came from the front of the house.

Drin pushed forward, as she'd seen him do before. He liked to place himself as a shield between attackers and the others, which made sense as he was the one within the nanites. Did she have that ability, too? Anais considered assisting, but she didn't want to try to push herself too hard. She still felt queasy and light-headed. Now wouldn't be the time to test the abilities of what Drin had given her.

Several Sekarans rushed through the wide archway leading into the room. They opened fire immediately, causing everyone behind Drin to duck, run, and scream. Drin's shield blocked the majority of the bolts, sending some ricocheting to the walls and ceiling. The walls sparked when the bolts hit.

The Skree and the three women with laser-repeaters took up positions to the sides of Drin, doing their best to return fire around his shield bubble. They managed to pick off the lead Sekarans advancing, but more enemies flooded into the doorway. There were too many of them.

One of the Sekarans grabbed a round object, pulling a pin from it.

"Grenade!" one of the Skree shouted.

Drin rushed forward, swinging his light sword toward the Sekaran holding the grenade. The Sekaran dodged and managed to roll it on the ground toward Anais and the others. Drin reached out with his foot, but he was unable to stop it.

The Sekaran used the distraction of the grenade to pierce through Drin's protective bubble, brandishing a curved knife and slashing at Drin's chest. The blade connected, but Drin stepped backward. The nanites created a heavy armor around his chest. "Move out the back!" Drin shouted.

There were guards on the rooftops outside, something Anais and the other women had run inside to hide from. Perhaps with the help of the Skree, they would have a better time dealing with them. It dawned on Anais the Skree might not know of the guards' presence. "There are guards on the walls and at the lookout post outside. We need weapons out first," she said.

The Skree didn't need to be told twice to move, as they backed toward the back door. But while they did so, the grenade on the floor went off with a *hiss*.

The grenade didn't explode as Anais was expecting, but smoke flooded from it. It was meant to blind them, not kill them. Anais moved to the back door as fast as she could but was crowded by the other women. Her back stung with each movement. How much of her wounds the nanites had been able to repair, she wasn't sure.

When the smoke filled the room, something strange happened. Protective goggles formed over her face. Anais reached for them, almost clawing them off in the panic. *What was going on?* Right, the nanites. She'd forgotten that they could form armor. The goggles allowed her to see clearly, even through the smoky haze.

Anais stepped back, letting the other women crowd the door ahead of her. The Skree who made it through the door opened fire upon the Sekaran guards on the outside walls. Those guards returned fire. The sound of laser-repeaters came from all around her now. She didn't have any way to escape from it. Still, with her ability to see where the others couldn't, it was best to let them move from the immediate danger inside the palace while she brought up the rear.

She turned her head to see Drin doing his best in holding off the Sekarans. They stayed back, out of the smoke, forcing Drin toward them. He could defeat the Sekarans, she was sure of that, but something inside her didn't feel right about the whole situation. They had to know at this point that Drin could handle anything they could throw at him.

Then she saw it. Several of the Sekarans had fallen to Drin's sword, crumpled lifeless on the ground. But the most recent bunch had all backed off, drawing Drin toward them. The smoke grenade's purpose had been to separate Drin from the others, to pull him out of their escape. A trap to kill him.

The Elorian stood, brave as ever, with his light sword in his hand, poised to fight. Anais had to sidestep to get a better perspective of what was going on. A lone Sekaran in flowing robes cut through the others as they fell back. Bright light radiated from him, coming from his hands in front of him. Trydeh, the battlemage, stood in the arch-way, and he was about to unleash a powerful blast of energy directly at Drin.

"No!" Anais shouted, which only served to distract both the battlemage and Drin.

She wanted to rush forward, but before she could, a hand grabbed her by the sleeve and tugged her toward the back door. Anais stumbled outside, where the women and the Skree had secured the area and were rushing for the slave quarters. Lyssa had her by the sleeve and dragged her away.

It was the right thing to do. She couldn't do anything but get in Drin's way as it was, but she still wanted nothing more than to reach out to her Elorian friend. She backpedaled as Lyssa forced her to move, trying to watch what was going on inside.

The battlemage's energy blast hit Drin with full force. He went flying backward into the doorframe, which cracked. Anais screamed as she was pulled away, unable to do anything to help him.

TWENTY-NINE

"Nice little insurrection you planned here, Elorian. But as you see, Eltu is with us, and it is written, 'no enemy shall withstand Eltu's might,'" the battlemage said. Another ball of energy formed in his hand.

The pain within Drin was like a thousand tiny supernovas bursting within him at every moment. The battlemage's last blast had scrambled his nanites, and they were in a state of recharging and refreshing. His light sword had dissipated. He'd been in this situation before but only when he had a full unit of Templars nearby to provide cover for him. This battlemage was strong. Without Anais's help, Drin would have not survived their last encounter.

The battlemage looked like he could sense Drin's fear. He had a glint in his eye, the confidence of impending victory. The thrill of someone about to spill the blood of his enemy. Drin knew that feeling well. But he couldn't let it end like this. They were so close to restoring the Skree to their rightful place in Altequine. If he died before they found the sheikh...

Another energy blast came at him. Drin lifted his arm to block his face, channeling all of the remaining strength in his nanites to shield directly in front of him. He hooked his leg around the doorway, pulling his body to the side. The blast hit, but at least it didn't pummel directly into him. The nanites fizzled, but Drin had protected most of his body from absorbing the impact of the energy.

He scrambled to his feet while the battlemage made his way out the door. Using the brief concealment of the palace's outer wall, Drin ducked, confusing the mage. He slammed his elbow into the man's gut, causing the most recent ball of energy to fizzle. Then Drin delivered an uppercut to the battlemage's jaw.

Much of his Templar training involved fighting without assistance from the nanites. He had to learn martial arts, boxing, and how to work with a real sword. The Templar training became invaluable in times like these. If he had relied solely on his tech, which needed time before it could come back up to strength, he would have been dead already.

The battlemage adapted to Drin's most recent attacks faster than would have been ideal. He was trained just as well by his Sekaran masters, if not better. Worse, he had a height advantage over Drin. Once the surprise assault passed, the battlemage was able to keep Drin at a distance with his own swings. With Drin on the defense, it allowed him to refill one of his hands with the Sekaran energy magic.

Drin's nanites were all but exhausted. There wasn't much for Drin to do but try to dodge. He lunged to the side and was struck in the thigh by the energy ball. It ate at his armor, evaporating and burning his flesh once it passed it. Drin sucked in a quick breath and spun to the ground.

He wasn't able to get a good look around him, but he didn't see the other Skree or the women nearby. A blessing not to have to protect civilians. Oddly, no Sekaran city guards came either. Anais had shouted about them. His allies must have been able to handle them on their own.

The battlemage was on him before he could move. He pulled Drin to his feet by the neck, keeping at arm's length, where Drin could do little to resist but squirm. The battlemage was impossibly strong, but then, it was a part of their magic. The Templars had never learned how the Sekarans did what they did. Such an insight would have given them a tactical advantage like the Sekarans had, knowing of the nanites and how to disable them with strong blasts of energy or electromagnetic pulses.

Drin choked, unable to breathe with the battlemage's fingers compressed on his windpipe. He flailed, but his movements proved futile. Finally, Drin was able to swing his weight far enough to deliver a kick toward his enemy. The battlemage saw it coming and dodged to the side.

It did cause him to ease his grip on Drin's throat. Drin gasped for air and pushed his body from the battlemage's grasp. He stumbled backward. There had to be some way to escape, to let his nanites recharge so he could have a chance against to survive this superior power. But with the walls all around the courtyard, and his nanites taxed as it was, he had no way out. If he ran toward the other build-ings, he would lead the battlemage directly to the women and the Skree. If he held his ground, he at least gave the others time to attempt escape.

To make matters worse, Sekarans flooded into the courtyard from the palace, the smoke from inside finally having cleared enough to allow them to get their bearings. They had their laser-repeaters pointed, and in Drin's weakened state, a simple blast from the common weapons might well do him in.

The battlemage held a hand up to his guards. "No. The Elorian is mine," he said, his voice filled with hate and vengeance. The destruc-tive energy formed over his palms again. He extended his arms toward Drin.

Energy shot from the battlemage's hands toward him, in a wide burst this time. It left Drin no way to evade. The wave hit him like a sky-bike crash, its force pummeling against Drin's body. He couldn't keep his footing and fell onto his tailbone. It cracked when he landed on the hard ground. Drin yelled in pain.

The battlemage stepped toward him, slowly and deliberately.

When Drin tried to sit up, the battlemage stamped his boot down on Drin's chest, pushing him hard against the ground again. His head snapped backward, and his skull thudded against the packed gravel. Everything seemed so bright. His vision blurred. A concussion. And his nanites couldn't protect him any longer, nor could they heal his wounds.

His whole body writhed in pain. The battlemage's boot dug into his chest and held him firmly to the ground. This was it. After all the battles, after all of his time and energy working to free the Skree people, it would end like this. Had God planned it all along? Would he be favored in Heaven as one of the martyrs and saints?

When the world compressed around him, and everything went dark, Drin prayed his actions had been enough to atone for the vows he forsook when he ran from the Templars.

THIRTY

THE SKREE WERE GOOD SHOTS, ANAIS HAD TO GIVE THEM THAT much. They targeted and removed the guards on the walls and the lookout post with ease. The Sekarans above fell to their deaths. The sheer number of guards still on the walls made her wish she and the women had been more productive when they fled the servant's quarters the first time. After the area was secure, the whole group gathered outside of the building, deliberating their plans.

The first priority would be to get the women to safety. Then the Skree wanted to go help Drin and find the sheikh, wherever that oaf was hiding. Anais liked the plan, but it didn't help them with keeping the women safe. The Skree turned to the wall, trying to blast a hole in it with their laser repeaters, but as thick as it was, it would take hours of chipping away at it to make an exit. It would also make far too much noise, which could alert other Sekarans in the city to converge upon them.

"If we had a grenade or something more explosive," one of the Skree said, "we could make an opening in single blast. I could guide the women to a safe place away from the fighting, and the rest of us could return to help the Templar."

"Sounds sensible," Anais said. But they didn't have a way to blast through the wall. Or did they? "What's your name?"

"I am called Reg-tel," the Skree said with the slight bow of his head. "I'm honored to assist you."

Nanites buzzed inside of her. Drin used them to project energy, at least in the form of a shield. If she found a way to make her own, what could it do to a wall?

The problem was, she didn't know how to use the nanites. The Elorian had years of training to be able to control and wield these things as effective weapons. Anais could make the wrong move and kill everyone around her. But she had to do something. She had the power, and as frightening as it was, she had a responsibility to try.

"Why don't you step back?" Anais asked the others, motioning around her to signal she needed a wide berth.

Reg-tel and the women did as asked. They had confused looks on her faces, but they didn't question her. Now it would be on her. She focused on the wall. *Energy shield!* she thought to herself.

Nothing happened.

Anais narrowed her eyes and clenched her jaw shut.

"You look like you're constipat—" Lyssa began.

But she didn't finish her words. The wind picked up around Anais, or perhaps it was the nanites on the move. Her ears flopped forward. Anais planted her feet in a wide stance. The wind became energy. She saw it rippling through the air. The others looked on in amazement. A faint pink ribbon appeared, then grew like a bubble. It pushed outward and expanded with incredible speed.

The wall in front of her blasted apart as if someone had planted dynamite at its center. The bricks split when the energy pushed at them.

The sensation dizzied her. Anais found herself spinning and could barely manage to stay on her feet. She stumbled to the side like a drunkard before Tarryh caught her in her arms.

"Easy there," Tarryh said. Then she looked to the wall, or at least where the wall had been. "Incredible."

Anais steadied herself enough to look. The debris settled, and sure enough, she had blown a hole in the wall large enough for the others to escape. Reg-tel pushed through first, pointing his weapon around to make sure they wouldn't be fired upon. He waved the women forward, who flooded through after.

Sounds of other energy blasts came from behind them. Anais couldn't help but look back toward the courtyard. Over a dozen Sekarans stood watching as Trydeh summoned energy into his hands. She couldn't see Drin, but judging by Trydeh's confident poise, the Elorian had to have been in trouble.

Tarryh tugged on Anais's sleeve. "Come on, we have to get going," she said.

Anais didn't look back but shrugged the other woman's hand away from her. "I'm not going. Drin needs me."

"Suit yourself," Tarryh said. Her footsteps padded away, along with the others, leaving Anais with the rest of the Skree.

The Skree leveled their weapons, but Anais held an arm up. "No, I've seen the battlemage in action. He's like a Templar. The weapons' fire will bounce off him."

"Then what do we do?" asked Reg-tel.

Anais bit her lip, considering. They had the element of surprise. The battlemage hadn't looked their way. He sent another blast toward the ground in front of him, the impact obscured by one of the buildings. Drin howled in pain as she'd never heard before.

What could they do? The battlemage was focused on Drin, and the Sekarans hadn't seemed to notice the women were a threat. It gave them time to do something, but what? Anais laughed at herself under her breath. If she could have told her younger-self she would be thinking about how to use an advantage in a fight, she would have called herself crazy. It was amazing how much this world had hardened her. Or was it the influence of the nanites, pressing her for survival?

It would be something for her to consider later. For now, she had to act. She narrowed her eyes, focusing hard. The pink bubble surrounded her, this time staying in a stable zone. It would protect her. But this sledgehammer of a weapon wouldn't be useful to take on Trydeh.

She needed a sword.

When she had summoned the energy shield, it took immense concentration. Whatever the nanites did to summon it made her dizzy, but she had to keep her focus and balance. She thought about the light sword Drin wielded. She willed one of her own, balling her hand in front of her as if she were gripping a hilt. Beads of sweat dripped down her face, but Anais was determined to create this weapon.

Shimmering from her hand as it came into form, the light sword flickered into existence.

The Skree behind her gasped, drawing the attention of some of the Sekarans behind Trydeh. Drin came into view, scrambling out from under Trydeh's foot when Trydeh turned his attention toward his guards.

This would be her chance. She ran forward, her feet bouncing on the ground, light, and with the speed only a Deklyn could manage, enhanced by the nanites flowing within her. The buildings blurred as she moved past them. She held her light sword high, steady and flat. Something in her mind told her not to swing it. Her arm strength wasn't like that of a soldier, or any of the other species she fought alongside. Her gifts were in speed, not strength. She used her momentum to carry the sword forward like a lance, hoping the force would be enough to pierce the battlemage's defenses.

The battlemage turned when he heard the screaming of his soldiers. Anais couldn't make out what they were saying. She moved too quickly, and she was too consumed in the moment for any distractions to register as anything other than background noise. Trydeh opened his mouth to shout at Anais. He tried to raise his hands, but it was too late.

The light sword struck with the force of all of her speed. It ran through Trydeh's neck, severing his head. The energy was intoxicating, but it also reverberated through her, giving her a sensation similar to hyperventilation. She pulled the sword out of Trydeh's neck and stepped back. The battlemage's body twitched for several seconds before collapsing, and his head rolled across the ground toward his guards' feet.

Anais's mouth hung agape. Was this real?

Before she could think about what she'd just done, the Sekarans opened fire, laser-repeater bolts immediately slamming into Anais's energy shield. Each blast tickled her, somewhat like the itch she periodically had in the back of her throat, impossible to quell. But if that's the worst they could do, the annoyance meant little. She knelt to capture Drin in her energy bubble, letting her light sword evaporate.

"How...?" Drin asked, struggling for breath.

"Talk later. We have to get you to safety," Anais said.

The Skree spread out behind, taking positions and cover to shoot at the Sekarans. A firefight ensued around her. Several shots connected with soldiers on both sides, bringing death.

Anais stayed focused on Drin, but she stayed still. Her people needed her as a diversion to draw some of the Sekaran fire.

"Go fight them," Drin said. "Run them off."

"I can't. That's not me," Anais said, shaking her head. She'd done what she had to in order to save Drin, but she wasn't a soldier, able to plow through people like a butcher at a slaughterhouse. All the carnage around her made her stomach queasy. Instead of fighting, Anais found herself burying her face in Drin's shoulder. They had to have looked ridiculous, two people lying on the ground together with a bubble of energy surrounding them. He said nothing, but held her in his strong arms while weapons' fire roared. His warmth felt good, even in the heat of the Altequine day.

After both sides fired several more volleys, the Sekarans fell back. The Skree pressed toward the palace and took positions along the doorway. "They're retreating! We've won!" one of them shouted.

Anais glanced up from Drin. Two of the Skree had met their demise alongside four Sekarans. So much death, but the Sekarans had retreated, ceasing their fire. It was over. Trydeh was dead, and he wouldn't come back.

"Help me up," Drin said.

"Don't you need to rest?" Anais asked. She pushed herself to her feet and then offered Drin a hand. He grabbed onto her. Even though he relied on her with his full weight, Anais found she was able to maintain her balance. The nanites. They gave her greater strength than she'd ever had before. A thrill of having such power ran through her. If she'd had this back on Deklyn, those soldiers would never have taken her, or anyone else for that matter.

Drin balanced himself carefully, releasing her hand. His facial expression was tight, but his eyes betrayed his pain. "I'll be okay. The nanites are recharging. What's important is we find the sheikh before he escapes or another battlemage arrives. If he does, all of this has been for naught."

He tried to take a step forward, but it was too much for him. Anais ducked her head under his arm and put her arm around his waist. "You've been doing this alone for so long. You don't have to anymore. Let me help you."

They made their way into the palace together.

THIRTY-ONE

THE DISCOMFORT OF HAVING A WOMAN TOUCH HIM SO OPENLY was almost worse than the wounds Drin had sustained from the battlemage. Each step pained him for a different reason. Anais had been right, he did need rest, probably several days of it, but he couldn't relax until the job was done.

On their way through the sheikh's reception room, Anais kept pestering Drin to stop and rest, but she didn't understand. If the sheikh managed to escape now, to tell the story of how he survived the clutches of a Templar, he would be able to rally Sekaran troops to his cause. The resulting force would in all probability be more than Drin could handle alone. Even with Anais who shared in his capabilities, he still had to consider himself alone. She had no idea the capabilities of the machines inside her, or even how to utilize them in a basic form.

They moved through the palace without a word. Drin grunted in pain every few steps. It would take time for his wounds to heal fully, but without too much strain, the nanites would keep him going as long as he needed. Worse come to worst, he could direct a surge of adrenaline at the right time.

Drin stopped. If the informants were correct, the underground safe room would be just below their feet. A rug with an intricate design sprawled across the floor, with no visible signs of a basement. "Take me to the wall," Drin said.

Anais helped him over as he'd directed.

Drin leaned against the wall, then pointed to the rug. "Roll that up, if you would."

"You know, you're not my commander," she said with a little sass in her voice. Moving over to the rug, she seemed to have a slight sway to her hips. Was she taunting him? Drin would never understand women. Despite her words, she crouched and complied with his orders.

Sure enough, a hatch lay directly where Drin had been told. He pushed off the wall and hobbled over to it. The movement exacerbated his pain. He grimaced but powered through it.

"You're not bending down to open that," Anais said. Half an hour earlier, she had been in worse shape than him, but her wounds were very concentrated, making it easier for the nanites to locate, isolate, and repair. He, by contrast, had scrapes and gashes all over him, and several cracked ribs, among other bones. Thinking about it made them ache worse.

Anais turned a small inset latch and tugged the hatch open. It revealed stairs that led down to a floor below, with a single, small glo-rod giving light. Beyond the stairs was a thick metal door with a complicated security pad.

Drin frowned. "If he's in there, we'll have to get through."

"How?"

"Use the light sword," Drin said. "It can cut through most metals. It may take a little for it to heat and melt through something thick, but it won't fail you."

Anais took a deep breath and, a moment later, a light sword appeared in her hand. It illuminated the basement with intense brightness, casting a long shadow behind her. She moved forward and drove the blade into the wall. Its tip disappeared, and then the rest of it up to her hands. She pulled downward, the metal melting around her hands and dripping to the floor before cooling.

The door swung open.

Drin scrambled down the steps, in case Anais needed help, but the quick motion tweaked his wounds, shooting crippling pain through him. He gritted his teeth together to try to focus on anything else.

The sheikh and a couple of attendants stood behind the door. They had no energy weapons, only their curved knives, which they pointed toward Anais.

"Eltu bless us!" one of the attendants shouted, charging Anais.

A pink ribbon of energy appeared in front of her. When the Sekaran ran into it, he jolted and stumbled backward. The ribbon stayed in place. Anais maneuvered toward them. Her raw ability to manage the nanites impressed Drin.

She learned quickly. Much faster than the Skree did. It made Drin appreciate her companionship more, though he shook his head to try to purge those dangerous thoughts.

He continued to monitor from the top of the stairs. If matters went poorly, he could handle the situation, despite his wounds. It didn't matter how much it hurt. He would protect her.

The Sekarans caught sight of him and glanced between her and him. The two guards around the sheikh dropped their weapons and lifted their hands up in the air.

"You're supposed to protect me!" the sheikh protested, pushing one of his guards forward.

"They know better than to sacrifice their lives for nothing," Drin said. Many Sekarans he had faced in his life had not had such wisdom. Their holy book was littered with praise for martyrs, and many took that fanaticism into hopeless battles, believing Eltu would bless them for their foolishness.

God would not. They would die, and they would spend their eternity in damnation for wasting their lives.

The sheikh frowned, and then his shoulders drooped. Drin had seen the look from leaders before, in the full knowledge of their defeat. The sheikh narrowed his eyes on Anais. "You were far more trouble than Watcher Tellah promised when he brought you to me."

Drin couldn't see her expression from his vantage, but she showed incredible restraint by not strangling him right there.

"You people shouldn't kidnap girls from other planets," Anais said.

First things first, Drin had to assess the battle situation. "I know there is a second battlemage on planet. We've slain your first. Where is the other?"

The sheikh's mouth clamped shut.

"Answer me," Drin said, fury in his voice.

It was enough to rattle the fat Sekaran. "He's escorting a shipment of rubies off-world."

"Good," Drin said.

The sheikh cast his eyes aside but said nothing for a moment. "Please. I can give you riches and titles. If you'd just let me go. What do you want? Name it, and it's yours."

The question caused Anais to look back at Drin, deferring to him. Drin considered. He certainly wouldn't be tempted by a desperate attempt to bribe him with worldly possessions or power. The only question would be what to do with him? They could kill the sheikh here, and bring his head to the square, but it wouldn't make for the best visual to have an Elorian invader enacting harsh justice. Instead, he reached into a pocket and produced a thumb-comm. "Sao-rin," he said to it, and the device connected to the Skree leader.

Static came through the other end, and then the sound of blasting laser-repeaters. "Hold on," Sao-rin's said on the other end.

Drin waited, watching the Sekarans and Anais. No one spoke, all eyes on him. The laser-repeater fire died down on the other end of the comm.

"What's happening? Do you need back up?" Sao-rin asked.

"No," Drin said. "We're fine here. We've captured the sheikh. Can you make it to the palace with some of your forces?"

Sao-rin laughed a deep laugh from his belly. "I can't believe it. I never thought it was possible."

"All things are possible through God," Drin said.

"Yes, yes. I think we can clear a path fairly easily from here. We'll meet you in the palace," Sao-rin said.

"Drin out." He tapped the device with his thumb and returned it to his pocket.

"What's that mean?" the sheikh asked, his voice tenser than before. The fear was setting in.

"We wait," Drin said.

DRIN AND ANAIS moved the group to the reception room, a larger area and better one for meeting Sao-rin and anyone else who happened to follow him. Drin knew the layout and the potential entrances and exits, so if there were any problem, it would be more defensible than being trapped by the basement stairwell.

The precaution proved unnecessary, as Sao-rin entered a moment later, a dozen Skree with him. He strode in with the confidence of leadership—victorious leadership. Drin had experienced a similar feeling after his first combat, though he never had the reward of a kingdom waiting for him at the end of battle. Only more fights. But such was the path of kings as well, whether Sao-rin understood or not.

Sao-rin nodded to Drin before taking the room in, surveying it. "Amazing work. It still feels like a dream. The usurpers took our palace, used the bones of our old palace and put their abominable aesthetics atop it. But the bones—the soul—is what matters, not the appearance. You taught me that." He motioned to Drin with his stump.

Drin stayed put, keeping close to the sheikh in case the fat Sekaran tried to run. Anais monitored the other prisoners in the corner of the room. Several of the Skree fanned out to assist her. This was now Sao-rin's kingdom, or would be soon. Drin wasn't sure what to do on the political end. In the past, he'd completed his mission, taken out the resisting Sekaran forces, and then stepped aside to allow the fathers, friars, nuns, and missionaries to do their work. In normal circumstances, he would be returning to the *Justicar*. But what would he do now? He hadn't planned for anything other than what he'd always known, the unending battle against evil.

Sao-rin stepped toward the sheikh. The contrast was stark between the two. The Skree was a tall, toned, muscular man. He had burns on his back from the battle, and his clothes were tattered. The sheikh appeared in the height of luxury in a white shirt with a purple sash, loose golden pants that looked like they would fall off in a combat situation. Sao-rin came face to face with him.

The sheikh shook with fear but held his ground.

Without warning, Sao-rin un-holstered his laser repeater and shot the sheikh point blank in the chest.

The blast burnt a hole in him. Drin tried to move, instinctively wanting to pull the two apart, but no brawl erupted. The sheikh had no chance, he wasn't ready and couldn't move fast enough. He stumbled backward, his own weight causing him to sway back and forth while he tried to regain his balance. The hole from the laser-repeater blast burned clear through his chest. Thick as the Sekaran's body was, it took time, but it eroded his skin and his insides. The sheikh gasped for air but, by then, he had no heart or lungs left to deliver. His eyes darkened, and he collapsed.

Anais yelped at the sight and turned away. The blast panicked the Sekaran attendants, who took off running. Several of the Skree tackled them before they went too far. The Sekarans struggled, but quickly understood they were outmatched. Once they understood their fates, they took to begging for their lives like cowards.

Sao-rin stood still over the body of the sheikh, staring down at him. He frowned. "It wasn't as satisfying as I imagined," he said softly, so only Drin could hear.

"It never is," Drin said. He placed a hand on Sao-rin's shoulder. "The way of Yezuah is to show compassion to one's enemies when they are defeated."

When Sao-rin turned to Drin, he had tears in his eyes, but he was also smiling. "Will He forgive me?"

"Of course," Drin said without equivocation.

"Good." Sao-rin wiped the tears from his face with his stump and laughed. "This isn't how I imagined myself appearing at this moment." He made his voice louder for the sake of the others. "Strike this from the history books."

The other Skree laughed.

Sao-rin turned and moved to the two Sekaran attendants. They squirmed against the Skree guards who held them, but Sao-rin moved to look them in the eye.

This was Sao-rin's situation to handle, but Drin found it difficult to suppress the urge to hold the Skree king back if he was going to do anything foolish. He clenched his fist.

"Please don't kill me," one of the Sekarans whimpered, eyes cast to the floor.

Sao-rin forced the Sekaran's chin up with one of his stumps. "Will you swear to learn of the one true God and repent your sins?"

"Yes. Yes, of course," the Sekaran said.

Sao-rin looked to the Sekaran's companion.

"Me too!" the other attendant said.

"Then let us show you compassion as Yezuah would have," Sao-rin said, glancing back to Drin. "Release them."

The other Skree didn't move at first, glancing between one another as if unsure of their king's order, but they released the Sekarans.

The two prisoners stood in shock, but once they had their wits about them, they hurried away. Whether they would come back and hold true to their word was impossible to tell, but Sao-rin had acted with compassion toward his enemies. It was the Skree king's first act on Yezuah's path. That word would spread through the city, and it would do good, regardless of what the Sekarans did with it.

"Now," Sao-rin said," "we have enough people here. Let's get the ceremony over with. I'm tired of my people calling me 'heir.'"

THIRTY-TWO

AFTER THE FIGHTING HAD DIED DOWN, THE SKREE MOVED THEIR people into the residences surrounding the palace, as well as the nobles' estates. There soon would be a new aristocracy in Altequine, but Sao-rin and his men had much to do to restore order to the city. The Sekarans proved to be willing to fight to the death for the glory of their prophet, something they considered a great service in martyrdom. Anais found it stupid. So many wasted lives, all in the name of... what?

There was a God. Someone controlling all of this. It only made sense. Whatever it was, the presence was real, and it brought her comfort. Drin would teach her more about it later. He had such conviction it still impressed her.

Despite her having the nanites flowing through her blood, Drin hadn't allowed her to rejoin the fight. "It's no place for a woman," he'd told her. With her wounds still fresh, she didn't protest. The nanites did a lot of work in patching up most of her skin, but it would be better not to tempt fate. Plus, she wasn't a warrior like him. This newfound power, it would take some reflecting for her to figure out how to use it in a way that she could both contribute and feel comfortable with.

When Anais moved into the palace, she had her pick of rooms. All she cared about was staying far away from the sheikh's bedroom. Sleep would have proved difficult there with the haunting memories of his advances on her.

Instead, she had chosen one of the guest rooms down the hallway. Once the thrill of the battle died down, she'd found herself extraordinarily weary. Rest was exquisite. The bed was so comfortable, and so were the sheets. The palace had every luxury she had been used to back on Deklyn, and the familiar comfort lulled her to a sleep far deeper than any she'd had since coming to this backward planet.

The sleep lasted three days, and when she awoke, the palace buzzed with Skree. They had set up a command center in the reception room. The slaves had become peacekeeping units, preventing crime and ensuring the trades returned to work. Most of the Skree would be in the same trades as before but, this time, they controlled their own destiny.

Excitement teemed in the palace. It'd been generations since the Skree had known anything but slavery. This was truly a new dawn for them.

By the third day since the sheikh's death, the Sekarans stopped fighting. Several came to petition Sao-rin—*King* Sao-rin—for the ability to return to work. He mandated that any Sekaran who wanted to work had to submit to the true God of Eloria and confess their faith in Yezuah as savior and lord. Most agreed, but whether they had conviction in their faith, Anais couldn't say. Those who didn't, unlike under Sekaran rule, were mostly left alone.

Anais stayed in the background, allowing the Skree to settle themselves. She was an outsider, despite having fought alongside them. It wouldn't do well for her to interfere. But when inter-city trade agreements were presented to Sao-rin, Anais stepped forward and offered to look those over. She hadn't much personal experience, but she'd tagged along on enough of her father's trade negotiations that she had a knack for it. Being helpful and having a purpose felt good. She could almost see herself living here, advising Sao-rin, though deep in her heart, all she wanted was to return to Deklyn. The Skree treated her as if she were some sort of saint. Word had spread of her having the same nanites in her body as Drin, which piqued their curiosities.

She hadn't activated them again. The nanites were as foreign to her as Altequine, and Drin warned her they could be as dangerous as they were helpful. With him having to go peacekeep along with the Skree police units, Anais didn't want to risk having a fatal error by activating them.

Another day passed, and this time, she woke to several shouts in the palace. The Skree scurried about as if the world were ending, stomping across the floor.

"They're coming! They're coming!" someone shouted from downstairs.

Anais rushed out of bed and over to a small arched window in her quarters to see what was happening. First, she looked to the streets, but nothing looked out of the ordinary. Skree walked about, manned the bazaars alongside a sprinkling of Sekarans, but all appeared peaceful. With nothing there, she looked to the skies.

Several transports and dropships loomed in the atmosphere, some closer to ground than others. They set down outside the city. Her heart fluttered in fear. Were these Sekaran ships, bringing reinforcements to subdue them?

She hurried down the stairs and into the reception room. King Sao-rin was deep in discussion with some of the Skree, and with Drin, who sat at his right-hand side.

"Those are my people," Drin said. He didn't appear to be too happy about the Elorians arriving. Was that dread on his face? But then, he always appeared to be brooding over something. It was so hard to tell what he was thinking or feeling.

"Excellent," Sao-rin said, a bright smile on his face. "They will bring us your holy words, and they will help us to restore order to this world."

Drin met Anais's gaze and then cast his head aside. "I hope this is the case."

"We'll send an envoy to meet them," Sao-rin said, scanning the room for others. "Err-dio, Sin-cho, Drin, and Anais."

Anais blinked, not expecting to be named in that group. "Just the four of us?" she asked.

"Better not to appear with a force. We want the Elorians to know we greet them in peace. Drin will help with that, but a small party also ensures they see him first." Sao-rin motioned with his stump. "Though some extra support may be advisable. Err-dio, take three of the palace guard with you."

Drin looked like he wanted to argue, but he kept his mouth shut.

Err-dio summoned guards, and Sao-rin dismissed everyone. The party set off together, out through the front doors, and down the streets of Altequine.

Skree police units patrolled everywhere. Compared to before the battle, the streets seemed much quieter. Most of the civilians hadn't seemed to acclimate to the change as of yet. The sight of so many armed Skree must have given the Sekaran population a sense of unease.

The group reached the city gates soon enough and moved outward. Over a dozen transports had landed outside of the city. "Your people don't do things in half-measures, do they?"

"We do not," Drin said, his somber voice filled with pride.

"But you're worried?" Anais said, edging closer to him. She accidentally brushed against his arm.

Drin stiffened and looked over to her. He slowed his pace, dropping back behind the Skree, and signaled for her to join him. The others continued ahead. "I am nervous," he confessed. "I... did not leave my people on good terms. I am a mutineer."

Anais blinked. "Wait, what?"

He told her a story of how he came to this planet. How he

panicked, unable to perform his duties. He didn't like war, despite the fact he was good at it. Being too good at it posed a problem for him because it felt like senseless slaughter and not a righteous crusade. "But after experiencing battle here, I now know my holy calling. I will have to ask for their forgiveness, as well as their permission to continue my work here," Drin said.

"What if these aren't Elorians you know personally? You could just tell them what you accomplished here," Anais said.

Drin shook his head. "I recognize the insignias on the dropships, even from this distance. It is my old ship, the *Justicar*."

Anais bit her lip. She didn't know how to console him. Her ears twitched at the sound of the ramps descending from the ships ahead of them. She shielded her eyes from the sun to see fully armored soldiers, several men in robes, and nuns in dark habits that covered their whole bodies. It struck her what Drin needed to say to them.

Drin tried to move ahead, but Anais grabbed him by the wrist. She turned to face him, and they stood close, much as they had several times. His body radiated heat by her, and the sensation stilled her breath. Just as it had every time since she'd encountered him. It probably always would. That was a feeling she would have to work out at another time. For now, he needed her to stand by him, and to give him guidance. "Trust in God, Drin. It's what you're always telling everyone else to do."

Shock crossed the Elorian's face. He'd never heard her talk like that before. *She'd* never heard herself talk that way. Call it divine inspiration, or simply her womanly understanding what he needed to hear, but it was the right thing to say. That much was certain.

"You're right. By Yezuah, you're right," Drin breathed. He brought his hands to her shoulders and rubbed her arms. "Thank you."

With one more nod, he turned to the ships and caught up to the Skree. They approached the Elorians together.

One of the robed Elorians came forward first. He clasped one of Err-dio's hands upon greeting the group. "Good tidings. We are from the church, the holy emissaries of the Lord God himself," the man said. "I am Father Cline."

"Err-dio, second to King Sao-rin of Altequine," Err-dio said.

Father Cline then turned his attention toward Drin. His face fell flat. "Templar Drin," he said.

Drin dropped to his knees before Father Cline. "Forgive me, Father, for I have sinned. I reneged against my duties to the Templars and to the holy church."

A tense moment passed when Father Cline released Err-dio's hand. He stepped to Drin, pity on his face. He made a sign with his thumb on Drin's forehead. "You are forgiven, my son. Now rise, and tell me all you have done here."

EXCERPT FROM SANCTIFIED

Continue the adventure with the NanoTemplars in Book Two, Sanctified!

Sanctified

Kneeling at one of the *Justicar's* hard sanctuary pews had to be one of the most uncomfortable experiences in Drin's life. He'd stayed in this position for close to an hour while Father Cline and the elders debated what to do with him.

"Meditate in prayer," Cline had told him. He'd done so, and his knees ached from his humble position on the wooden kneeler.

Footsteps sounded from the back of the sanctuary. Cline arrived, dressed in formal white robes that accentuated his green Elorian skin. He stopped in front of Drin.

Drin did not look up.

"Arise, my son," Father Cline said.

Drin stood. Only then did he look Father Cline in the eyes. "Forgive me, Father, for I have sinned."

"You are forgiven, but penance is required. The elders have

conferred." Father Cline paced in front of him, hands folded together, the sleeves of his robes draping over his knuckles. "Normally, a desertion would lead to excommunication, and the harsh removal of your nanites from your system."

Drin winced at the thought. He'd been prepared for it. He didn't dare pray for any other outcome. Whatever God's will would be was what would be done. He hoped the Lord conferred favor upon him for his other noble deeds.

"But," Father Cline said, unfolding his hands and raising a finger in the air, "one would have to be a blind man not to see the fruits of your good labor on Konsin II. The Sekarans had the Skree people enslaved, and thanks to your efforts in freeing them, they are now Yezuah's people. We have concluded it must have been God's will for you to come here, no matter the circumstances."

That is what I've been trying to tell the elders since the Justicar *arrived,* Drin thought. But he did not speak. It was not his place in this sanctuary.

"The lesson you must learn, when you have misgivings, or are not certain of God's path for you, is to speak with your brethren and with me. I am here to guide you, my son, and I am always here to listen."

"Thank you, Father," Drin said.

"But we must maintain order among the Templars, nonetheless. I mentioned there would be penance," Father Cline said.

"Whatever penance you would have me assume is a mercy, Father."

"While aboard this ship and not attending to your regular duties as a Templar, you will act as a vassal. Your station will be beneath the other Templars, and your duties will include cleaning the latrines, preparing meals, and other ship maintenance duties normally be beneath your station. This penance is meant to teach you humility, and to rely on the others of this Holy Church."

Not too harsh a penalty. Drin had never been averse to work. He enjoyed keeping busy so he could keep himself from fretting over the violence of the battles he engaged in as a Templar. Even after liberating the city of Altequine from the Sekarans, Drin found himself abhorring violence. Sometimes it was necessary, but the faces of the enemies he'd slain in the name of the Lord still haunted him. "Thank you, Father," Drin said.

Father Cline stepped to the pew and placed both hands on Drin's shoulders. He bowed his head. Drin did the same. "Lord Yezuah on high, absolve Templar Drin of his sins. Make him a clean slate and an offering to you and your glory so he may always do your will and never stray. Bless us and bless all of your holy servants, may we dwell in your kingdom forever and ever, amen," Father Cline said.

"Amen," said Drin, lifting his head again.

Father Cline patted Drin's arms, then stepped back. "Now that the unpleasantries are over, let's get to business. You still have your duties as a Templar we must prioritize above your penance. You're one of the best warriors and leaders we have, Drin, and I'm much relieved the elders didn't vote to strip you of your nanites and your power."

"I am, as well," Drin said.

"As you may be aware, Altequine is not the only city on Konsin II. It was a miracle that you led these slaves in a revolt and got as far as you did without Church support, but now we are here, and we should do all we can to ensure the rest of this planet is free from Sekaran heresy and abuse."

"My sword is ever ready to do glory to Yezuah's name," Drin said.

"Of that, I have no doubt. Our reconnaissance teams show the city of Shiraz is the next largest Sekaran stronghold on this planet, which is across the desert, into the mountains in the east. You will join your former unit in an assault there to remove the warlord tyrant and bring the gospel to the people of Shiraz."

"I am honored to serve," Drin said, bowing his head.

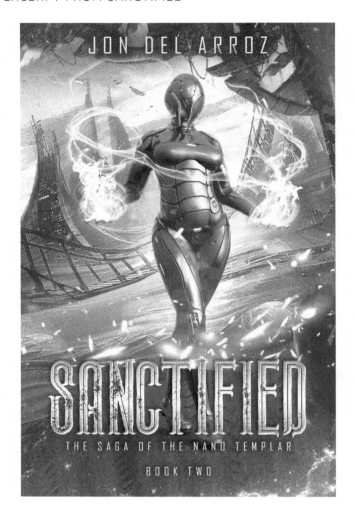

REVIEW REQUEST

Did you enjoy the book?

Why not tell others about it? The best way to help an author and to spread word about books you love is to leave a review.

If you enjoyed reading JUSTIFIED, can you please leave a review on Amazon for it? Good, bad, or mediocre, we want to hear from *you*. Jon and all of us at Silver Empire would greatly appreciate it.

Thank you!

ACKNOWLEDGMENTS

I want to give a big shout out to everyone who helped me on the journey of writing Justified. In 2017, I had a big idea to do a "Deus vult in space" concept, and the awesome guys in PulpRev kept me going and encouraged me through my idea to its completion. I want to thank them first and foremost. I hope I did you proud with this book.

Second, I want to thank everyone involved in editing and proofreading the book: Tim Marquitz, Avily Jerome, and Justin Tarquin.

It's been a crazy year in the business, and I definitely couldn't have done things without my Patreon/Freestartr subscribers. Thank you for believing in me and funding my dreams. It means a ton. Special shout out especially to Edwin Boyette for your tremendous support above and beyond.

I'd also like to thank Silver Empire Publishing for helping push my career forward. These guys have a lot of cool ideas that are unique in the industry and they're going to be major players before long (perhaps even before this book comes out).

Finally, this book was dedicated to my Lord Jesus Christ. A lot of this book was spent in prayer making sure I kept things straight. Even though this is an allegorical religion, set as if God came to a people in a distant galaxy rather than us, and made His sacrifice according to their needs, I wanted the message of salvation through faith to be central to the story, and I hope that came across. If you read this and want to learn more about Jesus Christ, please, don't hesitate to contact me. There's nothing more important in the world than your soul. God loves you and wants you to be a part of his kingdom.

ABOUT JON DEL ARROZ

Jon Del Arroz is a #1 Amazon Bestselling author, "the leading Hispanic voice in science fiction" according to PJMedia.com, and winner of the 2018 CLFA Book Of The Year Award. As a contributor to The Federalist, he is also recognized as a popular journalist and cultural commentator. Del Arroz writes science fiction, steampunk, and comic books, and can be found most weekends in section 127 of the Oakland Coliseum cheering on the A's.

Keep up with Jon on his blog.

JUSTIFIED

SAGA OF THE NANO TEMPLAR, BOOK ONE

By Jon Del Arroz

Published by Silver Empire

https://silverempire.org/

✹ Created with Vellum